Different Drummer

Different Drummer

One Man's Music and Its Impact on ADD, Anxiety, and Autism

Jeff Strong

Bestselling author of *AD/HD For Dummies*

To Stefanie

Welcome to the REI Provider family!

Strong
Institute

This book is for informational and entertainment purposes only. The techniques described are the author's and are not intended as instruction on how to play music therapeutically for any individual. The rhythms, music, and techniques described in this book are also not intended as a treatment for any medical or mental health condition or as a substitute for care from a qualified health or therapy professional. Neither the author nor the publisher shall be held liable or responsible to any person or entity with respect to any loss or incidental or consequential damages caused, or alleged to have been caused, directly or indirectly, by the information or Programs contained herein.

Strong Institute, 7 Avenida Vista Grande, #517, Santa Fe, NM 87508
Phone: 800-659-6644 • 505-466-6334
Email: contact@stronginstitute.com
Internet: stronginstitute.com

Rhythmic Entrainment Intervention (REI) and the REI Custom Program are trademarks of the Strong Institute, Inc.

First paperback edition published 2015.

ISBN-13: 978-0692372760
ISBN-10: 0692372768

Printing/manufacturing information for this book may be found on the last page.

For Beth

Acknowledgements

This book was a long time in the making and would not have happened if it weren't for a supremely long list of family, friends, teachers, mentors, colleagues, and clients. That said, there are a few special people whose support and contributions were instrumental in helping me develop my ideas and put them on the page.

First, I owe a debt to my wife and partner, Beth Kaplan Strong, who, from the first time she heard me play, encouraged my exploration of drumming and rhythm, especially the clinical work. She has steadfastly supported my crazy ideas even in the midst of the uncertainties inherent in a life of independent research, innovation, and creative expression.

I'm eternally grateful to my daughter, Tovah, who graciously puts up with my obsession with drumming, music and rhythm and who can always be counted on to offer insightful and considered feedback.

I am grateful to the many people involved in the development of REI. At the top of the list are my dear friends and sounding boards, Elizabeth King Gerlach, Michael Sheppard, L. Dee Jacobson, Jeanne

Bain, Philip Rampi, Denise Andes, and Therese Schroeder-Sheker, all of whom have guided me and witnessed my many stumbles while I was trying to understand and apply my music.

A special thanks goes to our chief tech/software engineer, Jacques Delyea. Collaboration has never been my strong suit (typical for someone with ADHD), but Jacques, like Beth, is sharp enough to keep up with my frenetic pace, while at the same time able to temper my tendency to shoot from the hip. His elegant code design speaks volumes about his ability to get to the essence of complex concepts and translate them into usable forms.

Also, my hearty thanks goes to the nearly 2,000 clinicians who made REI a part of their practices, many of whom generously shared their experiences to help me refine my Programs. Key early adopters include, but are not limited to: Lisa S. Matthews, OTR/L; Argie Criner, MOT, OTR/L; Jennifer Griffith, OTR, Heidi Pennella, OTR/L, Jane Soodalter, OTR/L; Kelly Zaros Berman, OTR; Kim Bell, MS, CCC-SLP; Kristen Clark, OTR/L; Diane M. Droescher, PT, Barrie G. Galvin, OTR/L, CIMI, IMC; and Kathleen Morris, MS, CCC-SLP.

Last, to my teachers and mentors: Thank you for sharing your love, wisdom, and support, even as I took liberties with the lessons you shared with me. Without your encouragement to integrate and innovate your teachings, I wouldn't be doing the work I am today.

Author's Note

Different Drummer is a memoir, drawing from my experiences with the drum from 1983 through 2014. This path is not exhaustive; rather, I use vignettes that I feel best represent the ideas I explore.

All events are true and clients are real. Quotes from clients are as written or spoken, with grammatical changes where necessary for clarity. Dialogues, in many cases, are not verbatim; instead, they are intended to convey the essence of my conversations. Mistakes or misinterpretations are mine alone. To protect privacy, I have changed names and identifying features of people, locations, and events.

I have been liberal in disregarding chronology in favor of creating a narrative that follows themes. In some cases, such as in Chapter 1, I present the time frame for clarity. Other times, when I don't feel the exact timeline is relevant, I leave it to the reader to get a sense of the chronology, so my focus can be the process rather than timing. This is especially the case in Part II, where I explore symptom areas.

I use two conventions in this book that relate to specific conditions. In the case of Attention Deficit Hyperactivity Disorder, I universally refer to all three variants of the condition as ADHD, rather than ADD (commonly used when hyperactivity is not present) or AD/HD (as listed in the DSM-5). In the case of Autism Spectrum Disorder, I prefer to simply use the term autism to refer to people anywhere on the spectrum. I also use the term Asperger syndrome for several clients, as that was their official diagnosis at the time, even though this term has since been integrated into the larger ASD diagnosis beginning with the DSM-5.

This is not an academic paper on drumming and rhythm; therefore, I have not included footnotes, references, an index, or an appendix. However, given that many readers may want more data explaining, supplementing, or supporting my ideas, I have included additional information on the book's website: differentdrummerbook.com.

I hope you enjoy reading.

Different Drummer

Contents

"Boom, Boom"
Billy, 27 year-old with autism

Part I
Development

Chapter One
Origins

Summer 1993

Stacey took my case from me as I walked into the house. She was excited, talking non-stop and peppering me with questions as we unpacked my gear. Did I see the latest Disney movie? What was that cord I was plugging in? What type of drum was I going to play?

At this point I was beginning to wonder why I was here. This child seemed so typical. She was curious, communicative, excited to meet someone new. She helped when I asked her to uncurl the microphone cable and watched intently as I tuned the drum.

Then the phone rang.

Stacey's mother left the room to answer it and Stacey panicked. She dropped my mic and ran screaming after her mother. She hugged her mother, pleading, "don't leave me, don't leave me".

Her mother ignored the phone and tried to calm her, to no avail because Stacey was inconsolable. She screamed and squeezed. Squeezed and screamed.

This was the behavior I was told to expect.

So, I did what I came to do. I played my drum. Quietly and slowly at first, then with more urgency, gradually building in tempo and volume until Stacey turned to look. Her mother guided her over to the couch near where I was playing and encouraged Stacey to watch me play. Stacey was uninterested at first, but as I played on she began to calm and occasionally glanced over at me as I drummed away.

I played for almost twenty minutes, the last half during which Stacey sat quietly on the floor next to her sister, who was thumbing through a book. Stacey spun a toy in her hands in rhythm to my drumming. She was calm and seemingly content. About fifteen minutes into my playing, the phone rang again and her mother left the room to answer it. Stacey didn't flinch. She continued playing with her toy while I drummed.

• • •

I was engaged in a tradition with a long history. In many places around the world drummers were employed to moderate behavior, to calm or excite, to soothe or provoke. They were the therapists, the psychologists, the psychiatrists. Drummers were the bridge to the unconscious and the unknown where the root of behavior resides.

I was called to play for Stacey because she was experiencing extreme anxiety that wasn't responding to more typical treatments. She also had autism. Hers was a mild case that is also referred to as Asperger syndrome. In this form of autism, language is present but communication is stilted, social interactions are one-sided and awkward, eye contact is fleeting or even non-existent. There are also other common attributes such as anxiety and ritualistic behaviors, both of which Stacey had in spades.

I met Stacey well into my search to understand the potential role of drumming techniques in therapeutic practice. Ten years earlier, while attending the Musician's Institute (MI) in Los Angeles, I had begun exploring the traditional use of therapeutic drumming around the world. I didn't discover these ancient techniques at MI. Rather, a chance encounter with a hand-drumming teacher I met in a park not far from my apartment in Hollywood led me down the path that I would spend the next thirty years walking, oftentimes blindly.

The Musician's Institute was a new school when I attended in the early 1980's. My class in the percussion program consisted of 16 graduating students. The program was arduous and demanding, but because of its intimate size, each student was encouraged to follow his passions. In class I focused on progressive jazz and Brazilian and Afro-Cuban styles. Outside of class I explored hand-drumming originating from West Africa.

Both my school and my apartment were in Hollywood. This was a great place to live while attending a music-based school, though, at the time, this part of town was a bit rough. There were lots of underground clubs and many artsy people hanging around. There were also quite a few homeless people and vagrants. Oh, and a few tourists on the main drag.

My apartment was just a few blocks from school, but the most straightforward, not to mention safest, route was past the Chinese Theater. The Chinese Theater, if you're not aware, was built during the height of the glamor years of Hollywood and contained the handprints of some of Hollywood's most enduring stars. In the courtyard you'll find the likes of Marilyn Monroe, Clint Eastwood, Steven Spielberg (not at that time, though), and many others. This site was the most popular tourist stop in Hollywood and drew hundreds, if not thousands, of visitors each day. And it was in my path to and from school. Needless to say, I quickly tired of wrestling the crowd. It didn't take me long to find another, more interesting route.

My trail-blazing took me off Hollywood Boulevard and onto Franklin Avenue, one block to the north. It was still a busy street for traffic, but few people walked so the sidewalks were clear (few people walked anywhere in LA in the 80's, probably don't today, either). This way only added a block or so to my commute and became my route of choice.

I should probably back up and describe why I chose MI as opposed to other, much more established, percussion programs. I could have gone to Berklee College of Music in Boston, a very good music school for traditional jazz, or perhaps the University of Miami for big band. I chose MI because my goal was to be a studio drummer and MI's curriculum was geared toward this goal.

I aspired to be like my heroes, Steve Gadd, Vinnie Calioutta, and my personal favorite, Jeff Porcaro. As it turned out, Jeff's dad, Joe Porcaro, was one of the founders and directors of the percussion program at the Musician's Institute, called the Percussion Institute of Technology (PIT). Aside from being able to study with Joe, I also looked forward to PIT's focus on Brazilian and Afro-Cuban drumming, collectively referred to as Latin drumming. These styles represent the roots of all popular music, especially the progressive jazz and rock that I loved. Unfortunately, I quickly found out upon beginning my classes at MI that, though the Latin drumming existed, it was only on the drumset. I wouldn't be learning to play hand drums.

Initially it wasn't a big deal because I had my hands full, so to speak, with the drumset work I was doing, but I longed to expand my horizons and learn these other instruments. It wasn't because of any sense of history or tradition, however. My reasons for learning hand drums were entirely practical: I felt that the more instruments I could master, the better chance I had of being able to make a living playing music.

As fate would have it, my route to and from school took me past a small park where a drummer often sat and played his congas. These are barrel-shaped hand drums that originate from Cuba, based on drums played for centuries in West Africa. Many days I idled by and listened as he played, intrigued by the variety of his sounds and rhythms. I could sometimes pick up bits and pieces of rhythms similar to those I was learning on the drumset, but many times what he played went way over my head.

After a month or so of hearing him play, I approached him and asked if he'd teach me. He said no, he wasn't interested in teaching anyone, especially a drumset player, saying that I would corrupt the drumming and wouldn't appreciate its roots. I assured him that I would be respectful, but he demurred.

Undeterred, I kept showing up and pestering him. I often resorted to hiding behind a nearby tree in the hopes that I could pick up some of his cool rhythms and techniques.

Finally, after a few weeks of this, he got sick of me stalking him and he relented. He agreed to teach me on the condition that I would take seriously the traditions he would share with me and follow his rules for how I was to use the information he would pass on.

I agreed, but I didn't really know what he meant by any of this. By this point, though, I wanted to learn to play hand drums like him so badly that I would have agreed to almost anything.

We set a schedule and I met with him a couple of times a week before my first classes of the morning. This began an intense period of study that involved me playing the drums or attending classes nearly every waking moment. I was so absorbed by my studies that I often forgot to eat. Over the course of about eight months I unintentionally lost close to 50 pounds. I wasn't big to begin with and I ended up barely over 130 pounds (at 5'9", I was thin). This, however, was the early eighties so my emaciated state was pretty on par for the young people hanging around Hollywood. I fit right in.

I have to say that the instruction at the Musician's Institute was top-notch. My teachers were first-tier drummers. Joe Porcaro could be heard on countless TV and movie soundtracks and almost all the live awards shows, including the Academy Awards. Ralph Humphrey, the other percussion program director, and his band, Free Flight, often played with the Los Angeles Philharmonic and he had played with the likes of Frank Zappa and on TV show soundtracks too numerous to count. My Latin drumming teachers (teaching drumset) were Alex Acuna and Efrain Toro, two of the most in-demand players in the genre, both of whom, ironically, played hand drums for their gigs.

But none of them held a candle to the understanding of rhythm and it's effects that I gained from this unknown drummer I met in a dirty city park. My teacher, Lloyd, came from a long line of drummers in his native Trinidad (and before that, West Africa). His was a tradition that dove deep into the roots of society, carrying with it much power. Where I studied reading and rudiments at school, I was learning history and responsibility from Lloyd.

He spent as much time schooling me on traditions as he did on techniques. I was learning the origins of my chosen instrument. I discovered that the drumset that I had spent the previous decade trying to master was a new invention, less than 100 years old.

This instrument that I revered was a cobbled together grouping of mismatched instruments used when there were too few people to play the drums individually. I was learning that the rhythms I was playing on my drumset were originally played by three or more drummers on separate drums, bells, gourds, rattles, or shakers. I was learning that the rhythms were an abbreviation of their original forms to accommodate the limitation inherent in using only one limb for each instrument or group of instruments.

Each of the traditional rhythm parts were much more complex than those that ended up on the drumset. For example, the kick (bass) drum part for the Brazilian Samba on the drumset utilized only the accented notes played by the big bass drum, called a surdo. The surdo's rhythms involve loud and soft notes and rim shots played with a mallet in one hand along with hand mutes and slaps to embellish, alter the pitch, and sustain with the other. The overall feel of a surdo's groove was much more driving and dynamic than anything that can be played with the kick of a foot pedal.

By learning the subtleties of the surdo's rhythms, I became a better drumset player and developed my own interpretations of the Samba that drumset players explored. So, from a musical perspective, studying the hand drums enhanced my abilities. But from a personal perspective, my hand drumming studies with Lloyd opened an entirely new world for me, one in which I came to understand the power of drumming and music and their profound effects on those listening.

Spring 1983

"Where are we going?" I asked, as I climbed into the waiting car.
"To meet a little boy," Lloyd said. We were on one of our many

"field trips" where Lloyd would show me a side to drumming that I, as a player of popular music, was unfamiliar with.

Over the previous six months, Lloyd had taught me the traditional rhythms he and his ancestors had used for centuries. He taught me their origins and was beginning to initiate me into the healing aspects of drumming. These healing powers, he described, were based on a connection to the sacred and tied to behavior. I'd learned to trust Lloyd and, though I was uncomfortable with some of the spiritual connections he talked about, I was traveling a path that many drummers before me had followed. Needless to say, I was enthralled by all I was experiencing. This field trip was my first glimpse into a world where drumming was used to affect behavior.

We drove along for about fifteen minutes before Lloyd said, "In our world, when someone is acting outside of the community's norms, they are said to have an illness of the spirit. It's our job as drummers to help keep people's spirits intact. We do this by using the power of the group, through celebration and ritual, to keep the community cohesive and to look for the signs that someone is not acting right. Then if we observe this, or a community member alerts us to inappropriate behavior in their daily life, we intervene. That's what we'll be doing today."

We drove along for another fifteen minutes before Lloyd added, "We're going to meet a boy who is aggressive, often violent, doesn't follow directions, doesn't communicate, won't be touched, and screams when asked to come out of his shell."

"So, how are we going to help?" I asked. "I know we can influence behavior by drumming, but this sounds like a mental disorder, not some spirit thing."

"Well, it is," he answered. "In Shango, we frame any acting out or non-conforming behavior as having a spiritual cause. This is a holdover from a time when we didn't have the language to describe these things in the way we do today. This is just another way of viewing what are now considered psychological or mental health issues.

Think of it this way: When you're feeling down sometimes you may say, 'I don't feel like myself'. In village culture your loved ones may say that you are suffering from an illness of spirit. It's the same thing. And it doesn't matter from our perspective. We do the same work either way."

"What's that?" I asked.

"We play the drum," he said. And that was the last he said until we arrived at our destination.

• • •

We were in an affluent part of town in West L.A. The house was large and imposing and was entered through a locked gate. There were two beautiful foreign luxury cars parked out front and the views of the L.A. basin and Pacific Ocean were astounding.

We were met by a housekeeper, who guided us into the house where a young family was seated in the sunroom. There was a boy of about six sitting on his knees on the floor pushing a Lego truck back and forth while rocking and humming to himself. The mother and father stood and we all said hello. The boy continued to sit, absorbed in his ritual.

"Ty," the mother said to her child, "Say hello to master Lloyd. You remember him, don't you?"

No response.

Lloyd leaned down and touched the boys shoulder. "Hello, Ty. It's nice to see you again. Do you mind if I play my drum for you?" he said.

Again, no response. No one seemed surprised by this and no one forced the boy to engage. Lloyd simply asked me to get the drums and set them up by two chairs. I did as he asked while he quietly chatted with the parents.

Once set up, Lloyd sat behind the conga and tumba and began playing. Slowly, quietly, he centered on muted tones, seemingly being careful not to startle the child. I sat and watched.

Lloyd played delicately for a while then slowly increased the volume and intensity, adding some slap tones and bass punches to the mix. I noticed that once in a while the boy looked over toward Lloyd.

Then after 10 minutes or so the boy got up.

He moved around somewhat aimlessly for a few minutes until he went over and sat on his mother's lap. Lloyd continued playing but toned down the rhythms a bit. The child sat rocking and humming against his mother while she held him. She began to cry.

Summer 1993

Stacey sat contentedly on the floor, still playing with a toy. Her mother returned from the kitchen, her phone call over, and settled onto the couch next to me. She smiled as she watched her daughter.

"I've not seen her this calm in a long time," she whispered in my ear after a while.

I nodded and took it as a sign that I should call this an end to our first session. I slowed my rhythms and progressively dropped the volume until my drumming faded away.

I've come full circle, I thought. Just a decade earlier, when he played for Ty, Lloyd showed me what it meant to calm an anxious, disconnected child with fast, complex drumming rhythms.

Spring 1983

"Hello, Ty," Lloyd said as we entered the house. Ty was spinning around the entry, eyes at the ceiling two stories above. Ty offered no response. Lloyd motioned for me to go to the sunroom and to set up the drums where we had the days before.

"Ty seems a little more settled every day," I heard his mother tell Lloyd. "Last night he went to bed without a meltdown. After his bath he climbed into bed and sat quietly while I read to him. Two books and I turned out the light. He slept until 5:30 this morning. We actually got some rest, too."

She was excited and Lloyd seemed pleased. I heard him mention something about the purpose of the drumming but I was essentially out of earshot and needed to focus on setting up the drums and preparing the space, so I didn't catch most of what he said to her. I could tell she was focused on what he was saying, often nodding in agreement and appreciation for what he was describing.

This was our fifth visit to Ty in as many days. This time I came prepared with a pocket tape recorder to document what Lloyd played. For the last four days I sat and watched as Lloyd engaged with Ty in a sort of dance where he would play a rhythm, or sometimes a series of rhythms, then Ty's behavior would change. Lloyd would switch to other rhythms and Ty would again change. I had been studying with Lloyd for several months by this point and knew all the traditional rhythms, but what I heard him playing was new to me. This intrigued me and compelled me to see if I could begin to understand what he was playing and how it might connect to Ty's behavior.

"Each rhythm has a purpose," Lloyd said as I asked him about this connection. "You have to find the right rhythm to draw your patient out. You play the wrong rhythm, or even the right rhythm at the wrong time, and you won't be able to hear your patient. Know your rhythms and you find your power."

As I played for early clients like Stacey and recorded and analyzed what I played for them, I remembered the urgency of Lloyd's words. I needed to find the patterns in the rhythms. I needed to understand the listeners' individual responses to the rhythms. This was a monumental task. And a task without a roadmap.

I've always been really good at seeing patterns. My job now was to look at the rhythms in a more focused and structured way—I needed to find the patterns in the rhythms and listener's responses.

Summer 1993

"Stacey slept in her own room last night," reported her mother when I showed up at her house two days after first playing for her. I tried to explore this further, but Stacey accosted me at the door.

"Hi Jeff," Stacey said looking past me and grabbing my drum from my hand. She struggled with the forty-pound case and nearly tripped over me. Unfazed, she continued talking. "Belle likes books. I like reading books too. Do you like reading books? I like books, Belle likes books," she said in a flurry.

Stumbling with my drums and recording equipment I said, "Umm, yeah, I like to read. Who's Belle?" I asked.

"Belle likes reading books just like me." she responded, not answering my question, while dropping my drum and grabbing a picture book. I disappeared from her awareness as she was drawn into the pictures and her own world.

I shrugged and continued setting up.

Belle, I later found out, is the main character in Disney's *Beauty and the Beast*, one of Stacey's favorite movies, one that she watched over and over and would talk about endlessly if you let her. She created an entire inner world with Belle as her friend.

Stacey was much calmer this day. She was not clinging to her mom, though I could see that she was acutely aware of where her mother was and at one point I saw her tense up when her mother walked toward the kitchen.

I decided this was a good time to start playing so I tapped a tentative rhythm with my fingertips, making sure not to startle her. Her sister, who was two years older and typical, came into the living room and sat down near Stacey to read a book.

They both sat quietly as I played a large variety of rhythms, tempos, and volumes. I played for about twenty minutes and really didn't see much of a response from Stacey at all. I noted that her mother wasn't in the room the entire time I played and Stacey didn't seem to care. She was calm the entire time.

Her lack of response was fine with me, as my playing wasn't always about getting a reaction. In this instance, I was testing out a bunch of rhythms that I would put on a tape for her to listen to everyday. With the goal of helping calm her down when she became anxious, these rhythms would hopefully provide a longer-term impact on her anxiety.

This long-term change concept came directly from my studies with Lloyd.

For the past year I had found a working system to help me formalize my exploration of the rhythms. I typically played for a client and recorded the session, taking notes about their responses to the different rhythms. Then I would come back two or three days later and play, again taking notes and recording my session. Then it was back to my studio to analyze the recordings and notes. From these, I made a recording of the rhythms that offered the most positive responses.

"Goodbye, Stacey," I said as I grabbed my gear and headed out the door. Just like last time, she was engrossed in a toy and didn't answer me or even acknowledge my exit.

• • •

Two days later, I returned to Stacey's house to drop off the tape.

"Are you going to play your drum today?" asked Stacey.

"Not today," I said. "I'm only here to give your mom a tape for you to listen to. Would you like to listen to a tape of my drumming?"

"Mommy, turn it on now!" she yelled.

She grabbed my hand and led me to the couch. "Turn on the tape mommy and we'll listen."

Stacey was insistent and excited and she listened intently for about 35 seconds before she was back on the floor with a toy. I moved to the floor with her to see if we could play together but she wasn't interested, pushing me away when I tried to interfere with her play. She spun a toy on a book over and over again.

I got up and said goodbye to her mother, leaving them with the tape and instructions to play it daily at bedtime or any other time Stacey got anxious. I also left a tracking form for her mother to complete. These notes would capture the patterns of Stacey's anxiety and her physiological responses to the tape.

Obviously, cassette tapes were not possible in the days that this drumming technique originally developed. In Lloyd's tradition, he would either move in with his patient or the patient would move in with him and he would play everyday for the person until the spiritual cause of the behavior was addressed.

Moving in was impractical for me. And, given that I worked in a recording studio, I had the equipment to be able to make a tape. The cassettes became my stand-in, the client's daily drumming session. Even though the recordings were static, my notes and live-session recordings allowed me to prepare rhythms that could have a long term impact on a client's anxiety.

Stacey's mother called me after 7 weeks, excited by an event that occurred the night before. She reported that Stacey had a sleep-over at a new friend's house, a first for her on several levels: First, Stacey had never been invited to a sleep-over before, second, she was able to separate from her mother to actually go on the sleep-over, and third, the next morning she was able to describe in proper sequence what she did at the sleep-over. These were major milestones for her.

Stacey was also perseverating less and engaging in more appropriate conversation. She was also making eye contact more often. After roughly 10 weeks, she was observed in class by the school psychologist who noted that, based on her behaviors, Stacey was "indistinguishable" from the typical children in the classroom. As a result she was mainstreamed into the regular (non-special education) classroom.

When I analyzed the recording and listened to the rhythms I played for Stacey, I was surprised at the complexity of the rhythms I was playing. Many times I had to slow down the playback to figure out what I had played.

This was something that continually surprised me.

Chapter Two
Otter Lake

"What do you think about doing a study on this?" asked Erik.

Erik was attending my African and Latin group drumming classes. I'd been telling the group about my experiences drumming for Stacey and other kids with developmental disabilities. Everyone was intrigued by the idea of using drumming for children with developmental disabilities, especially given the children were not asked to play the drum and only listen as I played. Erik, as it turned out, was the staff psychologist in a school district that contained what was considered one of the most progressive autism programs in the state.

"I think you have something here," he said. "Maybe we could do the study at my school. It has a great autism program and the director is progressive. I'll help you write a proposal and submit it. If we're lucky, we can do it this year yet."

"That sounds exciting, but I don't know how do write this type of proposal," I confessed. "What does it need to look like?"

Up until this point, I had written articles about therapeutic rhythm-making, but nothing along the lines of what I would need for a study proposal. Erik went on to describe the key points of a research proposal and I went to work on a first draft.

As I was writing the proposal, we hit a snag.

"You need a name," Erik said.

"A what?" I asked.

"A name. For your therapy," he replied.

"What do you mean? This isn't really a therapy yet. It's an idea. An experiment."

"I know, but the school board will want to it be more concrete. You can't just call it drum therapy. How about something more clinical?"

"Okay, let's see... AIT stands for Auditory Integration Training. That's a mouthful," I said, thinking out loud. "And it sounds clinical and serious."

AIT was an auditory therapy that was popular for autism in the early 1990's. I was aware of it mainly because my client Stacy had gone through AIT several times. Her mother was well-versed in the process and had explained it in detail to me. Stacy's mother was also a friend of the researcher conducting what would end up being the largest study done on an auditory intervention for autism.

It was the knowledge of AIT, along with my experiences with my drumming teacher Lloyd, that got me thinking that maybe I could be able to help with the condition.

So with AIT's name as a model, Erik and I brainstormed.

"What is the drumming doing?" asked Erik.

"Well, I think it's entraining the brain to a calm state," I answered.

"Entrainment is a fancy word for synchronizing," I explained. "There has been speculation that repetitive drumming can make the brain pulse in synch with the tempo." I was referring to a study I had just heard about that documented what researchers had been speculating for a couple of decades. In this study, repetitive drumming at four-beats-per-second induced a corresponding four-beat-per-second theta wave in the listener's brain. This discovery also fit with a series of studies where rhythmic pulsations, in the form of binaural beats, were shown to induce a similar effect. This effect is often referred to as brainwave entrainment.

"Okay, you use rhythm to entrain," surmised Erik. "How about calling it rhythm entrainment therapy? He paused and thought. "Not therapy. Intervention. Yeah, intervention. That's better."

"Rhythm Entrainment Intervention," I pondered. "I like it. But I think it should be Rhythm*ic* Entrainment Intervention, because the other entrainment approaches use beat frequencies. This sounds more precise."

"Rhythmic Entrainment Intervention... REI. I like it," Erik said thoughtfully.

So, we had a name. We had a study design and a protocol. Now what we needed was approval to do this in Erik's school.

Schools are notoriously unreceptive to experimental programs, especially where kids are concerned. First, we needed tentative approval from the program director and buy-in from the teachers. Then we would need consent from all the parents. From there, I was told, it would be on to the school board for approval. I was skeptical that we could do it.

"I'll take this to the director and I'll let you know what else we need," Erik said as he took the proposal.

The idea of a study intrigued me. I had been working with a lot of kids like Stacey over the previous year or so and had documented everything: The rhythms, children's responses, and effects of various recordings. This study would be another step toward trying to understand whether drumming had a place as a therapy for autism.

My teacher, Lloyd, had played for kids with issues similar to those exhibited by the kids I was playing for with autism. And I had watched Lloyd produce some pretty dramatic effects, especially with calming. I, too, had facilitated some great changes in anxiety along with improvements in other symptom areas; so I felt that this study may help me better understand the effects of the drumming, especially by collaborating with other people who had much more experience with this condition than I had.

Documenting case experiences and playing one-on-one were very satisfying for me for my own curiosity, but I really didn't have much sense of what I should do with my music beyond this. However, I made a conscious effort to follow whatever path formed in front of me. This study could be an interesting one, I thought. One in which, I was sure, I would learn a lot. And I was all about learning more without any real expectation of where it would lead me (a trait that has been my guiding principle throughout my entire career).

After only a week Erik called and said, "We got it."

"Got what?" I asked.

"Approval. Carol, the program director, looked over the study proposal and felt it was worth doing. We presented it to the teachers and they're all behind it. We're now waiting for the last of the parental consent forms to come back. I figure you can start playing for the kids on Monday."

"Wow," I said. I really wasn't expecting this to happen, and so quickly. "Okay I'll see you first thing Monday morning."

Now I was nervous. I had played for quite a few people up to this point, but a study? In a school? I was a drummer, not a researcher, at least not this kind of research. Up until this point, research was something I did by myself for my own interest. Now I had a school involved in my weird idea.

I mean, drumming. To help kids with autism. How strange is that?

Otter Lake Elementary School. 7:30am Monday March 7, 1994.

It was unseasonably warm, which was a good thing because the top on my convertible was torn and the heat in my old Volkswagen was never very good. Still, after a forty-minute drive I arrived chilled, my hands stiff. This won't do, I thought. I have to be limber to be able to play for these kids.

This was my first day of a pivotal study that would forever change my life and the nature of my work. I was at the elementary school where we were going to track the calming effects of drumming for 16 children with autism This school housed one of the most progressive autism programs in the state and, perhaps, the country.

"We received 16 parental consent forms back for the kids," described Erik when I met with him and the autism program director, Carol. "That's about half of the kids in the four classrooms. The kids range in age from 6 to 12, though most are between 8 and 11."

He handed me the forms and gave me a brief overview of each kid's issues.

"They are all so different," I said, showing my lack of knowledge of the many manifestations of symptoms, abilities, and behaviors of children on the autism spectrum. "Some can talk, some can't. Some are anxious, some are withdrawn. Some have seizures, some don't," I said, beginning to feel overwhelmed.

Could I actually do this? I wondered. Could my drumming have a noticeable positive impact on the kids? Sure, I had great success with Stacey and some other kids with similar issues, but the range of issues presented in these kids was astounding. I was feeling out of my depth. Who was I to think that my playing on a drum would help? For decades, professionals have been struggling to help kids on the autism spectrum. Even the multi-billion-dollar-a-year pharmaceutical industry was having limited results in being able to make a difference. How could I? And with a drum?

Erik could tell I was freaking out. So he tried to calm me by putting the study back in perspective.

"Just focus on the calming," advised Erik. "Try not to worry about having any dramatic effects. Just do what you did with Stacey and let whatever happen, happen. I'll be in the room with you the entire time."

I took a few breaths and we went to meet the teachers and aides. The introductions went well. Everyone was interested in seeing if the kids could be calmed. Anxiety and anxiety-based behaviors were the most significant and disruptive events during the day. So much of the teachers' and aides' time and energy went into managing these behaviors that very little learning actually occurred. Anything that could have a calming effect on their students, I was told, was a welcome addition to their classrooms.

The vast resources that go into managing anxiety and anxiety-based behaviors is the reason that the most accepted therapy for autism focuses on managing behaviors. ABA (Applied Behavioral Analysis) and other behavior-related approaches focus on re-directing behaviors through repetition, rote responses to stimulus, and an often arcane system of rewards and (sometimes) punishments. Behavioral therapies are time-consuming and labor-intensive—therefore expensive—and offer limited results unless implemented perfectly. A good behavioral therapist, working one-on-one with a client for 40+ hours a week, has to have the patience of a saint and the stamina of a marathon runner.

If this study could offer any observable improvement in calm, it could make the kids more at ease and receptive, potentially opening a door for learning and internalizing well-implemented behavioral approaches. Of course, thinking this way made me anxious again. It's a good thing that at this point I was asked to perform a little of the type of drumming I would be doing. The staff wanted to get a sense of what my drumming was about. Up until now, no one but Erik had actually heard me play.

This is always the fun part for me. In instances like this, I prefer to jump right into rhythms at my typical eight-beats-per-second pace rather than slowly speed up. This is partly for effect and partly because the sooner I can get the group to shift, the deeper I can take them in the few minutes I'm usually allotted for my demonstration.

Listeners always go through four distinct stages when they first experience me bang my drum. The first stage of listening to my REI drumming is disbelief, especially if listeners are expecting calm. Eight-beats-per-second is fast. And the drum I play is fairly loud (I can make it painfully loud if I want to, though I don't this day), so uninitiated listeners tend to get a little tense at first. This day was no exception. I actually saw some eyes go wide as I started playing. Several teachers looked over at Carol, the program director, clearly wondering what this was about. Carol, in turn, looked toward Erik, who just smiled and nodded in time to my playing.

After an initial shocker rhythm (yes, I can be provocative when I play—it makes people remember their experience), I settled into a calming groove based on the Cuban Son rhythm. This is a simple two-beat pattern that has a forward-driving feel similar in effect to a Mambo beat. Two-beats, by the way, are a two-quarter-note pulse, with me playing sixteenth notes. This means that there are eight individual drumbeats in this pattern.

This simple groove brought up the second stage of listening to live REI drumming: amusement. Some teachers smiled, some began to sway to the rhythm. I kept the two-beat pulse going until I saw most of the staff begin to relax and engage with me. Some of the same teachers who looked at the program director with concern now looked at her with what could be best described as, well, amusement. They were having fun, but didn't see how this was going to be calming for their students (or even themselves).

I began to morph my rhythm, turning this simple two-beat pattern into a complex arrangement of odd-meter variations that had no discernible beginning or end. Instead, it appeared to be a stream-of-consciousness improvisation with no real goal. There was a goal, however. And that was to usher in the third stage of dealing with my REI drumming: bemusement.

Now, nearly five minutes into my performance, I watched the gears in people's minds clog and jam as they tried to understand what I was playing. This was especially the case with those trained in music. What I was playing could not be understood intellectually in the moment—it was too unpredictable and went by too fast to analyze—so confusion fell across people's faces. At this point, I saw Carol look at Erik, questioning her decision to let me be there. Erik nodded reassuringly at her.

I took this as my cue to help drive my bewildered listeners to the final stage of the REI drumming indoctrination: surrender. Once the analytical mind surrenders and people stop "listening" and allow the drumming to waft over them, they let me take control of their brain. I'm just kidding (sort of). I'm not taking control in classic sense of leaving my listeners without a choice. I'm taking control in the sense they are open to allowing their brains to shift.

REI drumming does require the listener's brain to attempt to decipher the patterns I play. But REI also requires that the listener's brain entrains (synchronizes) to the pulsations of the underlying patter of my rhythms. This can't happen when people are trying to intellectually process what I'm playing. Many people will stop listening for understanding pretty quickly because they enjoy the feel of the music. Others, mostly people with musical training, will hold out until the constantly changing nature of my playing goes on long enough that they get tired of trying to count it out and make sense of what I'm doing.

Auditory driving research has shown that it can take a few minutes before the initiated brain synchronizes to the stimulus (I talk more about auditory driving in Chapter 5). This time can be shortened if I am able to break homeostasis. The brain wants to remain in its current state, but novelty and anticipation make the brain easier to influence. This is why I always start off with loud fast drumming—it shakes the listener and allows me to break homeostasis. Then I take my listeners on a journey from simple rhythms to progressively more complex rhythms until I have their brains engaged. This can happen in less than ten minutes.

I saw this shift take place as eyes drifted off of me and started to close or the swaying and tapping to the music stopped. This is my favorite part of my performances, because my listeners are with me, fully engaged with my drumming. And this is where I begin to see the calm. No longer was the staff looking over at Carol or Erik with concern. Most weren't really looking anywhere. They were just experiencing the drumming. I kept playing for a few minutes as I watched everyone settle more. Then I slowly faded out and stopped.

I sat quietly and didn't say anything for a while. Partly because I wanted everyone to be with their experiences for a minute and partly because I was speechless (this often happens to me when I play). I was calm. I sat with a big smile on my face. I tried not to, but I couldn't suppress it. I felt a deep sense of peace inside. I was finally ready to begin this study.

I went through the usual gauntlet of people thanking me for my playing and telling me their observations of their experiences, but I cut this short because I wanted to get to the testing room as quickly as I could in the hopes that I could remain in my own peaceful state.

I rushed to my room and set up my equipment while the kids arrived at school. Erik began the process of lining up which student will come at which time over the next two days. I would play for eight kids each day, recording the sessions and making notes, after each student leaves, of any thoughts and feelings I had as I played for them. Erik would keep the kids in the room and re-direct any behavior he saw as being disruptive to the process. He would alert me to any potential problems he may see coming or that I may have unwittingly initiated. He would also take notes of his observations of each child's reactions to my playing. From these recordings and our collective notes, I would go back to my studio and make a custom drumming tape for each kid.

"Steven won't be able to tolerate the drumming," his teacher said to me as she brought him to the room. "He is much too sensitive to sounds to be in this tiny room when you play that loud drum," she added, looking at Erik hoping, I think, for him to agree with her and let her take Steven away. Erik took Steven's hand without a word and guided him to a chair across the room from me.

"I'll play quietly and Erik will remove him if he is bothered," I replied.

She nodded but looked at me and Erik with doubt and concern. Reluctantly, she left, but stood by the door. Erik gave her a reassuring look as he gently closed the door and settled in a chair next to Steven.

Our testing room was small, about eight feet square, with cinder block walls, a suspended acoustical tile ceiling and a linoleum floor. Typical mid-century industrial drab construction. The reflective walls and floor created a booming sound with the bass of the drum and the tiny space made volume a real issue if I wasn't careful.

I was careful.

"Would you like me to play the drum for you, Steven?" I asked.

No response. He stood, left side facing me while looking at the wall and running his finger along the mortar line.

A scream erupted from outside of the room. Steven grabbed his ears and began to rock. His teacher, seeing this through the window of the door, started to enter but Erik waved her off and signaled me to start playing.

I tapped a slow bass tone, pushing my right palm into the center of the drum at a tempo in time to his rocking. He kept rocking and after a minute, dropped his hands from his ears. I continued this pattern for another minute or so and then added a quiet syncopation with my left hand in time to the bass tone. Simple at first, slowly growing in tempo and complexity. Steven turned my way.

I changed my rhythm to a faster triplet-based feel, one that often excited the children. I was hoping to get him engaged with the rhythm, so I added some bass and slap tones and played an odd meter variation on a Brazilian Naningo rhythm. This rhythm has a smooth half-time triplet feel.

Steven made his way along the wall and toward me and, more importantly, my drum. I added some bouncy fills to vary the rhythm. It took him a few minutes of moving along the wall, but soon he was standing right next to me when he stealthily moved his hand to the drum. He lightly touched the edge of the rim with his palm and let his fingers drape onto the head. He held it there as I kept playing this triple feel rhythm. He had a flat affect, showing no sign on his face of liking or disliking my playing as he stood touching the drum and it's head.

He stood unmoving for several minutes, so I switched to a calmer rhythm, one that many children have sat or lain down to, in an effort to elicit a response.

Nothing. He continued to stand facing the wall with his hand on the drum. I switched to a bass-heavy rhythm, knowing that he would feel a strong sensation in his fingers.

He smiled and moved his hand further onto the drumhead. With his hands in the way it was getting difficult to play and Erik, noticing this, tried to distract Steven and pull his attention and hand away.

Steven pulled back from Erik, keeping his hand on the drum. He began rocking again. I moved my hands to the edge of the drum and played a light soft rhythm, partly to get my hands away from his so

I could keep playing and partly because I wanted to keep him from getting anxious or reacting negatively to Erik's redirection.

Erik was eventually able to redirect Steven and have him sit quietly next to him as I continued playing. Once Steven was sitting, I increased the intensity and volume of my playing. Steven sat and listened. I kept building volume and rhythm speed. Steven sat quietly. Again, I raised the volume. Steven sat. With a volume that was high for the room and despite what I was told he could handle, Steven didn't seem bothered. I dropped the drumming to a whisper. Steven looked my way.

Encouraged by his response, I lightly tapped the edge of the head at a barely audible volume. Steven watched my hands intently as I fingered some double tempo patterns.

With Steven watching my hands, I stopped and placed my hands on the drumhead. He watched my hands for a minute and then got up and came over to the drum. He put his hands on mine and stood in front of me, looking off into the distance at the wall. We stayed that way for a few minutes until Erik came over and gently guided Steven back to his classroom.

I was feeling pretty peaceful about now and enjoying the silence of the room when a tornado came in. Her name was Nina. She was a highly verbal, highly anxious 9 year-old with Asperger syndrome.

Asperger syndrome is a subset on the autism spectrum and is the form of autism that Stacey (Chapter 1) had. Nina was a lot like Stacey. She had a large vocabulary that she felt free to use, though most of what she said was not appropriate or sensical. With Erik on her heels, she burst in my room and walked directly to me.

I introduced myself to her, showed her my drum, and asked if she minded if I played for her. She said that she didn't and then began vigorously beating the drum. So vigorously, in fact, that it was impossible for me to play at the same time. While I held the drum, I let her play for a few minutes until she seemed to settle a bit. She didn't stop on her own, however, and required Erik to redirect her before I could play.

This experience was a good introduction to Nina's overall personality and behavior. She, the school staff described, was an intense, uninhibited child. She was verbal and tended to perseverate on whatever came to mind. She talked almost constantly about anything and everything, much of it running together and making little sense. She was also highly anxious and sometimes aggressive to others. Her teachers noted that she was disruptive to the other students and they found it difficult to get her attention and keep her on task. It wasn't uncommon to need to separate her from the other children and to work with her one-on-one to get her to attend to her schoolwork.

When I began playing, Erik was playing a hand game with her while she continued to talk. She paid no attention to my playing initially, but after a few minutes she focused her attention on me when I began playing a rhythm that I often found helpful for people who were anxious or engaging in self-stimulatory behaviors. This rhythm, one that I had just successfully played for Steven, was based on a Brazilian Naningo. This pattern starts in a 12/8 time signature with accents on the first (bass tone), third (bass tone), sixth (open tone), seventh (slap tone), tenth (open tone) and twelfth (open tone) beats and evolves into a 23/16 rhythm by dropping the last beat of the second measure. This rhythm then drops another 2 beats to repeat a 21/16 time signature pattern.

After settling into this 21/16 portion, Nina sat down in a chair next to Erik and watched me play. I continued this rhythm and some variations on it for several minutes during which time Nina became quiet and attentive to what I was doing. I played for another six minutes using a variety of similar rhythms while she stayed quiet and sat in her chair, watching me play.

When I ended, she remained quiet while Erik led her back to her classroom. Her teacher later reported that she was calm the rest of the morning, until lunchtime when she became agitated by the change from the quiet of the classroom to the commotion of the lunchroom. The rest of her day was similar to other days, with her teachers struggling to keep her from acting out and becoming disruptive to the other students.

Nina was followed by her opposite: Marcus. Marcus was a small, quiet eight-year-old. Where Nina was high activity, high anxiety, Marcus was nonverbal, and largely non-responsive. Erik led him in the room and he sat, or more accurately, melted into the chair.

Like with all the kids, I started by playing very quietly for Marcus. He sat motionless for the longest time until, when I was playing a bouncy rhythm in a 19/8 time signature, he got up and walked over to the drum. He put his hands on the side of the drum as I played. I then switched to a simple samba-like pattern consisting of two bass tones followed by two quiet, open tones. This rhythm bounced along until I dropped a beat here and there to create a more syncopated samba-type feel. With the heavy bass tone pattern, Marcus lay down and crawled under the drum. He positioned his stomach directly under the bottom of the drum.

I dropped the volume a little so as not to hurt Marcus' ears, but kept playing an abundance of bass tones. Marcus stayed on the floor for the rest of the time I played.

When I stopped, Erik picked Marcus up and took him back to his room. He came back with nine-year-old Sammy. She came into the room and didn't say a word to me as I introduced myself. Erik had her sit next him and nodded at me to begin.

She sat quietly as I started playing the drum. After just a few times through a basic calming rhythm, Sammy looked at me and smiled. Over the next ten minutes, I played a large variety of rhythms, from simple, calming rhythms to complex, intensely focused rhythms. Sammy never stopped smiling. She did seem to prefer open tones on the drum and rhythms with triplet-feel (these types of rhythms tend to have an uplifting quality to them).

After I stopped playing and Sammy was taken back to her class, the teacher described that Sammy rarely talked, though she was able to express her needs and desires when prompted. She was also very socially withdrawn and difficult to engage, had poor eye contact, and poor motor control.

Next came Lucas, another eight-year-old. Lucas was somewhat similar to Nina in that he talked a lot, often not making much sense, and he could be aggressive to other children if he became overstimulated. He differed from Nina in that he rarely initiated contact with other children in his class, preferring to interact with his teacher and aide.

Lucas was told I would be playing a drum for him, so when he arrived he immediately approached me and asked me what kind of drum I was holding. I told him as I tapped it, then asked him if he'd like to play it a bit.

He touched the head as he tapped it with his fingers and talked and asked me a series of questions. The questions came as fast as he tapped, with no space for me to answer. But he didn't seem to want any answers. This pace continued for several minutes until Erik redirected him away from the drum. At that point, Lucas shifted his one-way conversation to Erik and I started playing.

I played quietly at first with the hope that he'd stop talking and focus his attention on the drum. I began with a simple calming rhythm that is a variation on a 2-beat long Brazilian mambo beat.

Short rhythms such as the mambo need to be varied for people on the developmental disability spectrum. Otherwise, they become annoying to the listener and defeat the purpose of calming.

In this instance, the variation I used created a rhythm in a time signature of 31/16 (the typical rhythm is in 2/4). Lucas shifted his attention to me, but continued talking as I played. After about ten minutes of playing various rhythms, I settled into a more complex rhythm and Lucas stopped talking almost immediately. I played this rhythm and some variations for a couple of minutes before Lucas came up to me and asked me how long I was going to play. I took this as a cue to stop.

Next came Tom. Tom, like Steven, was extremely sensitive to sound. He was very anxious and often aggressive. He was also nonverbal, which tends to contribute to anxiety and aggressive behavior for many children due to their inability to express their needs. Unfortunately, Tom often hit others without provocation. This was a problem and his teacher was hopeful that the drumming would help calm him down. She was concerned, however, because of his extreme sensitivity to sound, that he wouldn't do well with the rhythms. After my experience with Steven, I wasn't so worried.

With Tom's sound sensitivities in mind, I began by playing very quietly. Tom grabbed my hands and stopped me on several occasions, sometimes tapping the drum himself, seemingly to get comfortable with it and its sound. After about 4 minutes, he sat down next to Erik and watched me as I played.

I played a large variety of rhythms over the next 12 minutes and observed that he seemed to prefer rhythms that had a flowing regularity to them. The more complex, chaotic rhythms appeared to make him tense up a bit, though at no point did he cover his ears or indicate in any way that we was bothered by the drumming, even though there where a few times where I played very loudly.

By the time I stopped playing, Tom was sitting next to Erik and vocalizing along with the drumming. I couldn't hear him as I played, but Erik reported that Tom began vocalizing about two minutes before I stopped. In reviewing the session recording, I noticed that at that point in the session I had been playing a rhythm with repeating groupings of five. Tom stopped vocalizing after a minute or so of when I stopped playing.

He was the last person I played for that day. I left the school feeling pretty satisfied with the childrens' responses, hopeful that I could have a positive impact with this study. The next day I played for the rest of the children in the study and was again encouraged by their responses to the rhythms.

All the children were calmed and sometimes engaged by my drumming, which was a good start. But our goal was to see if listening to a recording of the drumming would elicit the same calm as my live playing. I spent the next week making each child their own cassette tape by playing rhythms I had mapped out from the live recordings and notes. Each recording would be twenty minutes long. The following Monday I brought everyone their tapes. It was like Christmas, at least for me, to hand them out.

Erik and I asked the teachers to play each child's recording once a day, preferably turning it on at a time when the child was anxious, then track their response. We would do this for four weeks at which time I would come back and see how everyone was doing.

I arrived at the school four weeks later, nervous. I hadn't talked to Erik or the teachers since I dropped off the tapes, so I had no idea how the kids were doing or whether these recordings were having any impact.

Erik wasn't able to be at the school when I conducted my four-week check-in, so we talked briefly on the phone before I interviewed the teachers and aides and met with each of the kids. Erik told me that he felt the autism classrooms were much calmer than before the kids started listening to their tapes. He also said he thought the tapes were having an overall positive effect on the kids. There were, however, some issues with teacher compliance.

"Very few of the children listened with the frequency that we planned," he said, preparing me for what I would soon discover from the teachers.

"What do you mean? How often did the kids listen? What a mess," I replied, clearly bothered, feeling my study was ruined.

"Everyone listened a different number of times over the last four weeks," he replied. After a short pause, "I know this seems like a problem, but we're still going to learn a lot from this study. It's rare that a study of this sort goes exactly to plan. And it's often in the unforeseen that we learn the most."

I was silent. I tried to process this new information, thinking I should have been at the school everyday to make sure the tapes were played the way I wanted them to be played.

"You couldn't have been there everyday, you know that. It would have been too disruptive to the classrooms," Erik said, reading my mind. "Just go in, talk to the staff, check in on the kids, and try not to worry. We'll make sense of the data when it's all collected."

"I guess," I said still trying to come to terms with how my study got sidetracked. I had never done a study before so I didn't know if Erik was telling the truth or whether he was just trying to make me feel better.

I stopped worrying about this when I arrived at the school for my check-in, surprised and gratified by the enthusiasm of the teachers and aides when I talked with them about their experiences the first month. They all felt that the tapes were having a positive effect and they described many instances where the music had made a big impact.

From a cursory glance at the tracking forms, it was clear that most kids were calmed when their recordings were turned on. I was encouraged by what I was hearing, but I was deeply touched when I met with the kids.

Nina was my first stop. She was sitting quietly in a private study room with her aide, listening to her REI recording. I observed her for several minutes while she worked: She stayed on task. I talked with her teacher and she mentioned that Nina was more compliant and less anxious than before starting REI. She did mention that Nina still got anxious and became disruptive and sometimes aggressive during the day, most often right after lunch.

The teacher said she felt that the transition from the unstructured lunchtime to the more structured afternoon class time seemed to be particularly problematic for Nina. Because of this observation, the staff developed the practice of playing Nina's REI recording a second time after lunch to help with this transition.

According to the tracking notes from her teacher and aide, Nina was calmed every time the recording was played. This calming effect generally appeared within 4-5 minutes of turning on the recording, though it was often sooner. They reported that many times Nina stopped her disruptive or anxious behavior almost immediately upon hearing the recording begin. It seemed that Nina often fell asleep during the recording, speaking to the toll that the anxiety was having on her.

It also appeared that listening to her tape twice a day was having an overall positive effect on Nina's behavior. She was less aggressive, more compliant to requests and directions, and was better able to attend to tasks.

My next stop was Lucas. This morning Lucas was uncharacteristically quiet, hardly talking to me at all. He sat in his chair and ringed his hands together while staring into space. His teacher told me that he had been having a hard time since his father moved out of the house two weeks into the study. She described that he had been arriving at school agitated, so they started playing his REI recording as soon as he got to school in the morning.

The tracking form showed that Lucas was calming down to the recording as it played nearly all the time (92%). This calming effect generally lasted through lunchtime. The teacher also noted that Lucas seemed to like listening to his recording and often commented on it.

Because Lucas was so quiet and was engaging in this hand ringing self-stimulatory (stimming) behavior, I decided to grab a drum and play for him a bit. I started with a rhythm that I often use for people who are stimming. This rhythm contains complex accent patterns in a time signature of 21/16.

Lucas glanced at me as I started playing and, over the course of three minutes, he stopped ringing his hands and came over to me. I switched rhythms to a loping Brazilian Samba-type pattern (this REI version consists of a four-bar phrase of a pattern played in a 15/16 time signature). Lucas put his hands on the side of the drum and held it as I played.

As I progressed through several other rhythms, he sat down next to his teacher and quietly listened. This continued for about four minutes until I stopped. At that point, Lucas came over to me and started talking. He was telling me about a game he liked—what it was and how it was played. This monologue continued as I walked with him back to his classroom.

When we arrived at the classroom, Sammy came up to me and gave me a hug. She stood next to me and smiled as her teacher told me that Sammy "loved" her recording and asked to listen to it a couple of times a day.

I noticed that Sammy was holding her tape and said as much to her teacher. Her teacher nodded and remarked that Sammy often carried her tape around with her during the day.

Sammy's tracking log showed that she was always calmed by the recording and often seemed "lighter" or "happier" after listening to it. The staff reported that Sammy seemed to be coming out of her shell and was beginning to engage more with the staff. She still had no interest in the other children, though.

I played for Sammy a little and she again smiled when I began playing. At one point I played really quietly and asked her if she would like to join me. The teacher led her over to the drum and she stood quietly in front of it for a minute or so, then put her hands on the edge of the rim as I played.

I played for several minutes while she stood holding the instrument. Even with very complex, intense rhythms and, at one point, an especially loud passage, Sammy stood and smiled. I should note that drums such as the Gonga I play can exceed 140 decibels at this close range—a volume that can match a loud rock concert, so it's important to be very careful and to keep passages such as these very short.

Sammy also looked me straight in the eyes for quite a while as I played, eye contact that I was told was very unusual for her. Once I stopped, she averted her gaze and let go of the drum. She continued to smile, though, as she left the room.

Tom showed up as Sammy was leaving, so I had the chance to play for him again. His response to my playing was similar to his first session—he wasn't bothered by the rhythms, tones, or volume of the drum, even with his sensitivities to sound. In fact, he seemed more engaged than the first live session, evidenced by his sitting quietly and watching me the entire time rather than stopping my playing.

His teacher reported that Tom had fewer aggressive incidents since starting his recording and the incidents he had were significantly less severe. His tracking log showed that he was calmed 98% of the time as it played. His tape was damaged by another student the day before my visit, so I had to make him a new one. Because of this, he missed three days in a row and listened to another subject's recording for these past three days. He was still being calmed by the other student's recording.

Next, I went to see Marcus. He was in the middle of working with his aide so I didn't get a chance to play for him. His teacher and I talked as I watched him work.

"Marcus doesn't really like his tape. It rarely calms him," said Therese, his teacher.

"Hmm," I said, thinking.

Before I can say anything Therese said "But there was something that we noticed. I'm not sure what it means, but he seems to calm whenever we play Tom's tape. Do you think one tape could be calming, another not?" she asked.

"I don't know, I suppose," I said. "Let's test this. I'll make a copy of Tom's tape that you can play for Marcus and we'll see if there is a difference in his response."

"Okay, I'll have Angela play Tom's tape until then."

"Actually, let's not. Has Angela been the person playing his tape and tracking his response?"

"Yes. Marcus does well with her."

"I think it would be interesting if Angela doesn't know that we changed the tape. Let's tell her that the tape was damaged and that I'll bring a copy in tomorrow. This way she won't expect a different response than she's been getting. If Marcus is calmed more or less this upcoming four weeks, we might learn something interesting."

So, that's what we did. After meeting with more kids in the study, I ended my day with Steven, the first child I played for at the start of the study.

When I entered his classroom, Steven was in a corner with his aide rocking and covering his ears.

"Could you turn on Steven's tape?" I asked his teacher.

"Sure," she said as she put it in the tape player and moved the player to a table near Steven.

She stepped back and we stood and watched. So far Steven had not noticed me because he was facing his aide with hands on ears and rocking back and forth. His teacher and I watched as Steven shifted his gaze to the tape player. Stilling holding his ears, his rocking became less chaotic, seeming to synchronize slightly to the pulse of the rhythms filling the room. Other kids in the room gravitated toward the tape player, some looking that way and others moving in its direction.

Steven's rocking subsided after about a minute and his hands came away from his ears. Less than a minute later he was settled into a chair in front of the tape player, listening intently.

"He almost always gets like this when his tape is played," his aide said.

His teacher handed me his tracking forms and, sure enough, Steven was calmed most of the time by his tape. Seeing firsthand how the tape calmed Steven put this study into perspective, a perspective I hadn't before imagined. I was used to seeing people calm as I played, but I had not seen firsthand what a recording of my music would do for such a diverse group of kids, especially as I looked around the room and saw that nearly everyone had calmed. Many children were also tuned into the music, either looking at the tape player or moving in time with the drumming.

This was a great way to end my day. I left the school and stayed out of everyone's way for four weeks, trusting that whatever data we collected would be enough to show me something about how my drumming may help kids with these types challenges.

At my next check-in, I was gratified by the enthusiasm of the students and staff. As I did at my four-week evaluation, I wanted to see each kid and talk to each teacher and aide to gather a more complete picture of their experiences than I would by simply looking over the various forms that Erik and I would collect.

I met Nina first, since she was my star student at the four-week point. Nina was alone, calmly working on her schoolwork with her aide when I arrived. They were in a separate room from the other students, as they had been at the four-week point. The aide reported that Nina had listened to the REI recording approximately two hours previously and that Nina had been calm since then. Her aide mentioned that Nina came to school agitated and was immediately brought to this room to listen to her REI recording. She was calm after about 10 minutes of listening to her recording.

Nina's tracking notes related that she was still calming to the REI recording every time it was played. Overall, Nina responded very well to her tape. Besides being calmed as it played, she showed some obvious changes in her behavior in general. Her teacher and aide both described that Nina was less aggressive toward staff and other students, she was more able to control her impulses, and was easier to direct and redirect if she was acting out than before starting REI.

Of all the children in this study, Nina showed the most significant change. She also heard the recording more frequently than the other participants, averaging 10 listening times per week.

Lucas was my second stop. His teacher described that Lucas "has been able to better express a variety of feelings as well as use quiet times to calm himself during anxiety. We also noticed an increase in group participation."

His rate of immediate calming for the second part of the study was still above 90% and his overall change was significant in several areas: His anxiety dropped 25%, aggressive behavior dropped 30%, his memory increased 35%, and his ability to listen and follow directions increased 60%.

I was looking forward to seeing Sammy again, especially after getting a nice hug from her last time I saw her (it's nice to be appreciated). As I expected, Sammy was consistently calmed by her tape.

Her teacher told me that "she loves listening to her tape. Aside from being calm, we have seen increased eye contact, less refusals and shorter latency to respond to requests."

According to the exit assessment, Sammy also showed improvements in motor control (coordination), eye contact, and social engagement. These were all good things to hear, but the best part was that Sammy approached me and asked if she could keep her tape.

I said she could. And she smiled and gave me another hug.

I checked back to see Tom and talk to his teacher and the school psychologist after four more weeks. They reported that Tom was noticeably calmer overall and that he was still calmed nearly all the time when the recording played. He showed significant improvements in several areas: His anxiety reduced by 45%, his sensitivity to sound reduced by 40% both for the intensity and frequency of his reaction to offending sounds, and his frequency and intensity of aggression dropped by 45%.

The staff noted that when he was without his REI recording, he listened to another subject's recording and found it calming while it played as well. This response caused us to begin looking at whether we could create a calming recording for people with autism that wasn't custom made.

Of course, this was followed by my meeting with Marcus' teacher and aide.

"Marcus did better with his new tape," Therese reported. "Take a look at Angela's notes."

"Wow, it looks like he is being calmed by Tom's tape twice as often as he was by his own."

Erik overheard this and said, "So, Marcus was calmed more by Tom's tape than he was by his own?" asked Erik.

Yes," I said. "The drum was the same. The recording process was the same. The tempo and the pitch were the same. The only difference between Marcus' tape and Tom's were the particular rhythms.

This is a pattern I've seen over and over again, I explained. One rhythm may be calming. Another may stop a stimming behavior. And another may engage and get someone moving.

From analyzing the two tapes, I noticed that Tom's tape had more odd groupings. "Remember during the initial session when I played that pattern in 13, then Tom sat down after circling the room? I put that and some similar rhythms on his tape. For Marcus, who was calm to begin with, I never played anything like that. Because he was so withdrawn, I played a lot of triple-feel rhythms. Those ended up on his tape. And he didn't like them when he was anxious. They weren't calming for him. Whereas the odd meter rhythms were," I said, thinking out loud.

"My teacher, Lloyd, used to talk about this. He said that each rhythm has a purpose and knowing what to play when was the key to having success with the drumming."

"This actually goes back to the origins of using drumming in ceremony where each rhythm is tied to a specific spirit or Orisha, as they're called in Africa," I added. "I saw this before when studying the rhythm-healing technique. The specificity of each rhythm is the

key to the traditions and the aspect of this that I'm most interested
in seeing hold true."

Erik and I examined the data and tried to make some sense of
it all. Most students were calmed most of the time, and those who
heard their tapes more than three times per week often displayed
improvements in their behavior. This study was encouraging, though
at the time I didn't know what to do with it. I felt out of my depth;
so when the study ended, I was unsure what to do next. I longed to
be on more familiar ground to allow this experience to settle in my
mind.

Within a week of going over the data with Erik, I was with my
partner Beth, in her Jeep, on our way to New Mexico and Arizona
to see if I could meet with native healers and gain more understanding of the rhythm traditions from that region. Unable to gain any
insights from anyone I talked with, we went from university to university in the region and dug through stacks of research journals,
looking for any studies on using drumming or rhythm for people
with neurological disorders.

In all our reading, I only found one article focusing on drumming and rhythm outside of its traditional cultural context. While
all other studies explored ritual and ceremony, one article examined
using drum solos for people with schizophrenia. The results of this
study suggested that unpredictable rhythms had an activating effect
on listeners.

This study, and frankly the lack of any others, reinforced my desire to continue playing for individuals, to look for patterns in their
responses to my drumming, and to further explore formal research
projects. I was intent on extracting the rhythm from the culture and
understanding the neurological mechanisms involved.

Chapter Three

Spirits

"Are you talking about spirits here?" a woman asked incredulously from the back of the room.

It was 1997, and I was in New Orleans giving a talk at the Autism Society of Louisiana's annual conference. My session was standing room only. Several hundred people were waiting for me to answer this challenging question.

"Historically, yes," I said, pausing to let my audience take this in. "But the language used then was very different than what we use now. Today we know so much more about human behavior and have an entire lexicon of terms for these conditions. We have no need to view aberrant behavior as having a spiritual cause."

I was in the heart of the Bible Belt, in the largest American city where vestiges of the African religious diaspora mingle with the conservative values and deep religiosity of the south. To top it off, New Orleans is a music town, lying at the crossroads of spiritual and secular music.

Blues, gospel and jazz, music that New Orleans is know for, each developed out of African spiritual traditions that blended with Catholicism to form musical styles that would eventually change the way we experience music in the West. Rock, pop, soul, R&B, hip-hop, and rap, all owe a debt to the spirituals sung by the slaves as they toiled in the fields of a new America.

The Africans that were brought to the new world had long and deep spiritual traditions that consisted of an intricate musical landscape. As is common with many cultures around the world, music was tied closely to their spiritual and religious practices. Most every religion and spiritual practice around the world has employed music to express and deepen one's faith.

For example, early Christian carvings, sculptures and paintings regularly show angels playing harps or drums, hymns are sung at nearly every contemporary service, and music has become an important addition to a church's identity. Even my Midwestern, conservative Lutheran church had a band that played contemporary Christian music to praise God. Other Christian faiths, such as Baptist and Evangelical, often put more emphasis on praise with music than my highly conservative Lutheran congregation. In fact, today the super-churches often spend enormous sums of money on their musical stages, equipment, and musicians.

Music touches us deeply and allows us to express ourselves, so it makes sense that it would be part of our connection with the sacred. However, many of us in the West are suspicious of music that feels too tribal. And nothing sounds as tribal as a beating drum. It's this association with tribalism and drumming that this woman spoke to. Her visceral response was that of fear.

Given the Hollywood images of tribal drumming associated with voodoo and the prevalence of voodoo in the consciousness of most New Orleanians, it made perfect sense. And because of this, I came prepared to answer her question.

I should say that this woman's question also spoke directly to my own concerns when I studied the traditions and developed my techniques. And it wasn't the first time I was confronted with others' suspicions of the drumming, especially when it was also connected to the sacred and spirits.

Several years before, when I was first exploring using drumming for calm, I worked with a four-year-old girl with a condition called agenesis of the corpus callosum (ACC). This rare condition, occurring in roughly one out of thousand people, happens when the bridge between the left and right hemispheres of the brain doesn't develop.

This child, Lily, had developmental delays, anxiety, and sleep problems, not unlike other kids that I played for on the autism spectrum. Due to my success with Stacey, I was asked if I could help Lily. She was a very anxious child, tantruming often, especially when asked to transition from one environment or activity to another. She also had a very difficult time getting to sleep and woke often at night. I had seen that I could help calm and also suspected that, by extension, I may be able to help with her sleep.

I played live for Lily in the same manner I had with Stacey and, like with Stacey, observed Lily calm down as I played. Her parents and I were encouraged, so I made a tape of rhythms that they could play when she was anxious and when she went to bed.

Lily fell asleep while the drumming tape played the first night. By the end of the second week, she was sleeping through the night most nights.

But then I ran into a glitch. At the same time I was playing for kids one-on-one, I was also teaching drumming classes, facilitating drum circles, and leading meditation classes using drumming to help people achieve a meditative state. Some of these classes were at holistic health centers, bookstores, and progressive churches.

The holistic health community in the Twin Cities of Minneapolis and St. Paul, Minnesota was fairly small and tight knit. If you taught at a center in South Minneapolis and your class was successful, you were often asked to also teach at a similar place across town. My classes were pretty well attended, so I was teaching everywhere. The community also supported a couple of wellness publications that were distributed through these and other grassroots, independent stores. Many of these publications contained articles by or about various teachers conducting classes.

While I was working with Lily, the largest local publication ran a special issue profiling a few of what they termed "visionaries", people doing something unique within the natural health community. I was one of the teachers featured. This publication got ahold of a photo of me in full musician mode—long hair, leather motorcycle jacket, handmade drums—and printed it. But even more, they put the focus of the article on the origins of my drumming work, including a generous dose of references to the shamanic and spiritual aspects of drumming.

Lily's parents saw the article. And they flipped out. I didn't hear this firsthand, though.

"Lily's parents mailed your tape to me and wanted me to tell you that they don't want her to listen anymore," Jennie told me. Jennie was one of my closest friends and the reason I was able to play for Lily in the first place.

"Why? Lily is so much calmer. And she's sleeping," I replied.

"Apparently, they read that article about you in the wellness magazine and became afraid of your drumming because of the article's references to the traditional spiritual side of drumming. They said they don't want to go against their religion."

"Seriously?"

"Yeah, they are concerned that your drumming is doing something spiritual to their daughter. "

"You know it's not. Besides, it was helping."

"I know, but what can I say? Their beliefs are important to them."

"Is there anything I can say to them that would allay their fears?"

"I doubt it. I tried telling them that what you do is not voodoo or pagan, but they couldn't hear me."

Speechless, I hung on the line trying to figure out what I could do to help Lily.

"I would let it go," Jennie added. "You can't help Lily."

Jennie was right. I tried calling Lily's parents, but they wouldn't talk to me.

In some ways, I shouldn't have been surprised. When studying with Lloyd, I dealt with this issue myself. Lloyd was very clear with me when he agreed to teach me how to play the drums the way he did: He would teach me respect for the instrument, the rhythms, and their origins. It wasn't long after I learned a set of core rhythms and techniques that Lloyd initiated me into a spiritual dimension of drumming that I didn't know existed and, despite his mentoring, found surprisingly unnerving.

My introduction into the sacred world of drumming came innocently enough. After I had been studying with Lloyd for several months, he invited me to play a gig with him and two other drummers, as they were short their usual 4th hand (or pair of hands, as it were).

We were to play at a church in the San Pedro area of L.A. It was a community gathering to help support an ill parishioner.

When I was in high school, I played for my church's praise band. My father was the treasurer and a deacon at our local church, and it was expected that my musical talents would be harnessed to help spread the word. When my church added contemporary music, I jumped in. I didn't feel particularly religious, but it was part of my community and, as an aspiring professional musician, I made a point to play at every opportunity I could.

When I arrived at the church with Lloyd I felt pretty comfortable, even though I was the only white person there. I had played in reggae and R&B bands for most of my professional career, so my being anglo didn't bother me, as I had often been in the minority. No one else seemed to care either. I learned that my presence with Lloyd was endorsement enough; no one was worried about an outsider, even a white one, attending their private gathering.

What did set me a little on edge were the instructions Lloyd gave me when we were setting up. He described that we would be an integral part of a special ceremony and we were responsible for its success or failure. We needed to play perfectly and we needed to watch everyone closely to make sure that no one acted out inappropriately.

Up until this point I had no idea that what I would play on a drum could have the kind of power, much less the responsibility, to make anyone "act" in any particular way, except maybe make them feel good and want to dance.

I really didn't understand what Lloyd was talking about. And I told him so. At which point he admonished me because, as he explained, he was schooling me on the proper etiquette when drumming. Did he not, he asked harshly, explain how each rhythm works?

I suppose he had, but I did not remember. Or I didn't understand. Or I wasn't listening. Or whatever. I don't know. Heck, all I wanted was to learn how to play the hand drums.

In the tradition that we were following, the drumming controls the intensity and direction of the ceremony (often called the "heat"). It was our job to make sure that each Orisha (spirit) was properly addressed. Our drumming was to be the bridge between the physical and spiritual worlds so the Orisha could, through the Manbo (priestess), facilitate the healing. We needed to play precisely in order for the spirits to appear.

We were four drummers. I played the tumba—a low pitched drum that provides the supporting rhythm of the group, much like a bass drum on a drumset, except with more complex rhythms than would ordinarily be played with the kick of a foot. One other drummer, Jimmy, played the conga, a mid-range-pitched drum that encompassed supporting rhythms that interlaced with mine to create complex polyrhythmic structures. Added to this was our third drummer, Sheryl, who played rattles, bells, and shakers, depending on the song and song section. She added a third counterpoint to our driving pulsations. We three would lay the foundation for Lloyd, our leader.

I should note that in traditional Shango, we would be playing different types of drums, those more akin to double-headed bata drums that you find in Cuba. But like many things related to the modern Orisha worship, we used the drums that were most available. As well, by this point Lloyd had only taught me the tumba and conga techniques. I would later learn the bata patterns and play them in ceremony as I continued studying with him and was initiated deeper into the traditions.

Both Jimmy and Sheryl had been studying or playing with Lloyd for quite a few years. In Sheryl's case, I was told that she was his niece and she started playing with Lloyd when she was a kid. Jimmy, on the other hand, had been playing with this group for roughly ten years. They, along with the drummer I was filling in for, often played for ceremonies like this. They also played as a complete band or as a rhythm section for other musicians, gigging several times a month in Latin and jazz bands.

This night, Lloyd played a quinto. This is a small, high-pitched barrel-shaped drum that played the main melodies and solos. Contrary to popular belief, drums can play melodies, though they are not in the same interval structure (pitch-wise) that you find with melodic instruments such as a guitar or piano. Drums offer an often-astounding array of sounds when played expertly in the hands of a master drummer, such as Lloyd.

As the leader, Lloyd's job was to make sure that we as a group supported the Manbo and led the dancers and other participants in the proper way to achieve the goals of this ceremony.

Once we were set up, Lloyd called us together and gave us the set list for the night. I was used to getting the set list just as I was about to go on stage, so this didn't bother me. Good musicians are able to sight-read charts and play an unknown song with conviction and emotion. This was actually one of my strengths. I was very good at sight-reading. So much so, that by the time I was 16, I was in a pretty heavy rotation of jobbing (freelance) musicians in the Minneapolis area. I think by the time I left high school I had played in nearly every country club and bar in the area, not to mention tons of parties. It's not glamorous work (nor highly paid); but for a kid, it was fun and it was a great experience.

I was ready to play any of the rhythms Lloyd had been teaching me, and I was pretty relaxed. But what set me on edge was what Lloyd said next.

"Pace yourself," advised Lloyd. "We'll start fairly slow and low and grow as we feel the heat build in the room. This is a complex ritual, so be prepared to play for several hours without stopping the music. Keep water close by. We'll have sections where you can sit out or play with one hand and drink. I'll signal you so you can take advantage of the breaks. Okay?"

"What? What about union rules? 45 on, 15 off?" I asked, half-joking, ever the smart aleck, my country club performing days coming back to bite me. Forty-five minutes of music followed by a 15-minute break were union rules at the time. I was used to them and paced myself according to this schedule.

"The spirits don't follow union rules," he replied with no hint of humor.

"I've never played that long without a break. I don't know if I can do it. What if I have to pee?" I complained.

"You'll be fine," he dismissed.

After a long pause (for dramatic effect, I think) he looked me squarely in the eye and warned, "Oh, and stay awake and be careful. Don't let Outo in."

Oh, shit, I thought. I had forgotten about Outo. This was the Orisha that possessed the musicians in the hopes of disrupting the ceremony. I would be especially susceptible to being possessed by Outo since I had no experience with the intricacies of the ritual and the physical demands of playing so intensely for so long.

Though Lloyd spent quite a bit of time in my lessons talking about the Orishas and their relationship with the music and the rituals, it never sank in.

"Orisha's are spirits or ancestors," he described. "They represent archetypes from which we can draw strength or important lessons. We invoke them to help us remember how to act or to guide us through challenging times. We also draw power from these spirits to heal."

"They can also wreak havoc in unstable minds. I'm sure you've heard stories of the possessed as zombies who mindlessly carry out the will of evil spirits or priests. These are distortions of the truth. Sure, there are Manbos that use their power to do bad things, but they are rare and they are not true Shango. Most people who practice Shango follow it for the same reason anyone follows any religion or spiritual practice: For a sense of belonging and for guidance on how to live a good life."

"Shango," he added, "grew out of the practices of my ancestors in

Africa mixed with our oppressors' Christian beliefs. Our spirits are often masked by the Catholic saints, but they are still our ancestors. We connect with our Orisha the same way Catholics seek out their saints."

When Lloyd first introduced the spiritual and religious aspects of the rhythms I was learning, I was uncomfortable. Okay, I'll be honest and say that it kind of freaked me out.

After all, I was a 20-year-old kid from a small town in Minnesota raised in the conservative world of Missouri Synod Lutheranism. Generally a pretty benign faith, the pastor of my childhood church was the fire and brimstone kind of guy. He believed in salvation through fear. Many of his sermons talked of all the ways you could go to hell. So, when Lloyd mentioned the spirits, possession, and the like, I was sure this was one of the ways Pastor Cook would say I'd be riding in the proverbial hand basket to the fiery depths.

I was already on the slippery slope, I figured, because I was a drummer and I often played in bars. This was just another step in the wrong direction. Oh, and I was living in one of the most degenerate of places, Hollywood.

In fact, even though I played for my church's band, I had some history of inviting disapproval within the community for my drumming.

I distinctly remember the day during the spring of my graduation from high school when all the seniors were asked to stand at the altar and declare to our congregation and community what we planned to do now that we were transitioning to adulthood. Most of my fellow graduates were off to college or trade school, a few choosing instead to take full time jobs, and me, well, I made it clear what I was planning to do.

"I'm going to play my drums," I said proudly when it was my turn to declare my future.

There was a chorus of gasps and laughs. My mom went pale, horrified by my blunt admission. I should say that I was a pretty decent student from a good family of college-educated professionals: My dad was a mechanical engineer and my mother, an artist. My brother was already in school for electrical engineering and I had a GPA in the upper 3's. Surely I was one of the college-bound graduates, expected to go into engineering, essentially the family vocation.

But I was cocky, already a seasoned professional, and determined to go on tour with a band for at least a year so I could decide how I wanted to approach my music career and, therefore, my schooling. Of course, I didn't disclose my plan beyond simply playing my drums. And I have to admit, it looked a little shortsighted. So after the service, our pastor pulled me aside and told me how irresponsible I was and how I was going to shame my family and community with my godless ways. He was also clear about his feelings toward playing popular music in bars and consorting with degenerates.

Had he only known that I'd also be consorting with spirits.

When Lloyd talked about the spiritual end of the drumming and the ceremonies, which relied on the drumming, I told him I was uncomfortable with this information. He was respectful of my hesitancy, saying that this aspect of the drumming was often misinterpreted. He also explained that, though the rhythms are tied to the spirits and ceremony, they are also used in secular music. He reminded me that I was learning rhythms on the drumset that have the same basic roots.

He also said that all music is tied to spiritual practices, whether it's the drumming I did in the praise band at my church, the songs I played at clubs or concerts, or the music we'd be playing in his church's ceremonies.

I understood. Still, part of me was sure I'd go to hell.

The ceremony was nearly ready to begin. The offerings and beginnings of a feast were laid out on table along the wall. People were filing into the sanctuary. The Manbo was finishing preparing an herbal tonic. And the sick woman was settling into a chair in front of the band.

Lloyd signaled for Jimmy and me to start the first rhythm. Slowly, at first, we set down a basic pulse. Sheryl quickly joined in and we vamped on (repeated) the groove for a few minutes while people gathered around the sick woman. The Manbo began a simple chant. The congregation began moving in time with the band and our rhythms grew in volume and intensity. Soon Lloyd added a simple melody followed by some solo riffs, which the Manbo played off of with her chanting.

Soon, the Manbo began a call and response pattern that the congregation enthusiastically joined in on. We followed the rhythms as they played us. The group became one singing, dancing life force, following the lead of the Manbo, who was actually taking her cues from Lloyd.

While chanting and swaying to the music, she grabbed fistfuls of the herbal mixture and smeared them on the neck, shoulders, and chest of the sick woman. The sick woman moaned and convulsed.

Lloyd coaxed the Manbo along with solos and chants of his own. By the now the din of the drumming, singing and dancing filled the room. Senses became blurred and the music permeated us at the deepest level, driving us all into another world.

I was starting to feel light-headed. I knew we had been playing for quite a while by this point, so I thought maybe I was getting dehydrated or something. I simplified my rhythm and took a long draw of my water.

Feeling better, I doubled-down on my rhythm. The band joined me, raising our volume yet another notch. The dancers followed suit, intensifying their undulations. Suddenly Lloyd stood up and played a kase', a fast and loud solo passage. Sheryl joined right in. I was startled, because I knew that he would only play a kase' if someone were acting inappropriately.

I looked out toward the dancers and immediately saw what had alarmed Lloyd. There was a young woman flailing around amidst the crowd. I was captivated by the woman's movements because she soon started jerking and moving to Lloyd and Sheryl's rhythms. Or was it the other way around? I couldn't tell.

Quickly they guided her down with their pulsations, starting with chaotic syncopations that matched her jerky movements, followed by smoother repetitive rhythms that settled her down.

This all lasted less than two minutes. No one else seemed to notice. I asked Lloyd about this later and he told me that the woman was beginning to act possessed. Possession is generally encouraged in Shango ceremonies. Because the spirit needs someone to inhabit in order to be present, it will often engage anyone who is sufficiently available. However in this ceremony, the Orisha is only allowed to inhabit the Manbo. Lloyd used his kase' to keep the spirit from entering an unwanted person.

The four of us kept playing. Sweat made our bodies glisten. I was so wet that drops were landing on my drum, stretching the cowhide head and driving the pitch even deeper than it naturally was. I enjoyed the sound so I started pounding my fist into the middle of the head, accentuating the deepest of the tones. Lloyd nodded approval, which was probably a bad idea because I decided that maybe I could do a solo, too.

I jumped in and jammed a few odd meter rhythms. I should say at this point that, although African drumming can appear complex, in the big scheme of things, the rhythms are pretty straightforward. African music, in fact most Western music as well, is either in duple or triple (triplet) feel. That is, you can evenly divide the measures into groups of two or three.

For example, most pop music can be counted 1 & 2 & 3 & 4 &, dividing each beat into two distinct pulses. This is duple feel. Blues or swing music, on the other hand, can be counted 1, tu, tu, 2, tu, tu, etc. (or 1 2 3 4 5 6, with accents on the 1 and 4), dividing each beat into three pulses. This is triple feel.

Traditional music from the East and Middle East often use odd groupings by mixing groupings of two and three beats, but it isn't part of the lexicon of African music.

During the development of progressive jazz and rock, musicians started creating grooves in odd time signatures that combined duple and triple feel in uneven ways. I grew up toward the end of the height of the progressive movement. One of my primary drumset teachers, Ralph Humphrey, was a master, having played with the likes of Frank Zappa and Free Flight. He also authored one of the pre-eminent books on odd meter drumming called, *Even In The Odds*. I was a serious student of his and intent on integrating odd patterns into whatever I was playing. I also had ADHD and was somewhat impulsive to begin with—a deadly combination in an environment like this, where there were very strict rules about what I was to play.

Anyway, at the height of the ritual, in my sweat laden, physically fatigued, possibly delirious state, I decided that I needed to channel my inner Ralph. I didn't get far before Lloyd admonished me with a series of slap tones and a hard stare, jarring me out of my reverie and pulling me back in line.

He later told me that Outo was pushing his way in, which impelled me to play inappropriately. I had felt oddly inspired to play out; but since I had a habit of getting carried away, I wasn't sure about the possession thing. Lloyd said he expected this possession, knowing this was my first ritual. He also knew I had an ego, an ego that he was intent on drilling out of me. I have yet to determine if he was successful.

Luckily, we were almost to the end of the ritual. The Manbo was back to leading a call and response chant. The sick woman was sitting comfortably and being cleaned up by several women. And Lloyd was signaling for us to slow down and switch to our final rhythms.

Once we were done, I never felt so exhausted, or elated, or, in some strange way, cleansed. We enjoyed a feast and upon getting my food I decided to go I outside for some fresh air. The sun was coming up over the hills. I was shocked to see that it was morning! We had played for over six hours! Non-stop!

For tens of thousands of years, drumming and rhythm-making have been used around the world for connecting to the sacred. Group drumming, also called community drumming (and in modern applications, the drum circle), has been used as a means to connect people, to create a common bond among its participants.

In Lloyd's ancestral tradition, the use of drumming within rituals was an extension of the role of drumming, dancing and singing to mark all important events. Music was used to celebrate the harvest, to mark life transitions such as birth, coming of age, marriage, death, and, as I discovered this night, to help connect with the sacred.

Tonight's ritual was designed to invoke a progression of spirits that allowed the Manbo to channel or, in the language of Lloyd's people, possess the priestess. When possessed, she would be able to intuit the cause of the woman's illness and to find a treatment. And in some cases, also heal in a spiritual way.

Treatments included the use of herbal remedies and energetic healing. As the band played, the Manbo smeared the herbs on the woman. At the same time, the Manbo's chanting and swaying connected to the patient's spirit. One of the first things the Manbo did was to see if the woman was possessed and, if so, drive the unwanted spirit out. If the woman's spirit had left her body, the Manbo would retrieve her soul.

Lloyd explained these details, but honestly this world made very little sense to me. Given my background, where the soul was God's domain and fiddling with it or with such things as possession was akin to worshipping the devil, I was very nervous. Lloyd was remarkably respectful of my trepidation and tried as best he could to alleviate my fear by trying to put all this spiritual stuff in a context that I could accept.

Still, my inability to accept the spiritual aspect of the drumming led me to seek an alternative explanation. This path toward an explanation quickly became my journey; I would spend over two decades exploring how rhythm can impact the brain and behavior. I would also come to terms with the spirits, though I prefer to think of them as inspiration and intuition.

• • •

I reflected on this as I answered the woman's question at my presentation for the Louisiana Autism Society conference.

The woman nodded and thanked me for the clarification and I saw the people in the room relax. This wasn't the first time I had confronted a query like this. By this time I had spoken at dozens of autism conferences and was pretty comfortable answering this inevitable question.

I suppose I could have avoided this type of question by simply leaving some of the historical references out of my talks, but I felt that it was important for people to understand that I didn't simply make up this technique. Rhythmic Entrainment Intervention is derived from ancient techniques and it is my responsibility to honor that history as I carry the tradition forward and morph it to meet my needs. Even if it means alienating some people who feel uncomfortable with the origins of drumming.

My talk was a success. So much so, that I was inundated with people wanting to talk with me after I finished and I missed lunch. My audience didn't focus on the scary spirit stuff, instead they took away a vision of being able to calm their children, students, and patients with recorded drumming rhythms. I also sold a ton of CDs, more at that conference than at any other.

Perhaps they weren't as concerned about the spirits as I was.

Chapter Four
Connecting

"Yes, that's right. Open your mind. Play what you hear," Lloyd said encouragingly.

I was in "trance" (whatever that means) playing the drum, connecting to the spirits he and other drummers have employed for eons. Ever since I asked to learn the rhythms he played for his client, Ty, Lloyd had been showing me how to contact the spirits and listen. I was discovering how to hear rather than think. This was a lot harder than parroting the right rhythm. It required having the skill and dexterity to improvise.

This must be what great jazz musicians do, I thought. Entering another state of mind where music is birthed, where sound without thought grows from the ether. This got me thinking about the clinics we had at the Musician's Institute.

Every couple of weeks a famous artist would come to our school and give a clinic. These were accomplished, successful artists from such rock bands as Toto and Heart; the drummer Bill Bruford from the bands Yes and King Crimson; session players like guitarist Tommy Tedesco, who was often called the most recorded guitarist in history; and jazz and blues greats like guitarists Don Mock and Robben Ford.

Inevitably, at every clinic someone would ask about soloing and improvisation. And each time the artist would say something like they weren't really thinking, but they were feeling the music and allowing themselves to hear what the song needs, or something to that effect.

Of course, this was pretty esoteric stuff for a bunch of young musicians. We wanted to know what techniques, rhythms, scales or chords they were playing. This kind of description didn't tell us what to play. And we wanted more than anything to know exactly what to practice so we could be as successful as they were.

Tommy Tedesco, the most pragmatic and helpful of the bunch, always emphasized that we study our scales, chords, and rhythms to the point that we could play them smoothly at all tempos and move fluidly from one to the other. From that basis, and through experience playing with others, we would develop a vocabulary of licks, fills and passages that we could use as the foundation to create something appropriate for the song. If we practiced a lot and got lucky, we may actually create something new.

To create a counter-point to this argument, Tommy also described that with his really fast guitar riffs he would choose a starting and ending note and just play anything in between to fill the space. He said that the notes went by so fast that, even if they were in the wrong key, it wouldn't matter because the listener couldn't process the music quickly enough to discern all the notes in the progression. As long as the first and last notes were in key, it would sound right.

He dramatically demonstrated this with some famous guitar licks played with a variety of on and off key middle notes. His presentation always elicited some laughter, but what he played always worked. Tommy was a genius, an expert guitar player, and was much more astute about music processing and perception than we gave him credit for.

Tommy gave clinics often and was always a hit. Even though I wasn't a guitar player, I found more inspiration and practical information on session work from Tommy than from any other clinician, with the exception of drummer Jeff Porcaro, who taught me what it meant to groove through interpretation of feel, something I talk more about in Chapter 8.

So, here I was, playing for Lloyd as he guided me to listen to the spirits; and I was thinking about how this must be what great improvisers do. Okay, maybe not the spirit thing. But the letting go of intellectual thoughts and trying to listen, to hear what should be played rather than thinking about what to play.

This is amazing, I thought. I was playing rhythms I had never played before, things that made no sense musically, but still worked.

"No, did you hear that," admonished Lloyd. "You're not listening. Don't try to steer the music. Let it carry you along."

I grunted and tried to clear my mind. No, it wasn't working. I lost it.

I stopped playing, frustrated.

"When the spirits come, you need to pay attention to them or they'll leave. They have no patience for your ego. You need to learn to keep it out of the room. You listen and you play. You don't think."

I grunted.

"Try again," he said.

I took a few breaths to calm myself and started playing again. I began with a variation on a Samba rhythm in an attempt to settle my thoughts, to get my head and my ego out of the way. Playing a repetitive rhythm that I know really well helps me focus on relaxing my hands and shoulders. This takes my mind off what I'm playing and opens me up to letting intuition, or spirit, or whatever, guide me.

Next I put Lloyd in my mind and asked myself what he needed, as he taught me. I watched him closely as I played, noticing any changes in his posture or expression.

"You have to connect with your patient. Create a dialog between his spirit and yours. The Orisha will help if you let them, but you need to find your patient's spirit in order to heal," he described.

I wasn't very good at this spirit thing; but I discovered that if I paid close attention to someone's response to my music, I could just let myself be there with him and play what provided the most positive impact. Sometimes, I couldn't tell if what I was doing worked; but if I then focused on playing as relaxed and fluidly as possible, I would get a sense of what to play next.

"Yes, you got it now. See how that feels? No thought, just flow."

This connection, whether inspired by spirit or not, would be the most challenging thing for me and would take me the better part of a decade to understand.

Lloyd and I traded playing for one another for many months. I learned to see how rhythms affected him and learned to feel for myself the rhythmic impact of his focus and intention on me. Once he was comfortable with my skills, of my ability to get out of the way, he let me play for other people.

Still, I didn't feel comfortable. Lloyd assured me that I would get it. That I would develop the sense necessary to connect and stay connected. The entire time that I studied with him, however, I never felt that I could do it. This is one of the reasons that I drifted back to a typical music career.

Over the years, though, what I learned and lived through with Lloyd tugged at me. I was determined to find a way to really connect, to be able to access the depths that he assured me were there for me if I could just surrender.

Several years later, as I happened upon another approach using drumming to affect the listener, I came close to completing the circle. This second technique was designed to allow the listener to go deep. When I had the opportunity to explore this approach I took it. Not without difficulties, however.

● ● ●

Why is this always so exhausting, I thought to myself. Here I was beating the drum again for hours on end. Whoever said that drumming was easy didn't play for these kinds of rituals. My arms were tired, I was thirsty, and I was sweating profusely. My head felt like it was going to explode and I was fighting sleep.

Fending off unconsciousness, I tried to maintain my job of keeping the steady beat of the drum going without stopping or even changing. My drumming was the tether that held Colin to this world. He was deep in trance; and without my drumming, he may not be able to accomplish his goal or to find his way back.

At this point, I had traded teachers. My studies with Lloyd had reached their end, and I now carried within me a centuries old lineage of drummers initiated into the Shango tradition. But I was a reluctant member of the lineage. And here I was, several years later, exploring yet another age-old drumming technique. A world where, instead of invoking Orisha to appear in our world, I was attempting to become a traveler in a tradition where the drum was a vehicle to other worlds, of places where mysteries unraveled and healing could be initiated.

This is the world of the shaman. And the vehicle for the shaman is the drum. I was playing the drum so that Colin, my teacher, could enter the shaman's world to access spirits to diagnose or facilitate healing. This tradition is one of the most prevalent in the world, existing on each continent in essentially the same way.

Shamanism involves using the pulse of the drum to shift his consciousness and drive him into an altered state, an internalized state where the shaman's spirit can journey into unseen realms.

When I first encountered Shamanism, I was as curious and concerned as when I studied with Lloyd. On one hand, I was intrigued by the idea that a simple beat of a drum could hold the key to a technique used for so long by so many people. On the other hand, I was again concerned with the focus on the spiritual dimension. There had to be another way to view this, I thought.

Colin, like Lloyd, saw my struggles; therefore, he let me play the drum while I gained an understanding of the shaman's role in the care of his patient. Ordinarily, the shaman would play his own drum and traverse both the shamanic and regular world in what is known as the Shamanic State of Consciousness (SSC).

I got up and began circling the room as I played. I'd been drumming for over an hour by this point and it was becoming increasingly difficult to continue. I figured moving my body would wake me up and recharge me. I kept watching Colin for a signal that he was ready to return.

So far, nothing.

I was concerned that I would fail. Even after over a year of studying with him, I still had not found my bearing with this approach.

Sure, the rhythms were easy. So easy that anyone could play them. Too easy. No skill needed. It didn't take a drummer with my technical abilities. What it did take was someone with a strong internal bearing—a calm mind and steady resolve. I was neither calm nor steady. This was my challenge and, honestly, one of the reasons I'd been sticking this out. I knew I needed to develop this skill of calming my unruly ADHD mind and controlling my thoughts.

Grumbling as I thought of this, I kept banging away, waiting for a signal that I could change up the rhythm and bring him back.

Finally, he signaled and I pounded out four half-tempo beats, then sped up the core rhythm as he stirred and awoke. He was back.

I played for Colin many times and he played for me, trying help me in the same way Lloyd did. Sure, I could play all day long (not without discomfort, but that's to be expected), but I just couldn't settle my mind. Part of it may have been my ADHD, but I was sure there was more to it. So I kept searching, looking for a way to quiet my mind. I eventually found it in the most unexpected place.

• • •

With trepidation, I drove up to a mid-century suburban house. I had been told that I couldn't hide anything from the woman inside. And at the same time, I wanted more than anything to be accepted by her. Needless to say, I was nervous.

I rang the bell and an attractive, petite, dark-haired woman in her mid-thirties answered the door.

"Come in Jeff," she said.

"Is Rachel here?" I asked, figuring that this couldn't be the wise old woman I was told to see.

"I'm Rachel," she paused, as she looked me over. My heart rate jumped.

"You seem surprised."

"No, no, I'm not surprised," I stammered, trying to be cool, while feeling a flush pass over my cheeks.

She gave me a skeptical look and guided me into her office, a spare bedroom with two chairs and a small table holding a cassette tape recorder and a lit candle.

"Sit. Relax," she instructed.

I did. I tried.

"And breathe," she added with a smile.

After a pause, "I'm going to spend a couple of minutes and check in. Then I'll ask you for your full name and date of birth."

I sat quietly, trying to breathe, my chest heavy. I was nervous. Rachel was a teacher and a spiritual intuitive. One of my friends had taken her class and said it was transformational. Rachel, I was told, could see things in the spirit world and, if she was willing, could teach me to see these things as well.

With my past failures to connect with spirits while I studied with Lloyd and Colin, I was hoping that Rachel could help me find that connection.

I struggled to keep calm, to keep my anxiety at bay. I worried that she would see through me, see the fraud that I was.

"Just try to relax. I'm not going to hurt you," she said with a warm smile as she turned on the tape recorder. She then recited the date.

"Say your name and date of birth."

I did, more nervous than ever. Not sure what to expect.

Rachel talked for almost an hour, peeling my world open in layers and leaving me naked, exposed, but somehow also healed. I felt elated—and whole—for the first time in my life.

She saw my needs, my fears, my deepest desires laid bare. I'd been in countless therapy sessions and I'd been to spiritualists before, but never had I experienced such a deep healing. I wanted to take her class. Needed to. I knew it would bring into focus all I had been researching with the drumming. I also felt, deep inside, that it would help me define and refocus my life.

For the last several years, I had been drifting, my sense of purpose and sureness with my career had faded. I was tired of touring for peanuts and working at night producing bands with the slimmest chance of success. I was recently divorced and dissatisfied. I hadn't been sleeping and often woke up anxious at night.

I also hadn't been drumming in the ways I had when I studied with Lloyd. When I left L.A. five years before, I left all I learned with him behind. His world scared me, and I felt like I failed at the spirit work.

Failed is probably not the right word. Rejected, is probably more accurate. I didn't believe. I saw amazing, mind-boggling things at the ceremonies and when playing with Lloyd's patients. I just didn't feel comfortable with the spiritual end of it. I felt way out of my depth and a fraud for thinking I could use drumming that way. And I suppose I was also afraid of what would happen if I did surrender.

It's not that I didn't think the drumming had power and could heal, but I didn't think it applied to me. And Lloyd told me that unless I could surrender and accept the spirit, I would never be able to do what he could. I'd never be able to access the power that the drum had to offer. I'd just be a musician, which was fine, he said, if that's the path I wanted. But I could have more if I was willing to open myself to spirit.

I couldn't.

So I gave up. I moved out of L.A. and followed a typical career in music. It was very satisfying for several years. I was busy playing live shows, many times with famous artists, and recording sessions with some amazing songwriters and singers. I taught both drum set and hand drums and produced up and coming acts. But as time rolled on, this path felt empty.

It wasn't me. But what was?

This was why I came to see Rachel and why I so desperately wanted to get into her class. I was told that she only took students that she felt she could help. And even if she accepted you, it wasn't uncommon to have to wait years to get into one of her classes, as each class was a year long and had limited enrollment.

I sat with my chest closing in on me as she finished with the reading. I was nervous that she wouldn't offer me a spot in her next class, which was starting the next week. If I didn't get into this one, I didn't know what I'd do.

"Breathe," she said as she chuckled lightly. Rachel, I would learn over my time studying with her, had a great sense of humor and could dissipate her student's pain and anxiety with a smile and laugh. She was also a tough nut; if you challenged her boundaries, consciously or not, she would put you in your place.

I breathed and relaxed a bit. I must have had a pleading look on my face, because she finally said, "You can't take my class unless you can stay in your own space," answering my unspoken question.

"You have potential, but you're all over the place. I can help you with that, but you need to promise to stay in your space."

Not knowing what the heck she was talking about, I said, "I can do that."

"Okay. I'm going to give you some homework. Let me show you how to gather your energy."

"Breathe. Now look up into the corner of the room. Imagine yourself there."

I tried.

"You don't have to try so hard. Just imagine yourself in the corner. No effort."

I breathed and just assumed I was in the corner, though I really didn't feel it.

"That's it. Do you feel that?"

"No."

"Alright," she smiled, I suppose, thinking I was kidding. I wasn't.

"Now let's get you grounded," she said. "Close your eyes and imagine roots growing from the bottom of your feet, running down to the very center of the earth. Don't think too hard. Just postulate that these roots go all the way to the center of the earth," she added.

I tried. Really hard. I think she saw me screwing up my face because she said, "No effort. Just let it happen. Surrender."

These would be words I heard lot over the next year and a half that I studied with her. No effort. Surrender. These were also words Lloyd and Colin used. There must be something to it, I thought.

"Good. Now that the roots are at the center of the earth, imagine neutral grounding energy coming up through the roots. Feel this energy in your feet, bring it up your legs, past your belly button and into a spot just under your sternum. This is your power center. Now let this energy flow through your body. Do you feel that?"

"Yes, I feel heavier," I said. This was amazing, I thought. I could feel the weight in my feet. I could feel the pressure of the chair against my body. I could even feel the tips of my fingers. I was grounded. It felt good.

"So is this what it feels like to be grounded?" I asked.

"Yes," she said and watched me curiously as I soaked in this unfamiliar feeling.

After a few minutes, she nodded slightly, smiled, then said, "Okay, do this every morning when you get up and every night before you go to bed. Class starts on Tuesday."

I was in! I left feeling hopeful.

Six months later I was deep into my studies with Rachel and already making big changes to my life.

"Jeff, get over to the club or you're no longer my producer. Or my friend," Ben's voice demanded from my answering machine. "I need you here. The sound man sucks," he added.

I'd just arrived home from my class with Rachel and knew that I needed to change my life. I couldn't go to the club. This was the best club in town, world famous actually, but I didn't have it in me to show up. I was tired of the noise and the false promise each of my artists were continually subjected to at the hands of club owners, managers, record labels, and producers like me. We strung them along saying we were nurturing their careers, all the while not having the tough conversations with them about their music or their prospects of actually getting anywhere in this field.

The phone rang again. This time I picked it up. It was Ben, of course. "Jeff, where are you, man? We need you here."

"I can't do it, Ben. I'm done producing. I'm sorry, man, but the sound guys there are top notch. They'll take care of you. I've worked with them dozens of times and, honestly, I'd just be standing there doing nothing."

"You can't just bail on us. I'll pick you up. I'll be in there in ten."

"Don't bother. I'm not going. I'm sorry, I'm done."

Asshole move? Yep, I was an asshole. And even after more than twenty years, I feel really crappy about bailing on Ben.

He wasn't kidding, by the way. I lost a friend that day. Two actually—Ben and his wife, who played bass in his band. Neither of them talked to me again.

Studying with Rachel changed my life. She pushed and challenged me and stripped away all the barriers that existed between me and my inner voice. From this, I started making changes to my work.

And I finally began to understand and integrate what Lloyd and Colin had been trying to teach me. For me, it ultimately wasn't about spirits. Perhaps it's my conservative upbringing, but I found that the language of spirits distracted and detracted from my understanding of what I could do with a drum.

Like the clinicians at my school, I focused on developing my skills to a point that I could play just about anything I could think of. Learning how to listen to a quiet inner voice allowed me to sense which rhythm, technique, or variation on a rhythm would work in a particular instance. My skill as a drummer allowed me to alter the rhythm in the moment in ways that I could not have planned beforehand.

Playing for someone is essentially composing music through improvisation. And my collaborators in this improv were not other musicians, but the very individuals I was playing for. Instead of using other musicians to play off of, I was using my powers of observation to see what to play next. As I played for more people and watched their responses to my drumming, I began to see the patterns in the rhythms and techniques.

My close observations of these rhythm patterns and their corresponding client responses allowed me to refine the rhythms to a very fine degree. This process led to the rhythms, algorithms, and protocols that form the basis of Rhythmic Entrainment Intervention. No spirits necessary.

Chapter Five

Auditory Driving

Closing my eyes, I began with a steady beat of the drum. The drum's rhythm filled my senses. I could feel it pulsing into the deepest recesses of my being. As the sound of the drum bounced off the walls of the small bare room, my ears started playing tricks on me. I heard one voice, then another. They spoke to me in a language without words, just vibration. Soon I heard more drums, more voices singing. Next, a chorus of angels. After a while I no longer heard the drum's beat, but felt it in my body as my temples pulsated to its incessant rhythm.

My body grew heavy. I felt like I was being pushed into the ground, while at the same time being lifted, drawn out of my body by the beat of the drum. This sensation faded as I rode the rhythm to a world much different than my own.

This is a proven way to transcend reality and enter the shaman's realm. And because of its absolute effectiveness, this technique has been steadfastly practiced for centuries. Ancient societies discovered this through years of experimentation, but modern man has labeled it, giving it a scientific sounding name: auditory driving.

The shaman's technique relies on a fundamental aspect of the human nervous system: Our brains are rhythmically organized. Brain activity is measured as electrical impulses, and the speed of these impulses—described as frequencies—determine our level of consciousness. There are four basic levels of human consciousness, each represented by different frequency ranges.

The slowest brain wave state is delta, which comprises frequencies up to 4 hertz (a hertz is one cycle per second). This state of consciousness is associated with unconsciousness and the deepest level of sleep.

The second level of consciousness, called theta, exists between 4 and 8 hertz. This state is where hallucinations and imagery take place and is the state we enter when we meditate or go on a shamanic journey.

The third state of consciousness is called alpha, encompassing brainwave activity between 8 and 13 hertz. Alpha is considered a relaxed-yet-alert state where we are aware of our external world, but we are relaxed.

The fourth level of consciousness is beta. Beta exists between 13 and 30 hertz and is our normal, wakeful state of being. High beta exists above 30 hertz and is associated with manic states and feelings of euphoria.

Our brainwaves can be influenced by external stimulus. When I was drumming, my brain began to pulsate in time with the beat. In this instance, the pulsations were roughly four beats per second, deep in the theta state of consciousness. This drove my awareness within and altered my sense of reality. As I drifted into theta, images crossed my mind and I entered into what Michael Harner, the grandfather of contemporary shamanism, refers to as the Shamanic State of Consciousness (SSC). In the shamanic state, imagery has a purpose and the traveler, hopefully, is able to have some sense of control over his experiences.

When successful, the imagery of a shamanic journey and the rituals that are part of the experience are immensely powerful. So much so that the marriage of imagery and ritual became the focal point of much research. The drum's rhythm became secondary.

For me, the rhythm was the focal point.

I should probably say that one of the reasons my work has taken the direction it has is because I'm not a romantic. Many musicians are romantics. Emotion drives creativity. The best songs are those written when the artist is in the throes of intense emotion. Love songs exploring the angst of a lost love capture the songwriter's heartache as he mines the depths of his despair.

Great artists draw from these emotions. They are romantics. Feel drives their art. I don't have it. Sure I feel, but it's tempered by something else—the need to understand, to see some connection to something beyond what's on the surface. I like to understand things in an analytical way. Focusing on the rhythm allowed me to do this.

When I was learning the rhythms and techniques from Lloyd, I was trying to understand how he chose each rhythm and how he worked with each client. With the shamanic technique, I began to explore why the drumming was used to facilitate journeys.

I sought out research that looked at how drumming could alter consciousness in the form of auditory driving. At the time (circa 1990), there was no data showing that the pulse of the drum altered a listener's consciousness; the first study wasn't published until 1994. This forced me to expand my research beyond drumming to find anything suggesting that music or sound is able to alter consciousness.

About the same time that researchers were looking at shamanic drumming (and focusing on the rituals or the imagery), other people were exploring rhythm in a different way. They did this through frequency, using a phenomenon called binaural beats or beat frequencies.

Binaural beats were first discovered in 1839 and relate to our ability to determine where sounds are coming from. The minor differences in phase from the sound going in one ear and the sound going in the other allows us to know where the sound is coming from. This ability also allows our brains to perceive slight differences in frequencies and to perceive them as pulsations. These are called beat frequencies or binaural beats.

Researchers discovered that when one sound is audible in one ear and another sound of similar frequency is heard in the other ear, the brain actually perceives the difference between these two as a sound pulsation, or third frequency. For example, if one sound frequency of 400hz is played in one ear while the other hears a frequency of 404hz, the resulting binaural beat would be 4 hz—the difference between the two frequencies. This third frequency is heard as a pulsation rather than a tone, allowing the brain to entrain. In this instance the brain begins to oscillate at the 4 hz frequency, resulting in a theta state of consciousness.

The use of binaural beats to entrain the frequencies of the brain was the primary outlet for auditory driving for several decades. The bias toward this approach over traditional shamanic drumming is purely cultural. Binaural beats are no more effective at inducing altered states of consciousness than the age-old drumming technique; however, as a culture we are more accepting of something that relies on a new technology over the low-tech. Add to that our suspicion of drumming in general and the scales easily tip toward binaural beats.

From a commercial standpoint, it's easy to make products containing binaural beats. All you really need is a tone generator and some nature sounds to mix with the tones. Then you can load the music into any number of devices. In fact, numerous mind machines have been created since the 1970's, all using binaural beats.

There are tons of shamanic drumming recordings available, but they tend to be more specialized, focusing mainly on traditional core shamanism or journeying rather than brainwave entrainment or cognitive enhancement. And because they are lower tech, they aren't perceived as sexy as machines that drive the brain. As well, binaural beats rely on technology and can be patented, as Robert Monroe did in 1975. His Frequency Following Response became Hemi-Synch® and the basis for dozens of products and programs.

• • •

As I drummed, I sensed that I was floating and at the same time, descending. Through the darkness I could see what looked like an arched stone tunnel with steps leading downward. It was damp. Cool water seeped between the stones in the walls, allowing ferns to grow along the steps and between the cracks. I was descending the steps, but seemed to be floating over rather than walking on them. After a while I approached large, ancient-looking wooden door with a rusty wrought iron handle. The handle was cold and wet. As I opened the door, I entered a forest of huge and grotesquely shaped oak trees. The trees were bare and so was the ground. Everything had a lifeless, gray tint to it.

I walked through this silent, barren landscape for a distance as a vibrantly-colored eagle soared overhead. I felt compelled to follow it and was drawn deeper into the forest. As I walked on, the trees became more dense. Serpent-like vines covered the trees and danced in the wind, sending chills down my spine. I soon lost sight of the eagle as the forest became so thick that I could barely squeeze through the undergrowth. Afraid and tired, I was ready to turn back when I got the feeling that I'd been here before. My heart started racing as I remembered why.

With a lump in my throat and tightness in my chest, I startled alert.

I had visited this place fifteen years earlier. For my twelfth birthday, I had received a strobe light and often sat in bed listening to music while I watched the light bounce off the walls. On several occasions when the music stopped, I realized that I was unable to move. Though I felt awake—aware of my room and everything in it—I was strangely conscious of another world altogether. Shadows on the wall became people in my mind, furniture and clothing seemed to move, voices came from nowhere. I found that if I closed my eyes, I was carried off into different landscapes. Occasionally, I found myself standing at the same door I saw in this shamanic journey; and upon opening it, I entered the same bleak forest with the same brilliant eagle soaring overhead. This landscape felt ominous to me. Each time I got caught in the thicket, I panicked and bolted awake.

Those experiences were my first encounters with the shamanic state of consciousness, though I was unaware of it at the time. I just thought it was the fertile imagination of a young and untamed mind. It wasn't until I saw these images while drumming that I understood that the flash of the strobe light, when set at just the right speed, had the same impact on my consciousness as the shamanic drumbeat.

Called photic driving, this effect was first described in 125 AD when Apuleius discovered that a flashing light could induce a form of epilepsy. This technique draws from the shaman's use of fire and candles during rituals and is triggered by the same mechanism within our nervous systems as auditory driving.

Both these techniques rely on the fact that sensory stimulus, once it enters the brain, travels to a nerve center at the base of the brain called the reticular activating system (RAS), also called the reticular formation. The RAS is our brain's internal volume control and sensory administrator. It dictates what sensory information is sent to the cortex and thalamus. The RAS distinguishes between the various sensory input, relates it to past experiences and beliefs, and routes this information to the appropriate part of the brain. The RAS also controls brain wave activity.

The repetitive nature of the shaman's drum beat or the pulses of a strobe light activate the RAS, eventually overtaking the primary rhythm of the brain, entraining the brain to its rhythm and causing a shift in consciousness.

Both the drum and the strobe light quickly drove me into a deep theta state, but something always pushed me out. I rejected the shaman's trance the same way I rejected the spirits when I studied with Lloyd. As powerful as the rhythm of the drum is at shifting consciousness, this shift won't happen if the journeyer's associations or beliefs are in conflict with the imagery or sensations present in theta.

Auditory driving, especially to the internally-directed state of theta, requires a surrender into the process. This was my problem. The images and feelings that I experienced were so otherworldly and in conflict with my deeply ingrained beliefs that I always bolted awake, in panic. My conservative upbringing wouldn't allow me to successfully navigate the shaman's realm. And until I was able to release this internal conflict, I wouldn't be successful in the shaman's world.

• • •

With the lights turned down low and a candle flickering in the corner, I started with a shake of a gourd rattle while standing in the center of the room. After that, I walked around in a circle, shaking the rattle and reciting an invocation. I knew it didn't really matter what I said. The important thing was to create an environment outside the participants' ordinary reality. To fulfill their expectations, this needed to feel like a sacred ceremonial space, for they were to embark on their first shamanic journey. I continued walking around the room. Then I picked up my drum and beat it rapidly between invocations; I stood over each of those present and pounded the drum in rapid succession for a few beats.

My goal was to break them out of their normal awareness of the world so that when I finally did start playing the shamanic drumbeat they would each be more susceptible to my rhythm and the shaman's trance. Although auditory driving is a powerful force and can effectively alter a person's consciousness, the human nervous system tends toward stability and resists change. Called homeostasis, this tendency often works against those trying to enter an altered state of consciousness.

Breaking the listener's brain out of its set pattern requires throwing off the sensory system sufficiently enough to allow for change. By turning down the lights and lighting candles, I was able to help them relax by reducing the amount of sensory input they had to process. Then by using the rattle and speaking ritualistically, I gave them a sense that something special and unique was about to take place. This heightened their attention to what I was about to do and further pulled them away from their normal, everyday world. By the time I started playing the shamanic beat, they would be eagerly anticipating the journey and more physiologically prepared for it.

Once I finished pounding the drum over everyone, I stood in

the center of the room and began playing the steady monotonous rhythm of the shaman. I glanced around the room while I played the drum. Most of them had no experience with shamanic practices and few had even tried meditation; however, all were serious about entering the shaman's realm, I knew that some of them would need additional help.

For the first several minutes that I played, many of the participants shifted their positions in an effort to get more comfortable. Most settled down quickly enough, except Jim, who was still fidgeting after five minutes. Jim was a self-described Type-A personality. During the introductions at the beginning of the workshop, he proudly announced that he liked to work hard and play hard. He described that he didn't have much patience for sitting quietly and was a miserable failure at his attempts at meditation or visualization. At the urging of his doctor, he was trying to learn to slow down.

As I watched him over the next several minutes, he seemed engaged in a bizarre ballet of sorts. An arm would move, followed by a leg, a hip, a twist of the head, or a shake of a foot. This all would have been funny except for the fact that he was truly frustrated with trying to relax and enter an altered state of consciousness. He seemed to be about ready to abandon it altogether.

There was nothing wrong with Jim. Everyone varies in his ability to experience the shamanic journey or meditate. Since the eighteenth century, scientists have recognized that some people are more neurologically susceptible to entering a meditative or hypnotic state than others. Cultural conditioning also has something do with it, as in my case. I was concerned enough about the spiritual end of things and how it conflicted with my religious upbringing that I was always resistant, therefore unable to successfully journey until I worked through my issues with Rachel.

When I first drummed the shaman's beat, I erected walls and resisted the drum's pull. Rachel helped me cope with my beliefs so that I could lower my resistance, and she helped me take control of my mind so that I could learn to trust my instincts. My analytic research of shamanic states allowed me to surrender into the process, knowing that I wasn't communing with the devil. I was simply allowing my brainwave patterns to shift and synchronize with the drumming.

I watched Jim as I played and knew that his struggles to enter the shaman's trance were not from a conflict of beliefs, rather it was an inability to focus his mind and eliminate distracting thoughts. I had a solution to this and quietly asked him to turn on the tape player that I'd given him before the session. He slid on the headphones and started the tape. This was my insurance for people like Jim who have difficulty focusing their minds or who put so much pressure on themselves to be successful that the stress keeps them from being able to relax enough for the drum to do its work.

The tape playing on Jim's Walkman (yes, a cassette player called a Walkman—this was in 1991) contained a narration of a traditional journey. In it, Jim was walked through a mental exercise where he was asked to relax one part of his body at a time. The narration took him from his toes to his head. Once he was relaxed, he was then guided through the journey by first imagining the entrance to the "underworld" (not the bible's underworld, rather, an earthly place). It could be like the door I entered, or it could be rabbit hole, a puddle, pond or lake, or a tear in the bark of a tree. From the entrance, Jim entered a shamanic landscape where he was asked to explore this world and observe what he saw, heard, and felt.

Narration is one technique that I've found to work for people who have difficulty with their first journey. Michael Harner, in his popular core shamanism workshops, also found that beginner journeyers often have more success while using a similar technique that he called a "simultaneous narration technique". In his technique, rather than narrate the journey for the participant, Harner asks the journeyer to verbally describe their experience as it unfolds. He describes in the instructions for one of his journeying CDs, "surprisingly, simultaneous narration usually makes journeying easier and often at least twice as vivid as when the person simply remains silent". This technique works well when journeying alone, but can be distracting when in a group. This is why I gave Jim a tape.

Jim seemed to settle down shortly after starting the narration. I glanced around and noticed another participant, Kathy, beginning to fidget. I started varying my rhythm a little by circling the head of the drum and deliberately making my pulse slightly erratic. She settled down again.

Kathy, like many people, was becoming habituated to the repetitive beat of the drum. Habituation, also called tolerance, occurs when the stimulus becomes too predictable. The nervous system treats it as "noise" and begins to block it out so other, potentially more important, stimulus can be attended to. Habituation is an important component of the primitive part of our brains. Our ability to screen out repetitive or non-threatening stimulus allows us to be alert to novel stimulus that may pose a threat to our survival.

For example, we become habituated to the constant stream of traffic passing by outside the window, the incessant ticking of a clock on our nightstand, or the torturous dripping of the faucet in the bathroom. Our ability to screen out these sounds allows us to be attuned to sounds that may demand our immediate attention.

Habituation is generally not much of a concern with shamanic drumming because of the variable nature of the drum's sound and the inconsistency of most shamanic drummers. The myriad of overtones and the inexact pounding of most drummers keep it at bay. Contrasted with the technologically precise binaural beats where habituation can be a real problem, the minor issues with the drum pale. The Monroe Institute, in order to avoid habituation, adds the sound of surf or other non-competing noises to keep the RAS from becoming habituated and shutting the sound out.

I stopped playing after about 25 minutes and all the people lying on the floor remained silent for several minutes. I slowly brought up the lights and, as the journeyers sat up, I asked them to write down what they experienced.

Processing the journey is an important part of the shamanic practice. It is the imagery seen by the journeyer that facilitates the healing, rather than the drumming itself. The drumming is an important component of the shaman's work, but it only acts as the vehicle to the realms where the visions take place.

Shamanic practices utilize the theta state of consciousness exclusively. Theta is thought to be the bridge between the seen and unseen world. Visual images predominate and intuition is heightened. In theta, the analytical mind becomes subdued and we are more open to the images and messages coming from the unseen world.

• • •

Still drumming, I finally settled back into my journey and found that I was still stuck in the gloomy forest where the eagle had disappeared behind the thicket. Afraid and tired, I was ready to turn back when I got a glimpse of the eagle circling to my right just beyond the thicket. I made my way toward the eagle and found a spot to crawl under the brush. Once through, the gray, desolate forest gave way to a fantastic meadow that stretched to the horizon and beyond. This meadow was filled with wildflowers of every imaginable color. Vivid blues, reds, yellows, and purples glowed against the emerald grass. Birds filled the air with their songs. I sat in the grass and started to cry. This is such a beautiful place, I thought to myself. I felt immense joy and love surrounding me.

As the sun warmed my body, the eagle circled then landed next to me. It was an enormous creature, but I was not afraid. I felt a deep kinship with this animal and reached out when it said, "You're not following your heart. Your world is like the forest, dark, cold, lifeless. You created this world out of your fear. Your stomach pains are your inner voice telling you that what you're doing is incorrect for you. Breathe into the fear and follow your heart. If you follow your spirit, you will find a world like this meadow, full of color, light and love. You'll create beautiful things when you trust your intuition and release your fear."

I sat, staring at the eagle as it flew off and disappeared over the horizon. I heard faint drumming in the distance. I walked through the meadow and along a stream toward this sound. The stream ended at a small pond. The drumming seemed to be coming from the pond, so I dove in and swam toward the drum's call. I swam for several minutes and realized that I could breathe in the water. Diving deeper, I noticed a cave to my left and swam into it. I was propelled upward in a spout of water. The drumming became louder. I suddenly awoke in the darkened room.

I sat up and grabbed my notebook, intent on documenting my journey in as much detail as I could. This journey was a powerful experience for me. It was my first successful journey where I actually saw things. All my previous attempts with the shamanic drumbeat left me either fidgeting like Jim or falling asleep. Like my attempts to connect in with Lloyd, my fear and resistance kept me from sur-rendering into the process. And because this journey was linked to visions I had as a teen, I felt I had finally opened the door to learn something profound.

According to many shamanic cultures, interpretation of the jour-ney is left up to the person having the vision. In fact, in many societ-ies, even sharing the contents of a journey is considered back luck. In our modern society, however, more and more psychotherapists are using the shamanic journey as a tool to uncover keys to a patient's psychological and emotional discomfort.

My journey was fairly representative of the archetype of the sha-manic journey. The eagle imparting wisdom harkens to the idea of a power animal or animal spirit, and the barren earth-based imagery suggests lack of clarity. But not everyone experience these types of visions. One participant of a workshop I led on shamanic journeying had this to say about her first journey:

"I tried to visualize a tunnel like you said but found myself walking down a corridor instead. It was a sterile environment, like a hospital or school building and no one was around. The hallway was straight and went on as far as I could see. Doors were lined up on either side and were all closed. Although I was completely alone, I didn't feel scared. I walked slowly from one door to the next, opening each one to see what was inside. Many of them opened to nothingness, others to empty rooms, but behind one door I found a torn and tattered doll. It was the same doll I played with as a child. I set down on the floor and held it close to me. That's when I heard the drum-signal telling me to come back. I put the doll down, walked out of the room, and back down the corridor the way I came. Then I woke up."

Not everyone has a visual experience in the shaman's world. In fact, only about 55% of the population experience visual images in their minds. The rest "see" in different ways, using different senses. Just as each person has a different learning style—some are visual learners, others auditory, and still others kinesthetic—so, too, everyone's imagery style is unique. Another workshop participant, Charlie, described a world in black and white with a very physical quality to it:

"When you started the drumming, I tired to see an opening in the earth but couldn't. After a while I just imagined that I was swimming, which is something I love to do. I could feel the cool water on my body and the force of the water against my arms and legs as I swam. I don't remember seeing anything, but I felt a sense of things floating by me. I decided that I had swum far enough and climbed out of the water to see if I could see the underworld. It was dark and out of focus. Again, I got a sense of things around me, but couldn't see them with my eyes. I heard something rustling next to me and asked who it was. 'I'm a duck', it replied. We talked for a few minutes until I heard the call to return."

Too often, beginners expect the journey to be visual. And when it's not, they feel like they've failed. Within the shaman's world, all of our senses come into play. We can see, hear, smell, feel, and even just get a subtle sense of something. For many people, multiple senses are involved, and for others, the senses change over time.

This was the case for me. As I let go of my contrary beliefs by studying with Rachel and practicing journeying with the techniques Colin taught me, I discovered that my senses became more attuned. My journeys became less visual and more simply a sense. I would discover that this is what Lloyd talked about when he asked me to listen to the spirits. According to Lloyd, I needed to get to the point where intuition (spirit) would whisper in my ear. At that point, I would be able to truly connect with the spirits.

Spirits or not, it became clear to me, as I studied the shamanic rhythm and its connection to brainwave entrainment, that my studies of African rhythm with Lloyd, particularly in ceremony, also relied on inducing a theta state of consciousness.

The shamanic drumbeat is played around four beats per second, at the low end of the theta range. Traditional African drumming (in fact nearly all traditional drumming and most music in general) is solidly within the theta frequency range.

Once we translate brain wave frequencies into musical terms and analyze their tempos with relation to these frequencies, we begin to get a sense of how these frequencies can be played and written as musical rhythm. Musical notation is described in beats per minute while frequencies are defined in terms of hertz—cycles per second. In order for the shamanic rhythm of four beats per second to be notated in musical terms, we need to do some basic math.

The most common time signature for Western music is 4/4. For this notation, the top number represents how many beats there are in each measure, in this case 4, and the bottom number represents the denomination of the note that receives one beat, in this case it's the quarter note (1/4). Tempo markings always correspond to the note that gets one beat. Again, in this case, it's the quarter note. Measures are divided up using various denominations of notes, which generally range from whole notes to sixteenth notes. For the purpose of this explanation, each beat of the drum will equal a single sixteenth note. Therefore the shamanic beat of four beats-per-second would be equivalent to four sixteenth notes per second, or one quarter note per second (there are four sixteenth notes per quarter note). This gives the shamanic drumming rhythm a tempo of 60 beats per minute in 4/4 time.

Using this formula, the theta range of four to eight cycles per second corresponds musically to tempos between 60 and 120 beats per minute when playing sixteenth notes in 4/4 time. Nearly all traditional drumming occurs within this range. In fact, most music lies somewhere in this range as well. For example, much of the andante sections of classical Baroque period music are played at 60 beats per minute while many of John Phillips Sousa's marches occur around

120 beats per minute. Likewise, most popular music lies between 90 and 110 beats per minute.

The shamanic beat is a repetitive rhythm, more variable than binaural beats, but still pretty regular. Because of the research done on brainwave entrainment using binaural beats, many people thought that a repetitive pulse was necessary to entrain. Research done in the early 1990's showed that a strictly repetitive drumming rhythm was not necessary to induce brainwave entrainment. Maxfield showed that both a repetitive rhythm—a traditional shamanic drumbeat—and a variable rhythm—syncopations at four beats per second—entrained the brain to the tempo of the drumming.

The fact that African drumming is not a steady, repetitive rhythm like the shaman's beat doesn't keep it from being trance inducing. The key with African drumming lies in the use of polyrhythms—more than one rhythm being played simultaneously—and the repetitive cycles they create. During the ceremonies with Lloyd, we played each rhythm for quite a while, upwards of an hour, though more commonly for 20-30 minutes. Their cycles became entrancing because of the cyclical nature of the pulses.

Melinda Maxfield experimented with non-repetitive rhythms using syncopated rhythms (irregular patterns). In her study, she came to understand that the subject's brain is able to fill in the missing beats as long as the underlying pulse (tempo) of the rhythm remained constant. It seems that the brain is able to read beyond the rests and ultimately entrain to the implied pulse, even if all the notes are not present or played as loudly as the others. This is an important key to the way I play the drum.

During my time studying with Colin, I was also re-exploring the Afro-centric rhythms that Lloyd had taught me, trying to understand their role in affecting possession. The feeling I had during, and immediately after, listening to the shamanic drumbeat was similar to what I felt when I played in ceremony with Lloyd. It was an altered reality. The math supports this, since all the ceremonial rhythms that we played were between six and seven beats per second.

• • •

Ty slid the toy truck back and forth on the floor as, first, his mother tried to engage him. He ignored her. His father then followed, going so far as to try to pull the toy away, getting only a tantrum for his efforts. Ty was fully absorbed in his rhythm.

Lloyd began drumming at a furious pace, as though pleading with Ty to engage. He had been building his rhythms for the past few minutes, while Ty resisted any efforts to draw him out of his reverie.

Lloyd's drumming became more intense, an intensity that I had not seen him use before. A minute or so at a breakneck pace pulled Ty's attention from his toy. The pace of Ty's pushing and pulling never changed, in spite of the speed of Lloyd's rhythms. The shift happened as Ty glanced over toward Lloyd then at his mother, who urged him to join her on a chair.

Lloyd dropped the intensity of his playing, though the speed remained. For the next several minutes, Lloyd settled into a groove. Ty's mother reached for Ty and he moved to her.

Ty's response—going toward his mother and finally sitting calmly with her—matched his response on the first day Lloyd played for Ty. This time, though, I was paying more attention to what Lloyd was playing than when I initially witnessed this. I noticed that Lloyd's rhythms were different than anything he was teaching me for ceremony. I also noticed that the tempo was faster. I asked him about it as we were driving home.

"Why did you play faster for Ty than we do for ceremony?" I asked Lloyd.

"I did what I needed to connect. His spirit wouldn't listen to my slower rhythms," he replied.

"But for ceremony, you said that we always had to please the spirits and they wouldn't appear if we deviated from the traditions."

"That's true, with ceremonies. One-on-one is different. You speak to your patient's spirit. Sometimes you need to play faster to get its attention."

I often thought about this as I was studying with Rachel. Why did Ty need faster rhythms? It was clear that he was unresponsive to slower rhythms, but what was it about these faster rhythms that got through to him?

I analyzed the tempos of the rhythms Lloyd played and discovered that when Ty responded, Lloyd was playing outside of the traditional tempos within the theta sate of consciousness. Instead, these rhythms were in alpha.

Alpha, I discovered, was the key to reaching people like Ty. He needed the stimulating effects of these faster rhythms. Rhythms at this tempo tended to have a more activating effect than those in theta, which makes sense because alpha is a more outwardly-directed state. It is also the state in which sensory processing is optimized. Most people like Ty, and me as someone with ADHD, have difficulty processing sensory information. We either take in too much and become overwhelmed, or we take in too little and are not able to distinguish subtleties of sensory information. (This is a topic I cover in more detail in the Sensory Processing chapter later in this book.)

This discovery became the cornerstone of my approach when I played for people. All the rhythms I use for REI employ alpha-tempo rhythms. You will find many tracks on Brain Shift Radio that use slower tempos, but those are primarily in the meditation category where theta is optimal.

Chapter Six
Stimulation

"Do you see that?" asked Beth.

"Yeah, let's see, what was I playing there?" I answered. "This is that 21-beat rhythm. Last time I played it the same thing happened. His stimming stopped."

"So how many is that now?"

"We're at over a hundred rhythmic patterns at this point. Could it be this specific?" I wondered out loud.

"Isn't that what Lloyd told you?"

"Well, yes and no. He talked about how each Orisha had a specific rhythm associated with it; so in this instance, the rhythms are exceptionally specific. He said that if you play the right rhythm at the right time, the Orisha will appear. Without the right rhythm, it won't happen. Even a minor variation in the rhythm doesn't work. And it won't work if you don't play the right rhythms in the right order," I explained.

"But when working one-on-one like this, he wasn't that clear. He talked about connecting in and following your inspiration. He said that each person would respond to the right rhythm for them, but he didn't talk about whether rhythms would work like this. When Lloyd drummed, the effects seemed more person-specific rather than behavior-specific. But the pattern we're seeing is unmistakable..."

I let this statement hang while I thought about the implications of this. Then I added, "But some of these rhythms are so bizarre. 21/16 is, even for me, a weird time signature to play. I mean, the rhythm kind of grooves, but it doesn't make much sense from a musical perspective."

We were analyzing the recordings and notes of my sessions with individuals on the autism spectrum to see which rhythms produced what response in the listener. This was the fun part for me. I loved seeing these patterns, but at the same time they baffled me. My discoveries were often in conflict with what I thought was possible.

Even though I had seen amazing things with rhythm, I didn't dare believe that playing a drum could be so powerful or that musical rhythm could have this specific of an impact. Yet, my partner Beth and I would repeatedly explore this pattern of discovery and analysis and come to the same conclusion: If you play the right rhythm at the right time, it can impact a very specific behavior or symptom and produce long-term changes.

Between 1992 and 2004, I played for over a thousand people and meticulously documented their responses to various rhythms. Over the course of this time, we were able to find over 600 rhythmic patterns that seemed to elicit very specific responses.

The problem was that, even though we saw these patterns and there was some historical precedent for using specific rhythms this way, there was no other research supporting the idea that musical rhythm can have an effect such as this on a listener. Still, the pattern was unmistakable. So I went looking for answers.

It was clear from the outset of our research that doing brain imaging was out of the question. First of all, we didn't have the money to do fMRI or PET. And even if we could do this type of imaging, the tests wouldn't likely give us accurate data, because the listeners would be confined and stressed and wouldn't be acting as they would in normal circumstances. As well, the types of conditions I work with, such as autism and ADHD, cannot be identified through these types of imaging devices.

Instead, these conditions are diagnosed and treated using behavioral measures, which matches the way I had been evaluating the rhythms. I continued down this path. I needed to understand how these rhythms affected the brain, how the brain processes sensory stimulus, and how these strange drumming rhythms may be impacting the very people I hoped to help.

• • •

At this time I was also exploring ways to deliver the rhythms without having to play live for each person.

I started my audio engineering career in 1985 doing MIDI (Musical Instrument Digital Interface) sequencing and drum machine programming. I wondered if I could use computer-sequenced drumming to make my performance more consistent. This approach could give me a standardized method for delivering my music, and I wouldn't need to play live for each person.

I should say that one of the reasons I considered sequencing the music was that the most popular entrainment approach at the time employed binaural beats. As I described in the previous chapter, binaural beats use a phenomenon of sound where the listener hears to two slightly different frequencies, one in each ear, and the brain perceives the difference between them as a pulsation. This pulse is referred to as a beat frequency or binaural beat.

With this idea in mind, I set up several experiments where we used a variety of different synthesized approaches. One used rhythms that I thought might be more generalized and therefore allow a series of rhythms to work with a large category of people, those on the autism spectrum, for instance. Another approach employed the specific rhythms recorded as MIDI data. The last used binaural beats to determine if the effects I was seeing were simply the result of entraining the brain to a calm state. These approaches were each compared to the results we were seeing with live drumming. In each instance, the live drumming produced better results.

Why was this?

This can be summed up in one word: Variability.

Our brains operate through pattern recognition and association. When we encounter a sensory stimulus, our brains become active. They look for the patterns in order to associate this stimulus with something in our previous experience. We are very good at this, better by a long shot than any computer.

Our brains love novelty. Difference and unpredictability activate our brains. And these are the characteristics of my drumming rhythms that allow the brain to stay engaged.

It takes no special skill to activate a brain. Though it can take quite a bit to achieve a sustained level of activation.

I saw this so clearly in the populations I worked with. And in my own brain patterns. Many people can force themselves to focus on mundane or repetitive things, but people like me on the ADHD spectrum can't really control our ability to focus. We either can focus or we can't.

I'm sure you've heard people with ADHD say that if something is interesting to them they can focus just fine; but if it's boring, forget it. This is because many people with ADHD don't have the same capacity to tolerate the mundane that most people have. Give someone with ADHD something interesting to do and you'll see some pretty spectacular things happen.

A focused ADHD brain is a work of wonder. Most people with this condition can make unexpected connections and be supremely creative when they are focused.

Because I was my first subject and harshest critic, I started with a level of rhythmic complexity and unpredictability that would be unnecessary for people without my particular challenges. My intolerance for repetition or predictability drove me to explore more complex rhythms than were historically used. Lloyd's rhythms were unusual, but not as strange as mine.

I should back up and say that I was a piece of work as a child. I was impulsive and disruptive. I got into a lot of my trouble because I couldn't control myself. Fortunately, I learned quickly (academically, not how to control myself), so my academic performance was never in question and many of my teachers were fairly tolerant of my outbursts as long as I got my work done (this was the '70's, after all, when kids were allowed to be kids). As well, by the time I hit middle school, I was a pretty accomplished drummer. I started my professional drumming career at 14; and by the time I had my driver's license at 16, I was working pretty regularly. And all of my teachers (and anyone within earshot, thanks to my impulse control issues) knew it.

This is all to say that when I started developing what would ultimately become REI, I was playing complex rhythms that I found interesting and bypassed my low tolerance for anything predictable and mundane. Few other drummers I knew were quite as interested in pushing the limits of rhythm as I was, probably because they didn't have my unruly brain.

When we tried to make the rhythms more mechanical or predictable, I found them hard to listen to and they didn't affect me in the same positive way as the hand-performed rhythms had. When I tested them with other people, I didn't see the same results, especially for those on the autism spectrum who seemed to decipher the rhythms more easily than others.

I don't believe that the early developers of binaural beats considered complexity or unpredictability, since they were working with generally typical brains doing fairly mundane things, such as facilitating meditation. One of the first explorers of binaural beats, Robert Monroe, was particularly interested in out-of-body experiences. Both meditation and out-of-body experiences rely on theta-tempo beats at similar tempos as the traditional shamanic drumbeat. At this tempo, the rhythm can be repetitive and still work.

From the outset of my personal journey of using drumming to influence the brain, I sped up my rhythms to the alpha-state tempo of eight-beats-per-second. Twice the speed of the shamanic drumming beat. I chose the faster tempo rhythms because theta-tempo rhythms made me feel sluggish, whereas alpha-tempo rhythms gave me mental clarity.

Early on, I learned that children on the autism spectrum seemed to "get" the rhythms in a way that other people did not. When I played really complex rhythms that most musicians would never be able to count, a young child with autism would be moving or fidgeting to the rhythm, seemingly in perfect synch. I also, more often than I could count, observed times when the rhythms went on too long and anxiety increased.

I saw this response first-hand in a series of double-blind, placebo-controlled studies I conducted in 1995 and 1996. In two of the studies, one with children with autism and the other with children with ADHD, approximately twenty percent of the subjects in the placebo groups dropped out of the study due to increases in anxiety from listening to the placebo recording. This recording used drumming rhythms at eight-beats-per-second like our REI recording, except the rhythms were not the complex patterns we use with REI; instead, they were traditional African rhythms. These rhythms, though appearing complex, were repetitive-sounding once the patterns were deciphered. It seemed that the children in these studies were able to decipher the patterns and, once they were understood, became irritated by them. Even the children who didn't stop the study because of increased anxiety didn't see any calming effects by the placebo recording.

Interestingly, all of the subjects that agreed to try an REI recording after complaining about the placebo (and after the study was completed) were calmed by listening to the REI recording.

Not only did I need to play incomprehensible rhythms, but they needed to change often; otherwise, anxiety or self-stimulating behaviors, such as hand flapping, would start.

This unpredictability and complexity became a cornerstone of my approach. Because binaural beats were developed to entrain to a deep meditative state where there is more tolerance for repetition, most binaural beat creators don't understand the need to include sufficient variability in their recordings. This is why binaural beats were essentially ineffective for entraining an alpha-state of consciousness.

To entrain to theta, a deep meditative state that Robert Monroe was trying to achieve, all you need is a pulse at the prescribed speed. It can be repetitive because the listener is entering a more internally directed state where she is less consciously aware of the repetitive pulse.

When you try to entrain to alpha, the listener is still alert enough that his brain needs the variability to stay engaged with the stimulus, lest the brain tunes it out.

This is what happens when we hear a dripping faucet in the next room. At first we tune into it because we hear a sound, but as we determine that it's a faucet drip, and it's not threatening to hurt us, we tune it out. The sound may still be there, but we don't hear it anymore because it's not important to us. Unless that pattern changes, say the drip turns into more of a flow, we continue to put it in the background (not everyone can do this, by the way, which is something I'll cover later on when I talk about sensory processing).

The repetitive pulse of a binaural beat, even if you vary the carrier frequencies, may initially engage the listener's brain; but it will become ineffective after a short time. This is called habituation. Our brains become tolerant of the stimulus, and after a while it takes more stimulation to achieve the same results. In the case of auditory stimulus, unless you can continue to vary the sound, the brain will shut it out. Habituation is a concern with medications as well.

I see this with some of my more simple rhythms, rhythms I use just to calm. One trick I have come up with is to change the pattern every ten to thirty seconds (often this is just one time through a pattern). Changing the pattern this frequently is not a problem because each one has a similar sound and these patterns are musical to begin with.

Which brings me back to the experiments I did looking at sequencing the music. I started this in an effort to find a way to stop playing live for each person. For a decade I played each client's recording live from start to finish. In one take.

In other words, after I met with a client, I sketched out the rhythms

I intended to use, set up my gear, hit record, and played without stopping. Twenty to twenty-five minutes for each client. I could do a couple at a time and a maximum of about five in a day before getting too tired to continue.

So, as I got busier, I was looking for ways to record each rhythm so that I could take those pre-recorded segments and line them up one after the other into a complete twenty-minute session.

I chose to use MIDI because I could record or program the rhythms as performance data and assign the sound later. This would allow me to record the rhythms once and change the drum later if I chose.

This was a great idea in theory, but it didn't work so well in practice. First, finding the right sounds was impossible. When I played a drum live, there were dozens of variations in tone and timbre; and even with the best samplers, I couldn't come up with sounds that were as expressive as the live drums. Second, I would record the rhythms and, because the sequencers at the time wanted to quantize the notes (automatically align each drum hit to a rigid timing grid), the minor variability and inconsistency in the rhythms was lost. Third, the volume (velocity) was not a high enough resolution so, like the timing, the subtleties were lost.

At first listen it sounded pretty good, but it lacked the human feel. And I quickly discovered that we humans need the human feel.

I didn't think sequencing would be a big problem because I've always had really good time. This goes back to my days studying syncopation and sight-reading. When I did my sight-reading, and ultimately every exercise, I used a metronome to keep in time. I did this so much that I have internalized the metronome pretty well. Many people have tested me on this by playing a metronome and asking me to tell them what tempo it is. I am almost always right. And if they play the metronome and I start clapping, then they turn off the volume and turn it back on again after a few minutes of me tapping, I am rarely off time with it.

So, even as good as my rhythmic timing is, it is still variable enough that listeners, especially those who are highly attuned, can sense the minor variability. And this variability, no matter how small, is important to keep a listener's brain engaged.

Binaural beats and sequencing through MIDI can't achieve this subtle variability, no matter how much people have tried. So, sequenced music was out. Drums, played live, were the way to go. The next step was to move beyond simple variability to some level of specificity. If there was a range of possible rhythms that worked for each symptom or behavior, I needed to find a way to categorize and organize them. I decided that stimulation had to be the key.

"How do we make sense of these?" Beth asked. "There are so many different rhythms and so many ways to think about them. And so many ways to arrange them."

"I think we need to find a pattern in them—a logical way to organize them into a system," I said, thinking out loud.

"When you play, what are you thinking?"

"I'm usually not. Most of the time I'm watching, looking for some sort of response. Then I just go with it."

"Each rhythm seems to produce a fairly consistent response. Like this rhythm here. You play it often when someone stims, and nearly each time the stimming stops."

"The rhythm seems to be associated with self-stimulatory behavior, particularly the hand-flapping; but where would it go in a recording? When I'm playing I just throw it in when I see the behavior. But if we're wanting to make recordings without first seeing the behavior, where would this rhythm go in relation to other rhythms we may want to use for someone?"

"How have you been doing it for the recordings you make now?"

"It's different. Since I played live for the person and saw how their response changed over time, I try to follow that same path with the recording. Same rhythms, same order. But if I don't have the live session to draw from, how do I plan it?"

"Maybe we need to take a look at the overall pattern of these live recordings. Not just the rhythms you played, but the order as well. Do you think there is a pattern to the progression of the rhythms and the person's response?"

"Could be. You're right. We need to go back and examine, not only the rhythms, but also their placement in a session. This is going to take a while."

And it did. Beth and I spent hundreds of hours going through recordings of me playing live for each client to see how each rhythm fit into a client session. After seeing patterns in rhythms and responses and noticing a consistency in overall responses to my drumming, followed by recordings of those sessions, we were hoping to find a way to systematize the process.

We were in the midst of conducting a series of studies where I would not have the benefit of meeting each subject, playing for them in person, and assembling a recording just for them. These studies were being conducted via the mail and with the help of several universities across the country. As well, in each instance we were asked to make one recording for an entire subject group. These would be placebo-controlled studies, so I needed to create a set of rhythms to cover the spectrum of each condition. We were administering the three studies at once—autism, ADHD, and chronic pain—and each of these groups represented a fairly large variability in subject types and symptom make-ups.

By now I had played for hundreds of people with each of these conditions and had seen a variety of responses to both my live drumming and the recordings that followed. But trying to translate that into a recording that would work for a group of people was a daunting task. One that I wasn't sure was possible.

• • •

"These studies are a mess," I said to Beth. "Responses are all over the place, as are symptom make-ups. There is no way we're going to be able to do a statistical analysis of this data; there are just too many variables."

"Why even bother? This isn't the best we can do."

Beth and I were on a walk trying to make sense of the results of the three double-blind, placebo-controlled studies we had spent the last six months working on. The subjects in the active rhythm group showed some good responses to the drumming, certainly better than the placebo group; but while we were conducting these studies we were also tracking, using the same evaluation process, clients who benefitted from live sessions followed by recordings of those sessions. The differences were startling.

People who I played for live saw significantly better results, so much so that we were convinced that a generalized recording made for a group of people was not what we wanted to do. So, we were on a walk to decide how we wanted to proceed.

"The best we can do... I like that. What *is* the best we can do?"

"Custom recordings."

"Okay, but if we really want to help the most people, I can't play live for everyone."

"Maybe you don't have to. What if we designed an intake similar to what we used for these studies and used that as the basis for creating a person's recording?"

"Okay, but we'd need to learn how to associate the questions on the intake to the rhythms I would use. This could take a while."

And it did. Beth and I spent eight years tracking people's responses to the rhythms I played live. We compiled several different intake questionnaires to create profiles that would allow us to predict which rhythms to use for a client. For each client, we started with an intake and then made a recording without my playing live, while comparing and contrasting the results to the cases where I played live.

"So, what's the pattern?" asked Beth.

"I'd say it's connected to symptoms. If we divide the rhythms and responses into basic symptom categories, maybe we can understand how to choose the rhythms."

This was the logic. Basically, in the process of my playing live for each client and documenting their responses, both in the short and long term, we saw patterns of symptoms and behavior.

After a lot of trial and error, in early 2004, just about the time that I was finishing my book on ADHD, we felt we had a pretty good handle on how this would work.

• • •

Stimulation relates to the difficulty a listener has in deciphering the rhythm. Aside from seeing connections between certain rhythms and changes in symptoms or behaviors, I also noticed some patterns in how people with different issues seem to "get" (understand) the rhythms. For example, looking at the developmental disability spectrum from mild learning disabilities, through ADHD, and on to autism, I noticed that the further on the spectrum—in terms of severity—the more complex the rhythms became.

I didn't design it this way, but I did notice that someone with severe autism became agitated with simpler rhythms if they were played too long; whereas someone with dyslexia could tolerate shorter, simpler rhythms. This became my basis for determining simulation levels.

My first step was to analyze all the rhythms according to a set of characteristics such as length, number of accented and muted notes, and relationships between types of accents, such as bass tones or slaps. I would also group them according to symptom categories and drum type. I use two types of drums: Each offers different tonal characteristics and, because I play them differently, each employs different rhythmic structures. I talk more about the drums I use in Chapter 7.

I assigned each rhythm a stimulation level between 0 and 999. The longer the rhythmic string, the higher the stimulation level. Likewise for the number or concentrations of bass or accent tones.

I also divided up the rhythms into ten symptom categories:
- Anxiety—Includes anxiety related issues.
- Attention/focus/hyperactivity—Includes attention-related issues including the classic symptoms of ADD and ADHD.
- Behavioral issues—Includes issues such as aggression, compliance, tantrums, and others.
- Cognitive issues—Includes symptoms related to cognition such as memory, reasoning, and others.
- Language/communication—Includes issues related to language and communication including speech and writing.
- Mood issues—Includes general mood issues as well as symptoms

of depression and bipolar disorder.

- Self-stimulatory behaviors—Includes behaviors such as rocking, flapping, toe-walking, vocal perseveration, and others.
- Sensory processing—Includes sensory-defensive and sensory-seeking behavior.
- Sleep—Includes issues related to falling and staying asleep.
- Social interaction—Includes issues related to social interaction and engagement.

Stimulation via these parameters was not as complex as I thought it would be, once I sorted the rhythms this way. Then it was a matter of associating rhythms with a listener. After my initial study (described in Chapter 2), I was lucky enough to get a call from the leading researcher in auditory interventions who helped me develop assessments for a series of controlled studies we conducted starting in 1995. He also invited me to share my research at one of his international conferences and mentored me on our first controlled studies.

These assessments were based on rating scales that were often used for diagnosis of the types of conditions I found myself working with: ADHD, autism, mood disorders, anxiety disorders, sleep disorders, and sensory processing disorders. Because I was using these rating scales in my controlled studies and my research playing one-on-one, by the time I decided I could categorize and rate each rhythm it was easy for me to associate each rhythm with a question or series of questions from the assessments.

• • •

"I think I can record each rhythm and build a system where I could just plug the right one in and not have to play live for each client anymore," I said to Beth as I was doing research for my second book on audio recording (*Pro Tools All-in-One Desk Reference For Dummies*, Wiley 2004).

"You think you could do it? What gear would you need?" asked Beth, ever conscious of the cost and the huge investment we were continually making in this strange work. We were ten years into the clinical research, and I had resorted to writing music books for a major publisher to help pay the bills and finance the ongoing research.

"Well, the tech is possible and it wouldn't require any new gear. I can use what we have. Though it would probably take months to record and edit all the rhythms."

It did. I spent the better part of six months recording then editing over 600 rhythms, using two types of drums, into two separate databases.

We decided to run with this idea. We finally felt as though we had enough experience and data to allow this approach to be available beyond the strict research setting that we had been operating within since the beginning. In fact, I was at the same time putting together a training program where we would recruit therapists to provide our Program.

We launched our REI Authorized Provider Training Program in November 2004, coinciding with the completion of the REI Custom Program databases and the release of my book *AD/HD for Dummies* (Wiley, 2004), which I co-wrote with neuropsychiatrist, Michael Flanagan, MD.

My first training, held in our home base of Santa Fe, consisted of a whopping three people. Yep, three. Not the most auspicious start.

This low-pressure situation, though, gave me a chance to refine my presentation. The feedback I received from these providers as they gained experience using the Program with their clients allowed me to quickly move out of the beta phase and develop systems that would allow us to handle working with more people.

My next training seminar, conducted in Boston during the worst snowstorm of 2005, was full and resulted in some provider relationships that continue today. Over the next two years, I traversed the country, conducting 26 seminars and training over 500 providers. Many of these early providers were instrumental in refining our protocols and helping us gather more data about the real-world implementation and effects of the Program.

At this point I was getting pretty busy making client CDs, since the creation of each CD was as much of an art as it was science.

Translating the intake form into CDs, even though I used pre-recorded rhythm snippets, was something that I was not able to show anyone else how to do. It took almost as much intuition as playing live from start to finish. This led to a problem.

"What happens to the Program if something happened to you?" asked Dana, a physical therapist, at a training seminar. "I don't want to invest time and energy into a therapy I recommend to my clients if I won't be able to fulfill their needs."

"I'm working on teaching others how to make the CDs," I replied. I honestly hadn't thought about it this way. Sure I was trying to figure out how to systemize the Program so I didn't have to make the CDs. I wasn't thinking about not being around or able to make the CDs. I was concerned with being able to keep up with demand. But this got me thinking and planning.

First, we stopped doing live trainings, both to slow down our addition of new providers because I had gotten super busy and to keep me from having to travel so much. I spent ten years on the road touring with bands in the 1980's and I didn't want to travel every other week to do trainings. Aside from being a hassle in the post-911 world, traveling every other weekend for months on end exhausted me and made it hard to keep up with client demand. I also had a young daughter I wanted to spend time with.

Then, we moved our training online in 2007. This freed me up focus on clients and to figure out a way to make the process of creating custom-made client CDs easier.

We never really considered not custom-making the REI Custom Program CDs. The other home-based auditory brain stimulation programs all used multiple CD sets of generalized CDs; therapists were trained to mix and match the CDs to get the best results for a client. Results were often dependent on the skill of the provider in their shuffling of the music. The manufacturer/creator of the CDs had little control over how well the CDs were implemented.

I wanted to avoid that fate, so I stuck to the idea of custom-made CDs. It took little skill from the therapist (who had other things to worry about) and allowed me to maintain control over the end result. As long as a client and/or his therapist kept in contact with us, I could ensure the best possible results.

So, as I was thinking about all this, I met a software designer who I clicked with. Several months earlier, the developers we had been using closed up shop. The three programmers each took jobs at trendy start-ups. Unfortunately, our website crashed just as they abandoned us. Luckily, a friend who ran a busy e-commerce site referred me to a developer who could rebuild our site quickly.

The rebuild worked so well that we decided to tackle trying to build software to automate the creation of the REI Custom Program CDs.

We started with creating the intake form. Rather than simply code the intake in, we decided that the best thing to do was to create a framework where I could add or change questions at will. Up until this point, our providers were using four different intake forms depending on a client's age and we had several alternate intake forms for things like sleep, chronic pain, and sensory processing. Including all of these possible areas meant that a single online intake would have hundreds of questions.

Based upon the variety of symptoms each client presented, we decided to build a framework that categorized each question according to age and symptom and have the client contact select the relevant categories, thereby narrowing the scope of the questions to only those that were relevant to the client.

Self-selecting categories was quickly dumped because too many people were calling to ask which symptom categories to choose. So, our current intake process only filters questions based on age. This means that there are often as many as two hundred questions covering all areas that we can help with. We then toss out the questions that receive a 'not relevant' answer.

Building this part of the online Program software was fairly easy. The next step was to decide how the rhythms would be chosen. I decided the easiest approach was to assign a rhythm to each possible answer on the intakes. This meant recording the appropriate rhythms for each question and possible answer. If there are 300 questions with

4 possible answers each, I had 1,200 rhythms to record. This satisfied the first track that would be chosen for someone, but what about adjustments for subsequent tracks?

We chose two approaches. First, we would build revision-mapping software which would choose the best rhythm based on the intensity of the rhythm in the big scheme of the Program. Then, second, we would have several databases of rhythms for each question, each factoring in the major symptoms categories and their associated needs. This ultimately meant that I would record eight separate databases of unique rhythms, each containing 1,200 rhythms. This totaled nearly 10,000 rhythms: 10,000 individual audio snippets anywhere from 15 to around 45 seconds long.

With the intake and rhythms connected to each answer, the next step was to develop the logic for the system to choose the appropriate rhythms that go onto a client's REI track. This logic is pretty complicated and took me several months to map out for our developers. Once this logic was in place, we ran into a problem when it came to actually assembling the individual audio files into one continuous audio file. It seemed no matter what we did, there was a short space placed between each rhythm file.

The solution we came up with was for me to cut about 95 milliseconds (about a tenth of a second) off each file so that when they were placed together by the software, the space it inserted was eliminated from the final file. Recording, editing, and then shortening each file took many months, but it worked. Flawlessly.

Next, was the track adjustment logic. Like I said, we decided to create a framework for intensity maps that re-adjusted the rhythms on a track. It works like this: The first track uses the intake to choose the rhythm files and assemble them in an order based on the weight of the symptoms detected by the intake. The subsequent tracks use the feedback from the client to select new tracks. The feedback looks at two main conditions: improvements and regressions. Within these conditions we also look at which symptom areas have improved and/or regressed. Then we also factor in whether someone missed an inordinate number of listening sessions and whether there were changes in medications, routines, or health.

The aggregate of these answers results in a particular intensity map being chosen. This map then selects the rhythms to be included and the order in which these rhythms are placed. As I mentioned in another chapter, the order of the rhythms is as important as having the right rhythms in a client's track.

We also built the software so that the intensity map and chosen rhythms, including database variations, could be manually selected. This was of critical importance because we were going to switch to this software without testing whether it did as good of a job as I did when I was selecting the rhythms by hand.

Imagine my delight when it went smoothly. We were initially able to test the software to make sure that the selection and compilation process was working. But we weren't able to ensure the logic was correct. This required real-life clients and their responses. Up until this point, choosing the best rhythms for a client was an art. In fact, I was the only one at my office that was able to do it. I tried to teach others, but no one else had the feel.

Building this software and logic required me to clarify how I made the choices I made. With the fairly open framework, I tweaked the first track selection logic and the adjustment intensity maps for the first year we were live with the online system. I can confidently say that the software is working better than I ever did by doing the Program by hand. And it's consistent.

The switch from my playing live, following handwritten notes, to selecting pre-recorded rhythm files eliminated the inconsistency of my drumming performance and represented a monumental shift and improvement in the Program. Yet, this level of improvement was nothing compared to what happened when we went from me hand-selecting rhythm files to letting the system do it, especially since we can factor real life results into the process to further improve the selection process.

Of course, I still hand-make tracks in the rare instances when the system doesn't get it quite right.

Chapter Seven
Drums

"I cannot lie," Carlos confessed, looking at the ground, "I think I threw away your drum. I'm sorry. I cannot work for you any more."

I stood, stunned. Carlos had been working for me for the past two years and had proven to be a hard and conscientious worker. He offered to quit after witnessing my desperate search for my favorite drum.

"There was a beat-up drum case in the back of the truck, and I threw it out with the rest of the trash," he explained.

"It's not your fault," I said with my heart in my throat. I realized he was right, but I also knew that I had put the drum in the truck. It was a lazy move. Rather than bring the drum into my studio, I transferred it from my car to the truck when I went to town the other day. And because I left it there, it went to the dump with the junk we were getting rid of.

"Are you sure that was the drum case?" Beth asked me.

"Was it a beat up case with grey duct tape on it?" I asked Carlos, knowing what he'd say.

"Yes, I'm sorry. I cannot work for you anymore."

"Don't worry about your job," I said. "It was my fault that the drum was there. And by the look of the case you would never know that it contained anything of value." Which was by design, I thought to myself. This drum had traveled the world. For years I took it everywhere I went: I wanted it to look so unappealing that no one would want to steal it.

Well, my disguise worked. Too well. Now I was without my favorite drum.

"Let me see if I can get it back," said Beth.

Beth can often make miracles happen. She spent the rest of the day trying to track down the drum. She started by calling the Santa Fe County waste transfer station where the drum was dumped. They told her that the bin had already been transferred to the county landfill. She then called the landfill. They had no information for her.

So she drove across the county to the landfill; and, bless their hearts, the employees drove her out into the landfill where the loads from across the county were delivered that fateful day. They even went so far as to use a land mover to dig through the waste, hoping to find the drum.

It was a heroic effort that was for naught. The drum was gone. So was a part of my soul.

This drum was one of three custom-made for me by the manufacturer. Even getting these drums was a monumental effort in itself.

I first discovered this type of drum on a spontaneous stop at Groth Music in Bloomington, Minnesota. As was my custom, I would stop whenever I saw a drum shop just to see if there was anything interesting. The day Beth and I stopped in I saw an unusual drum that looked kind of like an African djembe (a goblet-shaped drum often sprung with thin goat skin), but upon closer inspection it was actually a variation on a Cuban conga drum (a barrel-shaped drum outfitted with a thick cowhide head). This drum was unique in that it was one-third the length of a typical conga, with a telescoping chamber where the bottom two thirds of the drum usually sits.

According to the brochure, the Gonga's design was an innovation created by Gon Bops of California for the traveling congero (conga player) to put all three congas into one typical conga case, making it easier to haul them around. Every drummer will tell you what a hassle it is to have to haul their drums everywhere; they are always looking for ways to lighten the load.

Anyway, what was unique, no, magical, about this drum was not its space and weight saving qualities. It was the sound. It rang with such a clarity and depth, unlike any other skinned hand drum I'd ever played. And I'd played nearly all by this point.

Because of the shortened depth and the telescoping chamber, it created a bass tone, much like a djembe; except, because it had a thick cowhide head, its tone was much more controlled than the djembe. This drum had the punch and clarity of a conga drum. But the sound was warmer because it was made of mahogany wood instead of the oak or alder used for most congas.

It was the best of both drums. I played it and immediately fell in love. I bought the single Gonga this shop had in stock and grabbed a brochure, hoping that someday I could afford another.

This single drum was the only drum I played for five or six years. This is the drum I used for every client I played for live. I chose to do this partly because I loved the Gonga so much, but also because I wanted to limit the variables in the stimulus by keeping the drum the same.

I had longed for a set of three Gongas since buying my first one. The ceremonies I played with Lloyd, Jimmy, and Cheryl followed the traditional format of one drummer for each drum or percussion instrument. This was the traditional way of doing things; but just as the drumset was built with the idea that one drummer could play a host of different drums, hand drummers also grouped drums to cover multiple parts without having to add musicians.

In the 1950's, drummer Candido Camero was the first congero to combine the three conga-style drums—the tumba, conga, and quinto—into a set and play them by himself. Every hand drummer playing any style of contemporary music followed his lead and learned the conga drum parts orchestrated for one drummer rather than three. As someone who also played for popular music, having all three drums of a conga set was essential.

After moving to Southern California at the end of 1996, I decided to track down the Gon Bops factory to see if I could have a full set of three made for me. Even though they didn't generally work directly with artists, I cajoled them into making me the set.

The drive from San Diego to Chino became a monthly event for me for the better part of a year. I was told when I ordered my drums that they would take twelve weeks. Gon Bops was going through a major shake-up and was having trouble fulfilling my order; so after the initial time estimate, I made habit of calling once a week and driving up every few weeks to see if my drums were done.

My persistence paid off; because if I had not pestered them, I may not have gotten my drums at all. It turned out that my drums were some of the last made by Gon Bops before they went out of business. The smallest one, the Quinto, was, in fact, the very last drum they built.

These three drums became the cornerstone of my custom program, many of my CDs, and hundreds of tracks on Brain Shift Radio. Their clear, controlled sound and deep bass tone, allowed an expressiveness to my drumming that I couldn't achieve with the conga drum that I learned with Lloyd.

As fate would have it, the day I discovered the Gonga in Bloomington, I also discovered another type of drum that would be at the heart of my music. This other drum, called an Udu, is a clay pot drum originating from Nigeria. Imagine a round-bottomed, slender-necked storage vessel with a second hole in its side. This is an Udu. You play it by tapping and scraping on the sides and cupping the hole on top and the side to alter the timbre, sustain, and pitch. It's an incredibly expressive drum, albeit very quiet.

This drum, like the Gonga, offers a wide range of sounds, from a deep bass tone to a bell-like clang. I didn't buy one when I first discovered it, though. But this drum stuck in the back of my mind until I was at a NAMM, National Association of Music Merchants, show in Anaheim a few years later.

NAMM puts on a huge trade show every year for musical instrument and recording equipment manufacturers to showcase their newest and best gear. This show is not for the general public—you need to be invited, work at a music store, or be in the press to get in. Because I was a published author of music books, I was invited.

When I first played an Udu in Bloomington, I wasn't entirely blown away by the sound. It was just too quiet. But at NAMM there were a variety of different shapes and styles all outfitted with microphones fed through headphones. With the mics, I could hear all the nuances of the drum. I immediately felt that this drum had a place in my music.

The problem with the Udu, though, is that they are made of clay and, therefore, are very fragile. This is not necessarily a problem for many people, but I tend to hit hard. So hard that I broke a few before I learned to take it easy on them. For a while we planted each broken Udu in a garden in front of my studio as reminders of my tendency to be a little hard on my drums.

Though the Gonga and Udu drums became my preferred instruments, the unique tonal characteristics of these drums required me to find ways to record them that maximized their effects. Overtones detract from the main body of the sound and the reverberant characteristics of the room can impede with the impact of the rhythms, so I spent a tremendous amount of time exploring the best way to get the recorded sound to match what I heard in my mind. As the author of three audio recording books, this process was almost as engaging as my research into the best rhythms and drumming techniques to use.

After years of experimenting, I settled into recording in stereo. Everything in my studio is geared toward recording drums in stereo: my microphones, my preamps, and my converters. I am very happy with the recorded sound of my drums.

Initially my goal was to minimize the overtones of the drums and hone in on the purest tonal aspects of the instrument. This would eliminate any negative effects from harmonics.

Harmonic overtones are secondary sounds a drum makes and the main reason I didn't like playing a djembe. Djembes, with their thin goatskin heads, have a lot of overtones. This was also the case with all the frame drums I auditioned when I was looking for drums to use for my programs. Any drum with a thin skin is going to have these extra tones.

The overtones were the sounds I was trying to get away from. Uncontrollable frequencies are unpredictable and unnecessary. They aren't so much of a problem when playing live, but they can wreak havoc on recordings and negatively impact the effects of rhythms. I didn't want them.

Anyway, using drums that have a minimal mount of harmonic content is only part of the solution. At one point we experimented by my playing on a tabletop and the results were more immediate than some of the overtone rich drums. Tabletops were not expressive enough, so I happily settled on using the Gonga and Udu.

These drums still produced overtones, albeit not as many or as pronounced as thin-skin drums; but enough that I spent countless hours looking for the best combination of recording equipment.

In 2001, while I was writing my first audio recording book, I was doing some research for new gear. After testing dozens of mics and miking techniques, I settled on a matched pair of hand made mics from a Califorinia company named Josephson Engineering.

These mics are referred to as small diaphragm condenser mics because they have a very small membrane (the diaphragm) that sits in front of a metal plate that is charged with a small amount of electricity (the condenser) which captures the sound. This type of microphone is more sensitive than the dynamic mic I used for the original *Calming Rhythms*. Dynamic mics use a magnet wrapped with wire to pick up the sounds and, although very durable, they lack the clarity of a condenser mic.

Condenser mics offer an advantage over other mics. Being very sensitive, they pick up a pretty even distribution of frequencies, making a recording sound more natural than a dynamic mic, which has a tendency to accentuate the lower frequencies and attenuate the higher frequencies.

And compared to large diaphragm condenser mics, the smaller

diaphragm has a more even frequency distribution than the heightened low end of many large diaphragm condenser mics. As well, the smaller size better met my needs as I discovered my preferred recording methods.

There are a lot of ways to record in stereo. Most recording engineers are taught three methods: M/S, Blumlein, and X/Y. Blumlein and X/Y are pretty easy to implement, as they both use simple placement techniques. M/S, on the other hand, requires some decoding gear to make sense of the data. Regardless of the approach, all stereo techniques are designed to overcome issues with frequencies becoming distorted, due to the interaction of sound waves from the left and right tracks, when you play the music source back through speakers. Having correct phase alignment—making sure the hills and valleys of the left and right sound waves match—is critical in getting a natural, undistorted sound.

These stereo recording techniques work well once you get the hang of the basics of placement, but there was something I didn't like about each of them for recording drums. This was mostly due to the fact that I wanted to put the mics pretty close to the drums to minimize the sound of the room. This meant that the stereo separation wasn't that great. So I started looking for more esoteric solutions. Josephson Engineering suggested using a device called a Jecklin disc.

The Jecklin disc was created by classical recordist, Jürg Jecklin. His device was designed to act similar to the way a human head treats sound. Our heads absorb and block some sound as our ears pick up the music, something that traditional stereo miking techniques were unconcerned with. One of the top microphone manufacturers recognized this in the 70s. So they chose to build a head in which to place two mics, one where each ear would be. They reasoned that the shape of the head and the position and shape of the ears would impact the sound. It did. The first time I heard this binaural head mic set-up (also called dummy head recording), I was blown away.

I wanted to buy one, but it was beyond my budget at the time (upwards of $6,000). So I kept looking until I discovered the Jecklin disc. The Jecklin disc used a twelve inch disc covered by lambs-wool or foam with a mic positioned at a specific position on each side. The disc acted like the head in the dummy head unit by somewhat masking the sound coming from one side to the other side, making localization of the sound easier to discern. The wool or foam attenuated the higher frequencies, much like our skin, soft tissue, and hair do.

The result is a natural stereo image and, since I already owned microphones that would be appropriate to use, the cost was minimal. In fact, though you can buy ready-made Jecklin discs, most people who use one make it themselves. The process is easy and the cost is less than twenty dollars.

One of the wonderous things about the Jecklin disc is that I can place it just inches away from my drums and still get a beautiful stereo image. This is especially nice with the super quiet Udu clay pot drums.

Once I perfected my recording style, I discovered that I could successfully use thin-skinned drums for certain types of tracks on Brain Shift Radio (mostly those in the meditation, energy, and uplift categories). During this time I also began using an extremely inexpensive and indestructible frame drum made by Remo for my trainings, demonstrations, and workshops because I didn't want to risk damaging my precious Gongas by traveling with them, especially since they are irreplaceable.

If I'm going to use a thin-skinned drum, I prefer using drums with a synthetic head rather than a natural skin. Synthetic heads don't change in pitch due to temperature or humidity (and they won't split from extreme heat or dryness, ruining the drum). In fact, the drum on the cover of this book, a Bodhran made by Cooperman Drums, and the drum I play for Kylie, who I describe in Chapter 16, are each strung with a synthetic head.

I mention this because many people who attend my workshops start with a thin-skinned drum (usually one with a synthetic head made by Remo), something I encourage because the investment is minimal. As much as I love the Gonga and Udu, I also believe that they aren't the only drums that can offer positive effects.

After all, the rhythms are the key.

Chapter Eight
Ambient

"That's hard to listen to. Is there something you could add to the drumming to make it more musical?" asked Michael.

"I've been thinking about that. I don't know. I can't add anything too melodic or too harmonically complex otherwise it will detract from the effects of the drum."

This conversation with my friend and musical sounding board would be repeated for several years. I would try singing, chanting, didgeridoo, all to no avail. Nothing felt right. These instruments all sounded too new-agey, too melodic, or too unmusical.

As I explored the idea of adding something to the drumming, I reflected on one of the main issues I ran into when I was beginning my studies and talking with other music researchers who were exploring tribal or traditional music. Within the ethnomusicological world, a lot of emphasis is put on the songs, melodies, lyrics, and harmonic content. These aspects, coupled with the rituals and other cultural dressings, took the focus off what I felt was important—the rhythm.

It's easy to get distracted by the melodies or lyrics in music and believe that they are the essence of what makes the music powerful; but within the world I was exploring, melodies and lyrics were simply distractions. The true power lies in the rhythms. As one Macumba priestess describes:

"The rhythm is more important than the words [in our rituals]. The gods respond to rhythm above all else."

This is why Lloyd was so adamant that each rhythm we played was perfect. Not just the rhythms themselves, but, just as importantly, the feel of the rhythms. Feel is the key to making music move people. Feel is felt as the pulse of the music. And this is what affects the listener.

Each style of music has a particular feel. I'm not just talking about the rhythm, but instead, about the exact placement of the rhythms within the beat. There are essentially three ways you can place the pulse of the music against its metronomic beats. These three feels are: playing ahead (on top) of the beat, right on the beat, and behind the beat. Of course are there are infinite variations on how far ahead or behind you play. These are what make a piece of music groove or not. Each style of music uses these placements differently.

For example, R&B or Soul music are mostly played behind the beat. This gives the groove a sultry, laid back feel. Reggae music is played further behind the beat than these others, making it even more relaxed. An uptempo version of reggae, called ska, on the other hand, is played slightly ahead of the beat, creating tension and a sense of urgency.

I am steeped in R&B and reggae, therefore my default style is to play slightly behind the beat. It is often a struggle for me to play on top of the beat. For several years, as I played in a reggae band, I spent countless hours working with the bass player, trying to get the feel for the calypso songs we played. Calypso, like ska, requires an ahead-of-the-beat feel. It was a challenge, taking tremendous concentration, to create the driving, ahead-of-the-beat feel of calypso that makes people want to get up and dance.

Interestingly, early in my career I also played with a band that played 1980's post-punk "college rock" music. Think of bands like

The Smiths, REM, early U2. Their feel is often similar in pulse placement as calypso, that is, slightly on top of the beat. This feel is driving and optimistic, frenetic and energetic. Not my style. I can do it, but I don't particularly enjoy playing it. I love listening to this type of music, though.

Lloyd ran me through rigorous exercises so that I could develop a strong sense of where to place my beats against the other drummer's rhythms. Even within the group structure of the drummers playing in ceremonies, my job as the tumba player was to pull the music back just slightly. Not all the time, though, which is what Lloyd spent so much time drilling me on. While we played for ceremony, it was my job to push and pull the music. Yes, all the drummers were involved in this process; but as the bass tone element, my rhythms formed the foundation of the grooves. Therefore, where I placed each beat had a greater influence on the feel of the songs than Lloyd's or Jimmy's rhythms. In fact, often when I was pulling the pulse back, Lloyd was sometimes pushing it forward. By my playing slightly behind Jimmy and Cheryl, and Lloyd playing just ahead of them, we were able to create subtly varying levels of tension that would allow us to fine-tune the heat of the ceremony.

Controlling the heat of a healing ceremony, as I described in Chapter 3, is the key to having a successful outcome. For the ceremony I describe in that chapter, heat is intensity. Too much and the ceremony can get out of control, often resulting in someone other than the manbo engaging the spirits (or getting too hyped up). Too little heat and you won't be able to invoke the spirits. Because the overall heat is dependent on the entire community and not just the drummers, what works for one ceremony doesn't for another. Being able to interpret where the heat is at—and adjusting appropriately—is the art. One that requires experience and expert guidance. Both of which Lloyd had and was generous enough to share with me.

I played for many ceremonies where we were not able to build sufficient heat to accomplish our goals. But many more times we were on the edge of producing too much heat. This is where my tendency to play behind the beat was an advantage.

I knew many other drummers at the Musician's Institute who struggled with speeding up during songs. Their own internal tensions, anxieties or excitements (translated biochemically as adrenalin) caused them to speed up the song. Or if they weren't able to speed up, because the rest of the rhythm section held steady, they played on top of the beat. Slowing down and holding back were challenging for them. This has never been my problem, possibly because I don't get tense when I play. I am, and always have been, a very relaxed drummer.

With REI, because I only use one drum for clients and there are no other instruments to use as a reference point, adjusting the heat of the drumming through feel doesn't work. Instead I raise or lower the intensity of the music through the complexity and variability of the rhythmic structures. This works most of the time, but occasionally even the most simplistic or repetitive rhythms are too intense for some listeners. This is what my friend, Michael, was talking about. He found all of my drumming too much for his nervous system. And he wasn't alone.

• • •

"James is not sleeping."

"Alison doesn't want to listen."

"Damon gets agitated when the music plays."

These are comments I began receiving from our authorized REI providers once we started expanding the types of conditions we worked with. Comments such as these are all signs that the rhythms may be too intense, the heat too much for the listener.

Often in these cases, simplifying the rhythms doesn't work: First, it appears that each rhythm offers a specific effect on the listener. So changing or eliminating a rhythm reduces the overall effect of the therapy (Chapter 6 covers this in detail). And second, making the rhythms more repetitive can cause agitation (Chapter 9 goes into further detail on this).

So, the solution had to be adding something to the drumming

that could moderate its effects.

As it turns out, about this time I was also teaching an audio recording class at the Santa Fe Community College and routinely walked my students through different pieces of equipment as an introduction to computer-based recording. It was through this introduction that I realized that I should look toward my second love, synthesizers.

It made so much sense in retrospect. Drums and synths. These were my instruments.

Every classically trained percussionist is required to play a melodic instrument, generally mallets in the form of xylophone, vibraphone, and concert bells. I studied these through elementary, middle and high school; but when I got to the Musician's Institute, I traded the mallets for the keyboard. The scales and chords are the same. The only difference is that with mallet instruments you use sticks and with keyboards you use your fingers.

Playing keyboards is not to be confused with playing piano. Sure, many keyboardists are trained as piano players, but I am not a piano player. I don't have that level of technique. Mallets are limited to two limbs, even when you play using two or three mallets in each hand. You can effectively play chord patterns using three mallets with the handles placed between your fingers, but you are limited on melodic passages that you can play with your mallets. Piano players have four independent digits in each hand. Mallet players have one. Rather than learn piano, I focused instead on composing and programming synthesizers.

I also preferred the synths because they can play hundreds (and thousands) of sounds and are fairly easy to transport, whereas hauling around a vibraphone is a pain and you only get one sound out of it. Not to mention that popular music rarely, if ever, uses classical mallet instruments. Keyboards are everywhere.

Keyboards in the 1980's were analog, requiring a skill in understanding the various oscillators, envelopes, filters, and effects that comprise the myriad of sounds that these instruments are capable of creating. And because keyboard parts are often broken down for records, giving the composer and producers more control later in the production process, my skills were sufficient for all but the most complex passages (and those could easily be dealt with using sequencers, but I won't go there now). Most 88-key keyboards allow you to separate the lower and upper octaves into two different sounds, if you want to play the traditional piano way; but this wasn't the way I chose to work.

Instead, I often played the chords in one pass and the melodies in another. This process, called overdubbing, is the way music is often recorded nowadays. This process is not without controversy, but it is a legitimate way to make recorded music.

As you probably guessed by now, I'm not a purist. I'll use whatever tools or techniques I need in order to achieve my goals. I'm also willing to disregard tradition if I feel a new approach may provide better results.

When I started playing with the variety of synths sounds that were becoming available in the early part of this century, I was beginning to hear how I could enhance the drumming in a way that would give the drumming some support without negating its effects. In fact, I was learning that with the right mix of slowly evolving tonal changes (I hesitate to call it melody because of the lack of structure) and varying harmonic textures, I could actually fine-tune the effect of the rhythm.

The inspiration came when I discovered an old favorite CD left packed in a box from our move to Santa Fe several years earlier. This CD, called *Music For Airports* composed by Brian Eno and performed by the band Bang on a Can, was part of the ambient music movement of the 1970's. The premise of this style of music was to create minimalistic soundscapes to carry listeners on a journey. The masters of this field were breaking ground by ignoring musical conventions in the classical realm and, instead, giving the compositions space and letting the music breathe. They also often experimented with unconventional arrangements and sounds. The soundscape they created told most of the story. Melody and harmony carried less weight than did texture.

I listened to *Music for Airports* and other important compositions in this genre countless times, looking for their essence so I could find my voice.

Interestingly, when I was at the Musician's Institute, I didn't really fit with my fellow students when I composed. My arrangements, like my drumming at the time, were minimalist. I was, and I guess still am, a firm believer in using as few notes as possible to convey the message.

I know this sounds weird in some way because my programs and CDs all contain what one reviewer called, "rapid fire drums". I fill all the spaces at tempos up to twelve beats per second (that's fast by the way). This is a lot of notes, but they are all necessary to drive the brain the way REI does.

My ambient tracks, on the other hand, are open. They fill a void, but don't interfere. In exploring and researching the effects, I discovered that different intervals and progressions affect the brain in different ways.

I start building ambient tracks using a variety of synthesizer sounds, with many tracks consisting of layers and layers of sounds. Once I have a soundscape that I like, I then perform a twenty-minute composition that follows one of a variety of intensity maps that I created from the research. Each ambient track evolves in a unique way, with its harmonic and subtly melodic structures interplaying with the synth's sound design.

Some ambient tracks add intensity, some lower intensity and some alter the effects of the rhythms. For example, adding an arpeggiated pattern to a single drum track can add a focusing element. Whereas using a full-bodied drone with limited harmonic intervals and a slow, meandering melody can reduce the intensity of the rhythms and enhance the calming effects.

Over the last eight years I've created hundreds of ambient tracks to influence the rhythms in as many ways. We initially used quite a few for the REI Custom Program when a client needed its moderating effect, but as we've refined the stimulation, we find there is less need for them. The ambients are now rarely used in the custom program. Brain Shift Radio has become my main repository for these tracks.

After eight years of building ambient tracks and testing the mechanisms involved, I now have hundreds of ambient tracks for the seven categories of music on Brain Shift Radio. Each has their own flavor and neurological effects. Making these tracks is often the highlight of my day.

Part II
Practice

Chapter Nine

Anxiety

"We set up this room as a calm room," explained Neil. "We bring the clients in here when they are having a hard time. We could have your calming music play through the speakers in the ceiling. Have it cycling all day."

"Sure, we could try that," I said. "Is it practical to bring someone who is having a meltdown all the way in here to calm? What about playing the tape wherever they are at the time?"

"We could, but we already use this room to help with calm; here we could get a baseline that would help us evaluate how your tape works."

"Okay, so your clients are used to coming in here to calm. That means it won't be jarring to use this room to test the tape," I said thinking out loud. "How long does it generally take someone to calm down?"

"I don't know exactly. Obviously it varies, but I think if we take a couple of weeks and document who comes in and how long it takes for them to calm down just being in the silence, we'll have a good idea."

I nodded, thinking this would be a great little project.

"It would also be helpful to document the trigger for the anxiety or meltdown as well as its type and severity. Is that possible?" I asked.

"I don't see why not," he replied. "Could you create a form for us to complete?"

"Sure, I'll do that."

I was talking with the program director of a vocational training center for adults with developmental disabilities and cognitive issues. This opportunity came to me after I presented the Otter Lake School pilot study paper at the Autism Society of Minnesota's state conference.

Neil was impressed with how the drumming was able to calm the students and he wanted to do a variation on that study in his center. For this facility, I wouldn't be playing live for each person. Instead, this study would investigate the use of recorded drumming rhythms to elicit calm on their own. Additionally, I had not worked with adults with autism and had always wondered if adults on the spectrum could see the same results as the kids did. This opportunity would allow me to explore this idea.

Though Neil didn't question what we saw in my study, he was somewhat skeptical that recorded drumming would have the same effect without the subject first experiencing the live drumming.

"I think you create a bond with your client as you play for him," he said. "Then as he listens to the tape you made for him he remembers this connection and the way it made him feel so he calms down."

"It's possible," I replied. Everyone I've played for up to this point listened to me play live for them at least once. "What if we add another layer to this and I make a single tape that everyone listens to."

"That will be interesting,"

So, that's how we ended up in the calm room, talking about piping in my recorded drumming. I was again astounded by the generosity and enthusiasm of people like Neil who opened their lives to me and my drumming. Looking back, I see numerous situations like this that have guided me along the path that my work has taken. Had it not been for people like Neil and Erik, who made my first study possible, I would probably still be playing for individuals without any clear sense of the larger possibilities in the drumming.

I spent some time creating a tracking form that would be comprehensive enough for our purposes, but also fairly easy and quick to complete. I also needed to find a way to make a single recording out of all the different tapes I made for the students in my school study.

• • •

"Do you think you can make a single tape to calm everyone?" asked Beth, skeptically.

"I have no idea," I replied. "Let's listen to the tapes from the school study and see if there is a common thread. I'm concerned, though, that given Marcus' experiences with his and Tom's tape, we will find there are rhythms specific to each person."

I was referring to the school study I talk about in Chapter 2 where one student wasn't calmed very often by the tape I first made for him, but was calmed twice as often with a tape I made for another student. Because these tapes where made at roughly the same time, every aspect of the recordings—the drum's pitch, tone, timbre, the recording's mic and positioning, EQ and other effects—were identical. The only difference was in the particular rhythms that I played. This suggested that each rhythm was important and impacted each listener in a unique way.

As well, anxiety manifests in different ways, depending on the person and the circumstances. In the school study we saw anxiety in the form of tantrums, aggression, self-stimulatory behaviors, and sensory defensiveness. The question was whether there was a common thread to reducing anxiety, regardless of its manifestation.

"Do you really think you can make a common calming tape?" Beth asked again.

"I don't know," I said, my confidence fading. "But wouldn't it be cool if there was a way to make a generalized calming tape for people on the spectrum. The tape could be inexpensive and every school could have one and..." I said, getting ahead of myself.

"Slow down. Let's listen to the tapes from the study first."

So I listened. I spent dozens of hours listening and transcribing each tape from the student study and reconciling them with the tracking documents for each listening session. I was looking for several things: Were there consistencies between the effectiveness of someone's tape and the particular rhythms on it? Was the order of the rhythms similar? Were there rhythms, accents or tones that were common among the effective tapes? How about the ineffective tapes? Was there a pattern of calming related to the type of anxiety or behavior that responded to certain rhythms?

"I think I have it," I said to Beth a few weeks after our decision to explore each tape's rhythms. "This tape contains all the rhythms common to the ones that worked best and doesn't contain any of the tonal or accent patterns that were common to the tapes that didn't work as well. I think there is some room for error, so this might be a good starting point."

I turned it on, quietly.

Beth listened intently and after a few minutes she screwed up her face and said, "I don't think you have it. It's annoying. Why is it so different than the other tapes?"

"What do you mean?" I asked, somewhat offended. "The rhythms are all there."

"Okay," she paused, "but it sounds like you're playing a wet cardboard box in a gymnasium."

"I thought I would soften the drum sound and tune it down a bit. Then I added some reverb..."

"I think you need to tune it back up and remove that annoying reverb."

"I like the reverb," I said defensively. "What about the rhythms? They work, right?"

"I wouldn't know because it sounds like mud. I think you should try to keep the drum sound just like it was in the study. You can change the sound of it later if this idea works. Don't change everything at once, otherwise you're not going to know what does or doesn't work. "

"But I like the sound..." I muttered.

"You know what I think?" she said, cutting me off. "I think you're scared. I think you're so worried that your drumming isn't good enough that you're focusing on the wrong things. Go back to basics. Just focus on the rhythms and keep the sound pure. It will either work or it won't."

"But I like the sound." I repeated under my breath as I went back to the studio. I knew she was right, but I thought there must be a magic 'something' that this tape needed. It couldn't just be my drumming. It needed more.

In spite of my fear and because of Beth's insistence, I pushed through and made a tape that sounded almost exactly like the ones I made for the school study. I played it for Beth.

"That's better," was all I got from her.

But it was enough. I took the tape to the training center and we plugged it into the stereo and played it in the calm room.

Neil and I sat in the back of the room as the inaugural clients came in to calm down.

One client came in gripping his neck with both hands and rocking back and forth as his aide guided him to a chair. A few minutes later another man came in grunting and wringing his hands together. These men both exhibited behaviors similar to those I saw with the children in my school study. I started to think that maybe this could work. But after a couple of minutes, I wondered why it was taking so long for these guys to calm down.

I looked over at Neil, trying to get some sense of what he was thinking about it. Nothing. He was intently watching and giving no outward indication of what he thought. At this point I was nervous (the tape wasn't calming me), and I was convinced that it was taking forever for any of the listeners to calm down.

What if they didn't, I wondered? Neil and I sat as more clients came and went from the room with their various aides. No one said a word to me. I saw a few glances from the staff toward Neil and me, but I couldn't get a read on what anyone was thinking. This was maddening. I was convinced that I aged a decade while sitting there.

After about 40 minutes, Neil motioned for us to leave. We walked in silence to his office. He didn't say a word to me, clearly lost in thought as we walked. Once in his office, he called some of the staff that had been in the room with their clients. I'm sure that they were going to tell me what a waste of time this was.

"Jennifer, what do you think?" Neil asked one of the aides.

Jennifer stood silent for a minute, clearly trying to find a way to let me down easily.

"That was incredible!" she burst. "Michael has never settled like that before. I brought him in and he calmed down in about five minutes. You remember the other day when I was in there for two hours trying to calm him down?" she said, turning to Nancy, another aide.

Nancy nodded, "Yeah, and last week I spent over an hour trying to console him. James did well, too. Ordinarily, when he starts wringing his hands, I get a full-blown meltdown and he starts screaming and pulling on his hair. Not today. He just sat and listened to the music."

Neil and his staff continued to talk about the clients' responses as I stood there trying to take it all in. They were happy. How come I was not? The responses were too subtle to me. I didn't have a read on the clients. Perhaps this was because I didn't have a chance to get to know them first by playing for them. There was no connection for me. This brought up a lot of feelings. Was I ready to get out of the way and let my music speak for itself? Or was the process of playing for each person critical for my sense of accomplishment?

Neil looked at me. "I think you've got something here," he said, giving me a pat on the back.

I felt gratified, but we had a long way to go in this experiment. Because the staff was so enthusiastic, I decided that I would use this opportunity to try a variety of tapes to see if I could refine it. This meant that I wouldn't end up with a publishable study; but I would, I hoped, end up with a tape that Beth and I would feel comfortable using as a general calming tape.

My experience at the center ended with the development of my first calming tape, *REI for Neurobiological Disorders*. We sold this recording (cassette only—we couldn't afford to produce CDs) beginning in 1995 and continually worked on refining it. The second version, called *Calming Rhythms*, took two years to develop. When that recording came out we were finally able to afford to produce a CD as well as a cassette.

The success of the first calming tape allowed us to continue our research and also resulted in my presenting research at dozens of autism conferences around North America—in 1997 alone I spoke at 13 conferences. The response among these groups was extremely positive. However, some people didn't get it.

I'll admit that what I was doing, am doing, is unconventional. After all, I was using fast drumming to calm. This went against conventional wisdom on what it took to calm with music. This skepticism is best illustrated by a conversation I had a few years later with one of the most prominent people in the field.

"What tempo music are you using to help calm?" asked Don.

"Eight-beats-per-second," I answered, deadpan.

Don sat silently for a minute, trying to process what I just told him. I waited, knowing that he'd soon bombard me with questions. Partly as a challenge and partly because what I just told him flies in the face of everything he understood about using music to calm.

"Did you say eight beats per second? What is that in musical terms?"

"That's sixteenth notes at 120 beats per minute in 4/4 time. About march tempo," I replied.

He looked down at his plate, scooped a bite full of food onto his fork and ate as he pondered this for a minute. This was my first meeting in person with Don Campbell, author of numerous books on music and healing, including the breakout book, *The Mozart Effect*. This book put music as a therapeutic tool on the map, drawing from a study published in the early 1990's suggesting that listening to Mozart's music could improve cognitive function.

Together, Don and I had been on the faculty of numerous sound conferences over the years and had talked a few times on the phone, but this was the first time he and I had a chance to meet privately have an in-depth conversation. He asked for this meeting so that he could understand what I was doing with drumming. He was, at the time, working on what would be his last book, *Healing at the Speed of Sound*. Much of what I had been talking about for the previous twenty years was contrary to what conventional wisdom suggested about creating calm.

So calm was where we started our discussion. I was used to this type of questioning. In fact, several years before, I received a call from someone high up at a large publisher of music therapy books. He asked the same question: What tempo music do I use to calm?

In this instance, I received a hang up. Not just a hang up, but a scoff followed by an obscenity. Seriously, the guy scoffed, swore, and hung up on me. He didn't give me a chance to explain why it is that this fast drumming is calming.

Today, Don was giving me the chance to answer his questions. He was patient and gracious in putting aside what he knew about calming music to hear why fast drumming can have a calming effect.

"I understand you've been having positive effects, but how can drumming this fast be calming?" he finally asked.

"Well, first try to forget what you think you know about calming music." I answered. "Tell me, how would you compose music to calm?"

"I'd follow the 60-beat-per-minute music approach. Slow tempo, sparsely orchestrated, using major chords and non-dissonant intervals," he replied, summing up conventional wisdom in just a few words.

"Why is that combination calming? What's happening to the listener?"

"When this approach was first developed, it was believed that the heartbeat entrains to the music, calming the person down. But now it seems it's a result of what we call the relaxation response. This response is based on the idea that the music is soothing emotionally and that calms the mind and body. Most people find slow, sparse music to be soothing, therefore it is calming for them."

"Okay," I said. "So, how do you explain why many people with

ADHD say that heavy metal music is calming for them?"

"I'd call that catharsis. It hits them on an emotional level and gives them an emotional release, calming them down."

"So, the mechanism is essentially the same?" I asked.

He nodded.

"Both types of music create a relaxation response," I continued. "Each person has their own unique response to the music. You may find Bach calming, someone else may prefer Native American flute music, while I may like driving rock music."

"Sure, I can see that. But all music is psychological. That's the power of music. It moves us. Makes us feel."

"Sure, if it contains the elements of music that we respond to emotionally. So from this perspective, then, not everyone is calmed by the same music. It has to move each of us emotionally, right?"

I'm trying to help Don see music as I do. I am, after all, someone with ADHD. Rarely is conventional calming music calming for me. My brain doesn't like the emptiness and banal predictability of this 60-beat-per-minute music. It's not that I am a contrarian (though I can be, sometimes). It's because people like me, which represent between five and fifteen percent of the population, are simply different. Our brains operate differently. What works for us is different than what conventional wisdom suggests should work for everyone.

I wanted to show him this, mainly so he could see how I came up with the idea to play this fast in the first place.

Melody and harmony affect us emotionally. The effect of music on emotion is widely known. In fact, every composer instinctively understands that to push emotional buttons is the key to writing impactful music, so they quickly learn how to influence emotions with their music.

The root of our emotional response to music lies in music's melodic and harmonic content. The intervals between tones in music mean something to us because we rely mainly on association when listening to music.

All sensory input is weighed against previous sensory experiences. And it is through these previous experiences along with certain hardwired responses to pitched intervals that we feel the emotional impact. Separating rhythm or pure tone from the mix of melody and harmony largely strips the music of its emotional markers.

Even percussion-intensive tribal music contains sufficient doses of melody and harmony, through singing and chanting, to make this emotional connection. In fact, early ethnomusicologists focused on these aspects along with the words and rituals because these are the key to the emotional appeal of tribal music. Because I was not interested in the singing, or the melodic or harmonic components, or the rituals, I focused my attention solely on the rhythm.

Using rhythm alone requires a completely different approach. With drums you can't really create legato notes or passages. Drums produce sharp, short sounds. They are also not very melodic. Even if you were to tune your drums to pitched intervals, without a corresponding change in note duration, it doesn't carry any emotional appeal (unless you have certain associations with the drumming).

Drums, though disadvantaged in melodic or harmonic interest, have strengths that allow them to create calm without resorting to emotions. Percussion can directly influence the brain.

"REI is not like other music," I described to Don. "Because there are essentially none of the aspects of music that we respond to emotionally, we need to look at it in a different way. Are you familiar with brainwave entrainment technology?"

"Yes. Beat frequencies to drive the brain."

As I describe in Chapter 5, beat frequencies are a phenomenon of sound associated with our ability to locate sounds in space, where two slightly different sound frequencies interact to create a perceived beat or pulse equaling the difference between the two frequencies. Beat frequencies, when heard in certain circumstances, have the ability to entrain the brainwaves to the tempo of the pulsation.

"How about shamanic drumming to alter consciousness?" I asked.

"Sure. Maxfield's study from the 1990's showed that drumming induced a theta wave in the brain," explained Don. He was referring to a study where drumming rhythms played at four beats per second facilitated a corresponding four-beat-per-second pulse in the listener's brain.

"So, you understand they are the same thing," I said. "Both rhythmic pulses entrain the brain to the tempo of the pulsation."

"Sure, but it's not calming at the tempos you're talking about," he countered. "What did you say the speed of your rhythms are, again?"

"Eight-beats-per-second," I replied. "At the lower end of alpha. This a relaxed, yet still alert, state."

"Okay, I get that. But haven't brainwave entrainment technologies proven to be ineffective at alpha? If I recall correctly, tolerance is a problem. Because of the alertness of the listener and the repetitiveness of the pulse, the brain becomes desensitized to the stimulus and shuts it out."

"Yes, and this is where REI is different. Because it's drumming, played with human hands, using non-repetitive rhythms, there is a high variability to the patterns. This keeps it from becoming habituating."

"That makes sense. Novelty activates the brain." He stopped and thought for a minute while we each took a few bites of our food. "Tell me about your contention that each rhythm offers a unique effect. Didn't I hear you describe at the sound conference last year that if you don't play the correct rhythm you don't see a response?"

"Yes, I saw this even during my first study," I replied. Then I went on to describe the study (Chapter 2) where one of the students showed a definite improvement in calming from one drumming tape over another when the only difference between the two was the particular rhythms.

"Initiating calm in a typical person is pretty simple—play variable rhythms at eight-beats-per-second," I said, "But reducing anxiety, which manifests in a variety of ways, is more complicated. In this case the rhythms matter. Different forms of anxiety respond to different rhythms. Rhythms for generalized anxiety, for example, are different than those for aggressive outbursts."

"I see. So, you alter the rhythms that you use by focusing on the type of anxiety a person has," surmised Don.

"Exactly. This same process holds for all the symptoms my clients have. The trick is making sure the right rhythms are on a recording," I said.

My meeting with Don gave me a chance to see where most people get lost when thinking about how REI drumming can calm. I believe I learned as much, if not more, than Don during our short time together. I would also like to think that he left our meeting with a deeper understanding of the role drumming—even fast drumming—can have to calm listeners.

• • •

During my research, including my studies at the public school and the vocational center, I found that there was a fairly large range of rhythms that I could use. I learned that they couldn't be overly complex—that is, they needed to flow with somewhat predictable patterns—but they needed to be unusual and change frequently so that they didn't remain the same for too long.

This became my approach to anxiety in general. Episodic change—reducing anxiety as the drumming plays—can be done using the same rhythms from one episode to another. Whereas creating long-term changes in anxiety requires slowly building the rhythms' complexity progressively over time. I may start in the same place, but it isn't long before the stimulation levels get pretty high. It is the higher stimulation that seems to help with the chronic anxiety. I learned this early on when I was working at a center for people with chronic illnesses in the Minneapolis area.

"I feel that rhythm in my shoulder," said Kate as I played. "Now it's uncomfortable."

She had been directing me as I played, telling me how she felt at every turn of the rhythm. This was part of her process. Her anxiety, I was told, compelled her to verbalize what she was feeling at all times. This was helpful for me because most the people I played for were non-verbal or had limited language skills—even those that could talk had a hard time verbalizing what they were feeling.

"I don't like that one." I switched to a triplet-based pattern, one that was usually uplifting.

"I like that better." A pause. Then, "I feel pressure on the sides of my head. Please change the rhythm."

This was my fifth session with 32 year-old Kate; she had become a lot better in dealing with her anxiety in general. When we first met, she was at a low point and her anxiety was significantly impacting her life.

She also described that her sleep was poor. "I usually wake up two or three times a night. I can fall asleep pretty quickly, but I always wake up anxious and ruminate on all the things that worry me. I can't shut off the anxious thoughts."

She also experienced anxious thoughts throughout the day, the worst times were when she drove in her car. This anxiety often resulted in her getting disoriented and feeling lost even when on familiar roads. She also wouldn't travel on a plane. In addition, Kate was disorganized and often missed appointments.

"I slept in my car the other night," Kate said upon entering the room. "I was driving home and there was a construction detour and I got turned around and got lost. I freaked out. I don't know. I got lost and I freaked out. I had to stop and, you know, I couldn't drive so I climbed in the back seat and curled up under the sleeping bag. Like I used to all the time."

"How are you doing today?" I asked.

"I'm better, but still uncomfortable driving. I had to take the bus here. I'm also still waking up a lot at night with feelings of panic. I don't know exactly what I'm afraid of, but I get so anxious I wake in a sweat and can't get back to sleep."

• • •

By following her cues and adjusting my rhythms as I went along, my sessions with Kate offered me immediate feedback on how my drumming can calm a single listener. I also received important feedback from formal studies, such as those I conducted with the help of Neil and Erik. These avenues were only two (of many) places I was able to explore how fast, complex drumming rhythms can induce calm. I've also had many opportunities to test my theories with groups of listeners.

Over the last twenty years I've given presentations at research symposiums, trade conferences, schools, hospitals, yoga centers, and anyplace that will let me play my drum. In each instance, I give my listeners a chance to feel how specific rhythms can make them feel calm or agitated.

I begin with a five-beat rhythm that has two loud notes and three soft ones. At first people listen and nod. It's a little different hearing music played in five-beat-time, so people tend to tune in. But as I keep playing the rhythm I see my listeners first shift in their seats and then tense up. I usually play long enough that nearly everyone in the room is in this state of fidgeting before I stop.

"How does that feel?" I always ask.

"It's annoying." "I don't like it." "I find it agitating." "I'm certainly not calm."

These are the responses I invariably hear. This short, repetitive pattern is anything but calming.

I start up again with this same rhythm. Tension immediately fills the room; and before I have mutiny on my hands, I switch to a more variable and unpredictable pattern. It doesn't take long for everyone to calm down.

I have played this scenario in countless seminars and I always get the same response. Sure, there are some people who either don't become agitated by the five-beat rhythm or who don't calm down in the time that I allocate for this experiment, but the vast majority of listeners follow this pattern. This little exercise helps them understand, on a level beyond the intellectual, how rhythm can impact a listener.

I have even gone so far as to choose a much more complicated rhythm to repeat to see if I elicit the same level of agitation. It comes, but it takes longer.

Highly complex rhythms played at slower tempos, say six-beats-per-second, also often cause agitation. For these slower tempos, you need to find a groove and stick with it. Traditional rhythms in typical time signatures work best. If the rhythm is too odd or syncopated it doesn't work for calm. However, this same rhythm played at eight-beats-per-second can induce calm.

When entraining to theta, as rhythms at six-beats-per-second would do, having some level of familiarity and repetition is reassuring and allows the listener to relax into the altered state. Because theta is an inwardly-directed state, we open to otherworldly experiences and are less focused on the rhythm. This allows our brains to entrain.

Alpha, the state induced through eight-beat-per-second pulses, is a relaxed yet outwardly-directed state. In alpha you are aware and alert. You are also more attentive to your surroundings, so any repetitive stimulus that doesn't pose a threat to your survival must be ignored for you to be present for any stimulation that is a threat. Drumming rhythms are hard to ignore. Repetitive rhythms cause agitation if they go on long enough, whereas unpredictable, non-repetitive rhythms at the same tempo are calming because they keep the brain engaged.

The bottom line is that rhythms that would be calming in alpha are not calming in theta and rhythms that are calming in theta are not calming in alpha. Theta-tempo rhythms may work for a typical person, but when dealing with someone with autism, ADHD, anxiety, or sensory processing issues, alpha is a better state because the brain is more active and alert.

Of course, along with playing at the right tempo, it's important to play the right rhythm. At the right time. And it needs to be played quietly, if it's on a recording. If it's too loud, it masks the listener's ability to be aware of environmental threats, so it causes agitation.

• • •

Kate sighed as I settled into another rhythm. In a time signature of 37/16, it had the feel of a sultry half-time shuffle, which is a triplet-feel with a slow, arching pulse happening every six beats. These six-beat patterns happen five times followed by a turn-around beat in seven, totaling 37 beats. At eight-beats-per-second, this rhythm takes less than five seconds to complete. With a rhythm like this I'll often repeat it six to eight times, putting the cycle at around 30-40 seconds. Because I repeat the pattern, I try to make it a composition in itself; I'll vary the seven-beat part of the pattern every fourth time around. This keeps the rhythm from being predictable and makes it musical.

Musical form tends to follow certain structures; by following some of these structures in my playing, the drumming feels familiar. We all listen to enough music that we inherently know the structures even if we aren't musicians. Listen to any piece of music and you'll hear the themes and their variations and progressions. I've found that even though the rhythms I use are strange, including a sense of musical structure keeps them from feeling disjointed.

Kate was silent, a first for her. I could tell she was really relaxed by what I was playing. I'd used the 37 beat rhythm as the central theme of this passage and had been playing variations on it for the past five minutes, often returning to the core rhythm. The idea was to melt her anxiety by getting her used to this odd pattern while slowly making it odder.

This tends to reduce anxiety. I like to think of it as stretching the primitive mind. Start with something safe, somewhat familiar but not so much as to be agitating, and push the limits a little at a time; and slowly, gradually pull someone out of their comfort zone, occasionally returning to the safety spot if she starts to get edgy.

If you were to listen to any of my REI Custom Programs that focus on reducing chronic anxiety, you'll hear this type of progression. If you were to listen carefully to all of the tracks in an anxiety-directed Program, you'll hear this pattern play out in a progressive manner, with the first track using a somewhat complex rhythm and a handful of more complex rhythms.

The second track will pull one of the more complex rhythms from the first track into the first position and build complexity from there. It may also include the first rhythm from Track #1.

The third track will start with one of the more complex rhythms from track two and build from there, while also bridging back to Track #1's core rhythm. This progression will happen across all the tracks in an REI Custom Program. It is the progressive stimulation that makes the changes we see over the course of a Program.

We like to think of it as interval training or strength training where you slowly build endurance or strength by adding a little more at each workout until you reach the level you want. A client's musical workout can take time, but you can end up with a change in the way a person responds to a stimulus.

Kate listened to recordings of our bi-weekly sessions. After twelve weeks consisting of six live sessions and six recordings, each listened to once a day for two weeks, she was a different person.

Kate's anxiety centered on a generalized sense of worry or doom, so I could use her sense of anxiety as a barometer for how my drumming was helping. Many of the people I work with who experience anxiety manifest it through other types of behaviors. Ten-year-old Timmy tantrummed when he became anxious. This anxiety was most prominent when he was asked to change what he was doing. Transitions always elicited an emotional outburst: He would scream and lash out at whoever was close.

"This is our special needs room," described Sara as we walked into a classroom ringed by cubicle dividers. Each cubicle area was furnished with a small table and a couple of chairs. Some also contained a beanbag chair or a carpet on the linoleum floor. There was a large table in the center of the room with a dozen small chairs and two couches in the cubicle space directly across from the door.

"Why the cubicles?" I asked.

"We work with each student one-on-one for most of the day," she explained as she led me to the couches where we sat down.

I unpacked my drum, threw it on my lap and give it a quick tune as Sara explained, "Timmy will be coming back to the classroom any minute. He's usually pretty agitated."

She paused, then said, "There, you can hear him now."

Hearing a commotion coming from the hall, I started playing my drum. I jumped into a series of calming rhythms at a pretty high volume, not feeling a need to start quietly because Timmy wasn't in the room. Instead, I wanted Timmy to hear it from the hallway.

I was playing loud enough that I could no longer hear what was going on outside the classroom. I watched the door for him, ready to adjust my rhythms based on how he acted as he came into the room.

It took less than two minutes for Timmy to peek into the room. He did this by standing across the hall from the door. He seemed to look everywhere but at me. I ignored him as I played, waiting for him to get the courage to enter the room.

Timmy stayed in the hallway for a while, alternately standing where he could see me and moving out of range. I ran through a series of calming rhythms, hoping that he would come into the room. Eventually he did, slowly migrating from the doorway and around the perimeter of the room until he came to the couch. As he navigated closer to me, I dropped my volume until I was playing at barely a whisper as he stood before me.

I continued playing for another minute or two without looking his way. He remained planted a couple of feet from me.

I stopped.

Timmy surprised me by approaching me and touching the drum. He very gently put one hand on each side and looked past me. I tapped the head with my index fingers, creating a syncopated patter, still not looking at him.

His hands moved to the edge of the drum, then onto my hands while not disturbing my playing. I kept playing with just my index fingers, but edged-up the rhythms a little, increasing in speed and complexity. Timmy's hands gripped my two last fingers, which were hanging off the sides of drum.

As I morphed my rhythms over the next few minutes, Timmy's grip changed with each permutation. Harder, then softer. Back and forth in different intensities as the rhythms rose and fell. We were dancing the rhythms. This dance lasted several minutes until he abruptly let go and sat down on the floor. The connection was gone.

I dropped my volume and faded out. Timmy was playing with legos, his back to me. I packed up and left the room.

Sara followed me out and said, "That was cool. He doesn't like physical contact and here he initiated it with you."

"Yeah, it was cool," I replied. This connection, no matter how fleeting, was one of the reasons I loved playing live for kids and was something I never really got tired of. It was also something that didn't happen that often. However, as gratifying as it was, I didn't allow myself to spend much time on it. I was focused on what I needed to do in order for Timmy to become less emotionally reactive.

"Did he settle down quicker today than usual?" I asked, trying to get a sense of whether the rhythms I had chosen had contributed to his calming after the change in rooms and activities.

"Yes. He is usually pretty agitated for a while. But he seemed to connect with you. That calmed him."

"That was fun," I said as I wondered if this connection could be helpful in reducing his anxiety overall. Other kids I had played with seemed to carry that connection to their relationship with their REI recording. My work with past clients showed that this connection wasn't necessary, but I felt it always helped.

Sara and I talked more about Timmy's anxiety and she assured me that his parents were on board with him listening to an REI recording.

Sara felt comfortable using our online system, saying she preferred to play the track through her phone. I entered Timmy's intake data into our system and Sara was able to begin playing his recording in school the next day. She would enter Timmy's progress into her account and I would only lightly monitor it, letting our software take the lead in creating the tracks for Timmy.

The goal was for Timmy to become less emotional during the many transitions he experienced throughout the day.

Over the course of sixteen weeks, Timmy listened to eight progressively-created, custom-made REI recordings, each used once a day for two weeks during the school week. Making the recordings one after another, based on Timmy's responses, was the key to making overall changes to his ability to handle change.

Timmy responded immediately with his first REI recording. Sara chose to play Timmy's recording first thing in the morning because this was generally one of his most difficult times. The transition to school nearly always caused a meltdown. She also hoped that listening first thing would make the rest of the day easier.

The first day it took about five minutes for Timmy to settle in. Ordinarily he could be agitated for up to an hour. His calm lasted until lunchtime, when he had a meltdown in the cafeteria. I asked that Sara not play Timmy's recording more than once a day because I wanted to ensure that he didn't get overstimulated from the drumming.

Timmy's first two weeks continued with him listening first thing in the morning, calming quickly and remaining calm until lunchtime. At the two-week point, Sara called me to ask whether another time of day would be better from Timmy. She described that he seemed to adjust to the day easier and he was arriving at school less agitated. We decided that playing his recording right before lunch might be worth a try.

Timmy again responded immediately with this new schedule. Sara turned on his recording about ten minutes before it was time to go to the cafeteria and let it play as he got his food and began eating. She described from the first day that he stayed calm as he went through the transition from classroom activities to lunchtime.

It was obvious from the outset that Timmy would calm when the REI recording played. At the beginning of the Program, he would remain calm until another transition took place. Then he would get anxious. This pattern changed over the course of about six weeks. At first Timmy had the occasional time when he handled a change without issues, but after six weeks he would tolerate most transitions without a problem.

"Timmy is now self-regulating," described Sara at our eight-week check-in. "You can see him begin to get stuck in his pattern and almost have a meltdown, but then he collects himself. He never used to be able to do that."

Given that he was calmer and beginning to learn to calm himself and tolerate change, we had Timmy return to listening first thing in the morning. This was an easier time for Sara to play his track and we wanted to see how well he could navigate the day's changes without using the track during a transition.

The goal of reducing anxiety with REI is to get to the point where the listener is able to learn to self-regulate. As with Timmy, it can be helpful to use the REI recording when the anxiety is at its worst, but eventually it can become a crutch. The switch back to listening when a client isn't having an emotional reaction to change removes this crutch.

Timmy handled this change well. For the first few days, Timmy was agitated when transitioning to lunch; but by the end of the first week he was able to transition as smoothly as he did when he listened during this transition.

The last seven weeks of the Program were designed to integrate his self-regulation skills solidly enough that he would not need to listen to his REI recording everyday. He did this successfully. I talked with Sara a couple of weeks after he stopped listening to his last REI recording.

"Timmy is a new kid. He no longer tantrums when asked to move on to a new activity. His resistance has melted over the last couple of months and now all I need to do is let him know a minute or so before we make a change that he needs to get ready to do something else. You can see him preparing himself. He stops what he's doing for a few seconds and gets quiet. Then, when we ask him to switch activities, he does it without hesitation. He hasn't had a meltdown in several weeks."

Timmy illustrates the REI Custom Program path that many clients struggling with anxiety follow. The first track provides an immediate, temporary calm. Each progressive track extends the amount of time the listener remains calm after listening until we see some level of self-calming in situations that caused anxiety before beginning the Program.

Nearly every person I work with has anxiety. For some, like Timmy and Kathleen, it's the primary concern. For others, it's one in a long list of issues they want to address. Either way, I start an REI Custom Program by reducing anxiety, then move on to other symptoms, if there are any. This usually works well, because anxiety requires lower stimulation rhythms than other symptoms. As I build the level of stimulation for the anxiety, I eventually get to the level that the other symptoms can be addressed.

Of course, stimulation levels are only part of the equation. The particular rhythms also matter. This is something I cover in the chapters that follow.

Chapter Ten
Attention

I'm a drummer and a tapper. I drum on everything. All the time. It drives many people crazy (my wife, bless her, handles it really well, rarely telling me to stop). I always thought that my need to drum was just because of my obsession with music and rhythm; but as I was doing some research for an upcoming study on ADHD, I discovered that I'm not alone in my need to tap.

"Have you ever heard of 'fidget-to-focus'?" David asked, as we were talking about our study. David was a neuropsychologist. He worked at a progressive clinic in San Diego, and he was also a drummer. Although ADHD wasn't his specialty, he was excited about exploring whether my drumming could impact attention. We were planning a study using a Continuous Performance Test (CPT) to collect quantitative data.

"No, what is it?" I replied.

"It's based on a study done years ago on coping strategies people with ADHD develop to help them focus. This study was exploring why it was believed that ADHD was considered a childhood disorder that people grow out of as they reach adulthood. It turns out that people don't necessarily grow out of ADHD. Instead, many people develop strategies to help them function better. The ADHD is still there."

"So what does fidgeting have to do with it?"

"Well, it seems that fidgeting is one of the most common strategies people with ADHD use to keep their attention. Most are simple things like rocking, shaking a leg, playing with a pen or pencil, anything that uses a motor movement to keep them engaged."

"Like drumming."

"Perhaps. Do you suppose there is a higher prevalence of drummers with ADHD than other musicians?"

"I don't know. That's an interesting idea, though. Most of the drummers I know are kind of like me. In fact, I don't know any drummers who are not at least a little distracted, impulsive or hyperactive."

"That would be an interesting study to do someday. But for now, if we consider fidgeting to help with attention, musical or not, perhaps the rhythm impacts the brain in a positive way."

"It seems like the case to me, but what does fidgeting mean for our study?"

"Probably nothing, but maybe we can use the concept of fidget-to-focus as a basis for our hypothesis. Didn't you say that you started developing your therapy from your experiences playing the drums and feeling more focused?"

"Yes. I guess that would be like fidgeting-to-focus. Only I wasn't doing it solely to help focus. The drumming exercises were homework. And I wasn't just focusing better while I drummed, I felt more focused afterward. The residual focusing effect was the basis of exploring the drumming for focus. My goal was to see if listening to syncopated drumming rhythms provided the same focusing effect as playing my homework exercises."

I described to David that one of my challenges while attending the Musician's Institute was being able to keep up with the pace of my classes. The most difficult thing for me, and many percussionists, was music theory and composition. I spent a lot of time analyzing music, digging deep into the structures that were being used in rock and jazz music. To this day I can't listen to the Beatles and enjoy their music for what it is. I always find myself remembering the many hours spent dissecting their songs.

As someone with ADHD, focusing on the mundane analysis of music theory and composition was nearly impossible. Contrasted with this was my favorite class, sight-reading, which was always interesting and, as a result, easy for me to focus on.

Because I wanted to avoid music theory and instead work on sight-reading, I decided that I would reward myself for my theory and composition work by doing my sight-reading exercises before going back to some of the mundane work I was assigned. As someone who was somewhat impulsive and hated delayed gratification, I quickly decided to reverse this plan. Instead of theory first, I would allow myself to spend a half-hour or so doing my sight-reading exercises then dig into theory for 30 minutes, followed by another bit of sight-reading.

The reason I preferred sight-reading was that I was able to play continually unique patterns. One basic exercise consisted of reading rhythm patterns from a book on syncopation, called *Progressive Steps to Syncopation For the Modern Drummer*, by Ted Reed. The patterns were random combinations of 8th and 16th notes written across the page, page after page throughout the book.

My assignment was always to choose a page and read it in varying ways. Left to right, top to bottom, bottom to top, right to left, diagonally, whatever. The goal was to always be reading one or two measures ahead of where I was playing. By being accustomed to reading ahead, I could, when confronted with a new piece of music, comprehend and interpret it right away and convincingly perform it the way the composer intended. I loved these exercises. They gave me a rush.

Imagine my surprise when I also discovered that these exercises made doing my theory and composition work easier. After 30 minutes of sight-reading, I'd switch to theory and, to my amazement, could focus. The analysis was easier and the musical structures started making sense. I could even begin to appreciate the simple predict-ability of the Beatles' music.

And analyzing more complex music of some of the progressive jazz-fusion bands like the Mahavishnu Orchestra or Weather Report became rote. My grades for the semesters after discovering this sight-reading-then-theory pattern confirmed what I suspected. I was fo-cusing better and grasping complex concepts better.

I later discovered that the reason I had trouble focusing on the analytical composition work is that, as someone with ADHD, I tend to have an abundance of theta-wave activity in my brain, particularly in the frontal lobes where the ability to attend is centered. This theta activity is the reason that many people with ADHD are also sensi-tive, imaginative, creative, and are able to make connections between seemingly unrelated things.

Pervasive theta activity in people with ADHD is one of the rea-sons that stimulant medication is the treatment of choice for many people with the condition. Drugs like Ritalin increase brain activity, effectively reducing the amount of theta activity. This, in turn, helps with focusing. The syncopation exercises acted like brain stimulant medication by increasing the activity in the parts of my brain that usually hover in theta.

My experiences with the sight-reading were sifting to the back of my mind while I explored the techniques that I was learning from Lloyd. I never asked him his thoughts about my experiences, because it never occurred to me that they would some day be connected.

The connection came when I was teaching hand drumming several years later. Every Monday night I led a group comprised of students who studied privately with me. This class gave them an opportunity to practice with other drummers. This practice forced them to inter-nalize the rhythms, learn to listen as they played, and allowed them to learn how to play solos.

One night, to push everyone's techniques, three drummers were to lay down a basic groove at a much faster tempo than was usually played. In this case, a little over eight-beats-per-second. With the groove happening, the rest of the group took turns improvising on these grooves. We played for about 30 minutes. When we stopped, Gene said, "Wow, I'm in the zone. I feel really focused. Do you suppose that's the drumming?"

"Yeah, probably," I said. Then I went on to describe how I used the syncopation exercises, which are similar to improvisation, to help with my focusing at school.

"Would you play for my son?" asked Jan, jumping into the discussion. "I know you play for kids with autism. My son has ADHD and I wonder if listening to you drum would help him with his attention."

"Let's try it and see," I answered. Jan and I set up a time for me to play for her son.

The next week I went to Jan's house and met her son, Jamie. Jamie was nine-years-old and was having trouble focusing on his schoolwork. Jan and I decided that I would play for Jamie while he did his homework. To keep him from being resistant to the music, Jan told him that I was there to play for her and that she wanted him in the room so she could keep an eye on him.

The session didn't start out great. Jamie was interested in the drum, so getting him to attend to his schoolwork wasn't easy. We decided to let him focus on the drumming for a while until it became less of a novelty to him. This took about ten minutes. During this time he danced around the room, came up to the drum, held it, tapped it, and pushed my hands off so he could play. He basically showed his hyperactive side.

I tried playing every calming-type rhythm I knew, but it still took a good ten minutes before he settled down.

Jan stood by, letting him go through his paces until the novelty of my drumming wore off and he could be directed to the table. She began by drawing with him, something he loved to do. They sat at the table while he drew and I played. During this time, about ten minutes or so, I sped up my rhythm a little and began introducing more complex patterns, in the hopes of helping him focus.

A couple of minutes before I ended, Jan brought his math homework to him. She got him started on it by helping with the first couple of problems. I was playing quietly so it wouldn't be a distraction for him. I continued playing for about five minutes at a low volume as he did his homework, then faded my playing out over a couple of minutes and stopped. I quietly got up and joined Jan in the kitchen, where she had retreated once Jamie was settled into doing his math.

We stood in the kitchen and watched through the door as Jamie kept up with his math. After about fifteen minutes we became bored watching him work, so we sat down at the table and talked.

"He never spends this much time on his math without getting distracted," she said. "Ordinarily, he gets up every five minutes or so and I have to steer him back to his work."

"He does seem content," I said.

"Content? He's never just content. You saw him when you started drumming. He's always like that. Endlessly moving. I call him my energizer bunny."

"So his settling like that and staying with his work is not typical?"

"No," she laughed. "This is something I've never seen. Not even when he was little. He has always been such a terror." She paused. "I think I could get used to this."

"Oh, I'd be surprised if this lasts. For me, each time I needed to focus I had to play the syncopation exercises. I would think if listening to the drumming helped, he would still need to listen next time he needed to focus."

"Could you make a tape of this that I can play for him everyday?"

"Sure."

I met with Jamie again a couple of days later with a tape in hand.

"You were right," said Jan when I arrived. "Jamie didn't focus any better yesterday when I asked him to do his homework. He was up every couple of minutes and needed constant re-directing. Could we turn his tape on now?"

"Yes, I'd love to see how it works for him," I said.

Jan wrangled Jamie into his chair at the table while I turned on the tape really quietly. My work with Jamie was about a year before my study at the school. At this point, I had never had the opportunity to watch as someone responded to a recording I've made for him. I was excited and curious.

Jan and I stepped away as Jamie started by squiggling on his paper. We sat on the couch and quietly watched as the tape played in the background. So far, Jamie had not mentioned the tape or gotten up and moved around. He spent a few minutes doodling on the page; and then after four or five minutes, he tackled his first math problem. Then the next.

He diligently worked on his math for the next fifteen or so minutes while the tape played. It wasn't long after the tape stopped that Jamie was up and running around.

"Well, it looks like he was able to focus to the tape," I said.

"Yeah, that was great. It was almost like the day you played," she said, but added thoughtfully, "But he seemed focused for longer after the live drumming."

"I'll bet the live drumming was more powerful. Still, this is encouraging. Could you play this everyday and see if he still focuses well while it plays and also see if the focusing lasts longer after the music stops?"

Jan did, and kept me updated every week at drumming class. It seemed that Jamie was focused most of the time as his tape played. It also seemed that the residual effects of the tape grew over time.

She also noticed something else. "This may not be related, but the other day at church several people came up to me after the service to say how well-behaved Jamie was. So, I got to thinking about it and I think they were right. We were able to stay in the sanctuary for the entire service this week. I usually have to leave with him because he gets disruptive. Do you think that could be from the tape?"

"That's pretty cool. I don't know. I guess it could help. I've noticed that the calm tends to build as people listen to their tape everyday. It's almost like they learn how to regulate themselves," I described. "Maybe there is a similar effect with focus."

Jan continued using this tape and Jamie continued doing well with it. My work with Jamie was the beginning of what would become a long exploration of listening to drumming for attention.

Because my playing live for someone with ADHD was more of a

distraction than a benefit, I directed a lot of my attention on what it would take to help people focus with a recording of the drumming. For four months, I worked with a group of children with ADHD using recordings like the one I made for Jamie. I also compared my recordings to a placebo recording of traditional drumming rhythms.

For the kids who listened to my REI recordings, I also initially played for them to see what effect it would have on their behavior. Like with Stacey—my first child client who calmed to my playing— most of the kids calmed down. I wasn't looking for focusing while I played because it was such a distraction.

One child, a ten-year-old named Jessie, did well with this recording. I talked to her mother after four weeks of listening.

"How is Jessie doing?" I asked.

"She has had very few temper tantrums since starting the listening," Martha replied. "She is also developing the ability to stop herself and calm herself down, usually within about one minute of when the tape starts."

"Interesting. This is something I've seen with the kids with autism but never considered for ADHDers."

"Her teachers in school have noticed a drastic change in Jessie over the past month," she added. "She has had a behavior chart in school where every 15 minutes the teachers would mark a plus or a minus for her behavior. Before starting the tape, many days she would have 10-15 minuses. After listening to the tape for the first two weeks, she started having a day here and there of all pluses. At the end of the first month on the tape, she had seven consecutive days of all pluses."

"Were her teachers aware she was listening?" I asked.

"No, I didn't mention the drumming to them. I wanted to see if they noticed any changes without expecting anything. They said that she was paying better attention in school and staying on task. I also noticed that she's not bringing as much homework from school, mostly just study guides for tests."

"That's exciting. I'm glad her teachers didn't know about the drumming," I said, encouraged by this revelation.

Not really expecting anything else, I asked, "Was there anything else that you noticed with Jessie's behavior?"

"Well, she has been getting along much better with her brothers and sisters," she added.

Jessie wasn't the only child in that study who saw improvements in focusing and in behavior in general. Overall, the results were on par with what I had seen with other kids who listened to me play my drum live and then had their own tape to listen to daily.

The most interesting thing I saw with this study was that none of the children who listened to the traditional drumming tape showed any increase in focusing abilities or improvements in other behaviors. On the contrary, a few were actually agitated by the traditional drumming. It seemed that the traditional drumming tape didn't contain the type of rhythms that could induce calm. After listening closely to the traditional recording and comparing it to the REI tape, I noticed that the traditional rhythms were fairly simple and they repeated for anywhere from four to five minutes each, too long to tolerate. Calm, as I described in the previous chapter, requires variability.

Focus requires this same variability as calm, but variability isn't enough. I discovered that the rhythms for focusing were more complex than those for calm. And I learned that I needed to change the rhythms more frequently for focus than for calm. For someone needing calm I could, for the most part, keep using the same tape for four or more weeks. For people with attention problems, I found two to three weeks was the maximum length of time they could use the same tape and continue to make progress.

If I were just using the recording to help someone focus while the tape played, the same tape could be used almost indefinitely; but if I expected any long-term or growing residual effects in focusing, I found that I needed to change the rhythms regularly.

Much later I also discovered that I could use variable tempos of rhythms to help with focusing. Changing the tempo slightly, along with changing the rhythms, meant that the same recordings could be used for even longer periods of time without seeing the effectiveness of the recordings drop. These variable tempos are a key to many of the tracks I created for Brain Shift Radio, my streaming music service.

Children like Jessie did well with the drumming. I also discovered that adults could benefit from the drumming, too. In one recent case, I had the opportunity to work with a 33 year-old man who had a classic case of ADHD.

Jim had difficulty sustaining focused attention, was restless, had trouble getting started on projects, and was impulsive. He also had trouble falling asleep and had significant anxiety, addictive behaviors, and mood issues.

Jim began the REI Custom Program soon after we launched our online system, which allowed me to create a new track every week and progressively build the stimulation levels in a way I couldn't when making and shipping CDs. The immediacy of delivering tracks online eliminated the time-lag that happened when shipping CDs. Jim's experience with this new system showed me that this approach was perfectly suited for people with attention issues. Because of his ambitious list of goals, Jim's Program was set to provide a new REI drumming track each week, more frequently than the two-week-per-track schedule most Programs employed.

Jim wanted to put an emphasis on attention and his addictive behavior, but also on his mood and anxiety. The stimulation needed for this mix of symptoms is somewhat at odds. Eliciting calm and focus at the same time meant using less complex, therefore less stimulating, tracks at the beginning of a Program than I would if I were only working on attention. As well, including the attention element into these first tracks meant that changes in sleep and anxiety wouldn't be as immediate or as pronounced than if I was able to start with just calm.

I mentioned this trade-off to Jim and he was okay with going slower on the anxiety and sleep if he could focus a little better sooner. He was preparing to begin graduate school and needed to be able to sustain his attention on his intensive reading schedule.

Jim's first week on track one resulted in a more stable energy level and mood throughout the week. He still had some anxiety and depressed negative thinking (due to circumstances and life changes).

But he was less impulsive in his decisions and was able to refrain from addictive behavior. He also found some improvement in focus, but still had some difficulty focusing in meditation and schoolwork. He did not see any improvement in his ability to fall asleep or in his pattern of waking early in the morning and being unable to get back to sleep

The next two weeks provided a similar effect with improved ability to maintain his focus, especially on his reading and writing. He was able to start projects and work on them without frustration. He had fewer feelings of anxiety during the week and found it easier to redirect himself and refrain from addictive behavior. His mood was still better and more stable. Jim's sleep hadn't improved yet and his resulting fatigue was beginning to be a problem, so we decided to adjust Track #4 to see if he could fall asleep easier and stay asleep longer.

This track brought an incremental improvement in sleep. He described, "for a few nights this week, I did not feel stuck in a tired state of being unable to fall asleep." By the end of the week he was falling asleep while his REI track played and was less tired than he had been since the beginning of the Program. His ability to focus when studying also continued to improve. He reported fewer addictive thoughts and actions compared to the previous week and was less anxious overall.

On the flip side, this track brought up emotions, including "some intense anger, frustration, moods and thoughts with resentment and bitterness."

It is not uncommon for adults to feel emotional during the process of an REI Custom Program. This often seems due to a greater self-awareness rather than an actual increase in emotional reactivity. These emotionally intense periods were short-lived and didn't pose a threat to him or others, so we proceeded on the same path we had been on, expecting him to move through this phase fairly quickly as other clients have done.

After a week on Track #5, he stated:

I realized this week that I have had long term anxiety problems

in addition to ADHD (my father also has had anxiety problems). I felt intense feelings of frustration, anger, and resentment earlier in the week, each of which were significantly reduced by the end of this week. My mind has slowed down, with fewer racing thoughts and intense moods.

The next five weeks showed a progressive improvement in all areas including, attention, sleep, mood, addictive behavior, and frustration tolerance despite moving out of state and beginning graduate school, "which brought about a resolution to a long, difficult period of change."

During this period he reported:

I was starting to see an overall consistency in all areas. Less anxiety, more solid sleep, more stable moods, better focus, and attention. Almost no feelings of anger, resentment, and frustration compared to a few weeks ago. Did not see any clear regression in any areas. Still having some problems with impulsivity towards addictive behavior (listening to music and internet activity). A couple of nights it was harder to fall asleep. Better focus when reading, but my mind will wander off. Focus could be better in meditation.

Three weeks before the end of his Program Jim reported:

I had the first major test of my focusing abilities this week, being in a classroom and studying afterwards. I was able to remain calm and focused during work and class. This is a very noticeable difference and change from earlier time periods doing school-work. I do not recall any anxiety and my moods were quite stable overall. I am generally more calm and centered.

Jim completed his Program and felt that he had an "overall much more centered and focused mind, stable moods and energy compared to the beginning of the Program.

Jim's experience on the REI Custom Program is fairly typical of the changes I see with both children and adults. He was somewhat unique in that he was exceptionally diligent in offering feedback—I only included a small sampling of the notes he provided me throughout his REI Custom Program. His response gave me a lot of insight into his daily progress and reinforced my commitment to dynamically-adjust each REI track during the Program. I discuss the dynamic process of an REI Custom Program in more detail in Chapter 18.

• • •

"I'm going to conduct a study in my school. Could you tell me what CD to use?" asked Niels. "Also, could you make a 'fake' tape of drumming?" he added, looking for a placebo recording to use as an alternative stimulus to the REI drumming.

Niels was headmaster at a private elementary school in the Netherlands. He was also a client who was, at age 44, recently diagnosed with ADHD. He was excited about REI because he just had his attention tested while listening to his custom CDs.

Niels used the Test of Variable of Attention (T.O.V.A.), a Continuous Performance Test (CPT). I was excited to see what results he would find, since David and I wanted to use this test but were unable to conduct our study due to my move out of the San Diego area.

Niels' psychologist tested him using the standardized T.O.V.A. under three conditions: 10mg of Ritalin (an ADHD stimulant medication), 20mg of Ritalin, and while listening to his REI recording.

His score with 10mg of Ritalin was a well-below normal score of—6.60 while his 20mg Ritalin score showed a significantly improved, though still well below normal, score of—3.47.

His score when listening to the REI focusing music, the same tracks you will find in the Focus category of Brain Shift Radio, were a near normal score of—1.87. This improvement was nearly 50% greater than the better of the Ritalin scores.

"It's nice to see the difference. I must say I was happily surprised by the effect of REI," Niels described to me in an email.

These results encouraged Niels to conduct a fairly large, controlled study in his school.

His study examined 100 elementary-aged children in a randomized, placebo-controlled format. Students were divided into two groups (an active and placebo group) and each would perform four separate CPT's, consisting of two tests with no music and two tests with either a placebo (fake) music recording or REI music tracks. Children were randomly assigned to the placebo or REI test group.

I didn't hear from Niels for several months and essentially forgot about his study. It is not uncommon for me to receive a call or email from someone planning to do a study on my music to only later learn that the study was not completed for any number of reasons. So, I was surprised and excited when he sent me a copy of a paper he had published on his research.

In this paper, he described that his results showed a significant improvement in attention for those who listened to the REI recording over both the silence and placebo conditions.

According to the translation that Niels sent me of his study (the original was published in Dutch), the children who listened to the REI drumming focused longer and showed improved academic performance.

Niels' studies and subsequent results got me thinking as I was digging around in the databases for our streaming music site, Brain Shift Radio.

"Did you know that over half the listening on Brain Shift Radio is in the Focus or Brain Boost categories?" I asked Beth, as I gave her a tour of the database showing user activity and engagement.

"I'm surprised it's that high," she said.

"You know, I was thinking..."

"Uh-oh."

"We could do an attention test on BSR." Beth looked at me with a mix of confusion and concern. "Remember those studies that were done on REI in the Netherlands using Continuous Performance Tests?"

"Um, yeah..."

"Well, the CPTs are computer-based tests. I'll bet we could add one to BSR and show users how much better they can focus with our music compared to silence."

"That sounds expensive," she said, ever my tether to reality.

"Maybe not. These tests aren't that complicated. They're just a simple trigger and response compiler. We've already built much more complicated software with both the Custom Program and BSR. Let me sketch this out, run it by Jacques (our chief software engineer) and we'll see."

CPTs are used to track attention. They present a simple trigger, like a sound or an image on a screen, and the test-taker responds. The test tracks whether the correct response was given and at what speed it was given. An algorithm compiles the test-taker's response times and accuracy and offers a score. These tests are often used to track the efficacy of treatments, such as medications, for attention. There is a lot of data on these tests and quite a few that have been proven to be accurate, like the T.O.V.A. that Neils used in his studies. All it took to create an accurate test was to follow a few rules.

Analyzing various tests gave us a clear framework from which to build some software, so we decided to build a test out. This process went quickly and took less than two months from idea to beta. During this short time frame, we built two different test types, an intake process to choose the best music for a test-taker's test, and algorithms that help BSR use the test results to optimize testers' subsequent track selections.

"What if they don't work?" I asked, finally doubting myself after completing the build. This is fairly typical for me. I come up with an idea and work through the process of realizing it. Only then do I stop long enough to wonder if it was a good idea or not. Some people call it impulsivity; I prefer to call it unfettered creativity. Whichever it is, I suppose, depends on your tolerance for risk. Mine is pretty high. Beth's, less so (though compared to non-entrepreneurs, still fairly high). We both realize that jumping at opportunity and following inspiration is necessary, though she is less comfortable with the financial needs of following some of these ideas.

"I mean, we built these attention tests and put them out there without knowing if they will show that the music actually helps." I added.

"The goal was to make the most objective, accurate test possible, wasn't it?" asked Beth.

"Yeah, that's the thing. We made sure the test is the best we could make. We factored in randomness, unpredictability, and simplicity and we adjusted the algorithms to eliminate any learning improvement. We even built in an intake that would choose music best-suited to a person's age, gender, and self-perceived focusing abilities. The test will accurately show whether BSR's music helps or not. The problem is, what if the music doesn't help?"

"You worry too much. The Dutch studies used tests like this with our music and they turned out well. Besides, in all the testing you've done with the prototype, there was an improvement, wasn't there?"

"Yes, but, both the Dutch studies and our development tests were just a small sampling. We don't know what will happen when just anyone can take the test."

"It'll be fine," she reassured me.

She was right.

I watched the first hundred tests as closely as a meteorologist watches a hurricane approach shore. I analyzed each test and stewed over those that didn't offer the results I was hoping for.

After six months and thousands of tests, our median results showed a 34.7% reduction in error rates. This represents a significant improvement in focus.

More exciting than these results, the data enabled us to improve listeners' experiences with the BSR music. We saw what types of focusing tracks produced the best results and began to identify which approaches worked for various segments of our users. We were also using a person's test results to help choose better music for them.

We have now launched what we are calling the Music and Cognition Project, a platform where other researchers can use our CPT framework to explore the focusing effects of music, whether it's our music or not. These researchers can have us plug any music into the tests and track their results. As we compile data about these various forms of music, we can start seeing how different styles and individual components of music contribute to enhanced attention.

Even though Brain Shift Radio's music was designed to explore episodic (temporary) enhancement in attention, the results from the CPT has also helped me enhance the effects of long-term improvements in attention of the REI Custom Program by refining the stimulation I provide in each of a client's custom-made REI tracks.

Chapter Eleven
Tics

"How would you like to do a study on Tourette syndrome?" Laurel asked me.

"I don't know anything about Tourette syndrome. Is that the disorder with the tics?"

"Yes. I work at a summer camp, and I talked with the staff about what you've been doing for my daughter. They asked if you wanted to come play for the kids. Maybe it will calm them down."

"Sure, I'll play for anyone."

"Come to the camp on Monday, and I'll show you around. We'll have some kids available for you to play for. Maybe you can then make tapes for them to listen to. Could you send me the parental consent form you used for your other study?"

"I'll drop it in the mail tomorrow and see you on Monday."

I'd heard of Tourette syndrome, but had never worked with anyone with the condition. I knew that it involved tic behaviors that were sometimes motor-based and sometimes vocal-based.

So, I did some research. From everything I read, tics were often present with anxiety and attention issues. Many professionals, I read, think of Tourette syndrome as ADHD with tics.

The anxiety piece made sense to me; and since I felt pretty comfortable helping reduce anxiety, I thought that I could approach the tics from an anxiety-based perspective.

I arrived at the camp first thing Monday morning and was greeted by Laurel and a host of kids between eight and twelve years old. I could see many of the tics manifesting as I said hello to the kids. One blinked repeatedly, another cleared his throat, and yet another shrugged his shoulder. All were very calm, though.

This gave me pause. Perhaps my idea of calming the tics wasn't the right approach. I wondered if the attention piece was connected. I didn't have long to ponder, because I was led to a cabin where I would play for each child like I did for the public school study I explore in Chapter 2.

Laurel brought each boy (they were all boys at this camp—most people with Tourette syndrome are male) to the cabin, and I played for them one at a time, recording each session.

Fourteen boys and no change in tics. They all enjoyed my drumming and many wanted to play with me, but I didn't see any change in tic behavior as I played. I was a bit discouraged, but agreed to make the tapes so that each boy could listen everyday. Perhaps repeated listening would make a difference.

"Anything?" I asked Laurel after the kids had listened to their recordings for four weeks.

"No changes in the tics," Laurel said. "But your boys were calmer and more focused than the other campers this summer. We all noticed. The director even asked me what we were doing differently, because my group was so compliant and present. I think the drumming had something to do with it."

"That's interesting," I said. "I'm not really surprised that there were no changes in the tics, because I didn't see anything as I played. It seems to me that if I could help, I'd have seen something during the live sessions. I'm encouraged by the attention and calm, though."

Tics, I later learned, are a difficult symptom area for me. Sometimes I see a steady, progressive change and sometimes the process is drawn-out and meandering. One client who stayed with me for almost two years gave me a tremendous amount of information on tics and REI.

Nate was a twelve-year-old boy with anxiety, attention issues and tics, mostly motor but some vocal. His motor tics consisted of a shrugging and head leaning motion, and his vocal tic was throat-clearing.

When I started working with him, his mother and I talked about whether I'd be able to help with the tics. She felt that if I could reduce his anxiety, his tics would reduce.

"His tics are lot worse when he is stressed," she said to me. "They are also more prominent when he is sick. He has allergies and they make them worse, too."

She paused to think for a second then said, "Anything that stresses his system sets the tics off. Do you think you can help?"

"I'm pretty confident that we can reduce his anxiety a bit and probably help with the attention, but I don't know what to expect with the tics."

"That's okay. I'll take whatever you can offer."

And she did. She was exceptionally committed and diligent in working with me. She was also able to see the subtleties in how each REI track worked for Nate.

"His tics were down for a couple of weeks and then he caught a cold. The tics came right back. Do you think you could change the track?"

"Sure. How is his attention? And his anxiety?"

"He's been doing better at school. His grades are up, so his attention is improving. And he's feeling more confident. But his tics make it hard socially. It's not that anyone makes fun of him, it's that he's aware of the tics and can't control them. So, when the tics get worse, he gets more anxious."

"I'll see if adding some more calming-type tracks can help with the tics."

"Oh, and can you add one of the ambient tracks? He seems to do better when it's included."

The ambient track, I learned with Nate, is a key to reducing the tics. No matter what I did with the rhythms, if the ambient track wasn't there, the drumming didn't help.

This didn't mean I could just choose any rhythms or skip the rhythms altogether. I still needed to choose wisely. But if I didn't put a particular ambient instrument on Nate's REI track, I didn't see any improvement in the tics.

My work with Nate had been a long road. Nearly every time I made a new track, I saw a reduction, and many times an elimination, of his tics. But the effects were temporary.

The tics would come back anywhere from six to twelve weeks after making a new track. They were usually triggered by either allergies or an illness. I had yet to see Nate not have a cold or allergy incident every couple of months. And I had yet to see the tics come back without the additional presence of the allergies or cold.

I was beginning to think that the tics were dependent on his physical health and not related to anxiety, mental stress, or mood.

I continued to work with Nate. His mother was happy to continue playing the REI tracks for him, with me adjusting the track each time the tics came back. So, I made new tracks and tweaked my process for as long as it took.

Even though it took almost two years, Nate ultimately did well. He became calmer than when he started the REI Custom Program and his grades were significantly better. He also got to the point where his tics were pretty well under control as long as he continued listening to the most current track I made for him. Whenever he stopped listening for more than a couple of days, the tics came back. Even when playing his REI recording everyday, the tics occasionally reappeared when he got sick with a cold or flu or if he was under more stress than usual.

Fortunately, not all children with tic behavior respond as slowly as Nate. Another child, Michael, started the REI Custom Program with a lot of tics. At 11-years-old, his tics were both vocal and motor and impacted his life significantly. His vocal tics included grunting and throat-clearing, while his motor tics consisted of lip-smacking and picking, neck-rubbing and finger-bending.

At the beginning of his REI Custom Program, Michael's tics were present most of the time. Starting just an hour or so after waking in the morning, they continued unabated throughout the day until bedtime. The degree and intensity of his tics seemed to be related to his anxiety and energy level. If he was tired, he exhibited more tics. Likewise, when he was anxious, his tics were more pronounced.

Aside from his tics, Michael also had difficulty sleeping, both falling asleep and waking at night. Generally it would take him one to two hours to fall asleep and he would often wake once at night, usually between 3 and 4 am. Most of time he was able to fall back asleep by having a parent lay with him. Other times, approximately one or two times per week, he would not be able to go back to sleep. The days after staying awake were often times when his tic behavior was much worse.

Michael also exhibited high levels of anxiety, which centered around his fear of new places, unexpected events, and separation from his parents. On a good day, he was able to go to school without clinging to his mom, and he displayed only minor trepidation toward new or unexpected situations, such as an unscheduled trip to the store or an event outside his normal routine. His anxiety exhibited itself as clinginess, crying, and tic behavior, most notably vocal tics.

In addition to the tics, anxiety, and sleep issues, Michael also showed classic signs of ADHD. His symptoms included restlessness, inattention, impulsive behavior, and low frustration tolerance. Given that Tourette syndrome is often referred to as ADHD with tics, this wasn't unexpected.

In Michael's case, the tics were very pronounced, whereas his ADHD-type symptoms were less significant than is usually the case when tics and ADHD are combined. His psychiatrists felt his attention issues were not severe enough to warrant an ADHD diagnosis.

Michael did our online REI Custom Program not long after we launched it. This Program differed from the methods I used when working with people in the 1990's. First of all, I didn't meet with him before making his Program recordings. It also differed from the REI Custom Program we offered through our early REI Authorized Provider years (2004-2010) in that we'd refined the online custom Program to consist of 12 recordings that were custom made in a progressive fashion, with each new track created based on the results we saw from the previous track. (I described more about the various iterations of the REI Program in Chapter 6).

The new online system offered enhanced feedback options, more closely mimicking the days when I played live and checked in personally with the family as they used the recordings. And true to the data the online system was capable of capturing, Michael's mother was very good at completing the feedback and keeping in close touch with us as she went along. This meant we could expect better results than if she wasn't so engaged.

The goal for Michael's REI Custom Program was to improve his sleep and reduce his tics and anxiety. Additionally, we intended to improve his ADHD symptoms. This was a lot to accomplish; so the key was to prioritize the focus of his Program by starting with anxiety and sleep and moving on to his inattention, impulsivity, and frustration tolerance as he moved through the Program.

Sleep is essential in moderating any of these symptoms; therefore, improving his sleep would likely also improve some of his other symptoms. As well, according to Michael's intake, his tics were more frequent and intense when he was tired.

Anxiety was a major issue for him in general and also exacerbated his tic behavior. Reducing his anxiety would not only help with the clinginess and crying incidents, but would also help with the tics.

Michael began listening to Track #1 at bedtime. The first night he was calmed while the recording played, but he didn't fall asleep right away. According to his parents' feedback, he was calm enough that his dad was able to leave room and turn off the light without incident, even though he took a while to fall asleep. This pattern continued for most of his first week. At about day eight, he fell asleep while the recording played and slept through the night.

During this first track, Michael exhibited less anxiety over everyday changes where he was separated from his mom, such as going to school or therapy sessions. His vocal tics were slightly less frequent, while his motor tics remained pretty much the same.

Tracks #2 and #3 continued to improve his sleep and reduce his anxiety. He was able to consistently fall asleep while the recording played and only woke up two nights. He was able to fall back asleep both nights that he awoke. This was a significant improvement over his historic sleep patterns. His anxiety was better than before the Program started, but still manifested as separation anxiety in some situations.

His tic behavior was variable, with some days being better than others. According to the tracking documents completed by his parents, his vocal tics were overall less frequent than before the Program. His motor tics were largely yet unchanged.

For most REI Custom Programs, there is a significant jump in the stimulation level of Track #4 as we adjust the focus of client's Program to encompass different symptom areas. This was the case with Michael. Because he showed improvements in sleep and some changes in anxiety, I decided that this REI track would focus more on his tics, particularly the motor tics, which up to this point had only marginally improved.

The first three days went well—his tics, both vocal and motor, decreased significantly in frequency. He had periods during these days when there was no visible tic behavior. Unfortunately on day four, he began waking up at night again (something he had not done for almost three weeks). This trend of improved tic behavior and night-waking continued for the remainder of Track #4 (six more days).

Because of Michael's change in sleep patterns, I chose to reduce the stimulation level of Track #5. This was a trade-off between his improving tic behavior and his sleep patterns, but it was chosen because good sleep was important not only to functioning well in general, but also because his tics often became worse when he was tired. Also, disrupted sleep patterns during the REI Custom Program usually indicate over-stimulation. The best way to counteract this is to reduce the level of the stimulation.

As expected his sleep improved; but also as expected, we observed an increase in his motor tics. His vocal tics remained nearly non-existent. His motor tics, though higher than they were toward the end of Track #4, were still below the level that they were at the beginning of the Program, so we were encouraged by his overall progress.

During the six-week period of Tracks #6 through #8, we continued the dance between uninterrupted sleep and reduced tics. At times his sleep was off (Track #6) while his motor tics abated. And at times his sleep was good, but the motor tics increased (Track #7). This was an interesting development because I always felt that good sleep contributed to fewer tics. The problem was that it appeared that the type of stimulation needed to help with the tic behavior was disrupting his sleep.

By Track #8, I decided to go with the stimulation that would help with the tics and add a track to play at bedtime for sleep. I asked Michael's parents to play Track #8 (and the rest of his REI tracks) during the day and additionally play a special REI Program Sleep Track at bedtime. After a few days settling into a schedule that worked— they chose to play the custom REI track during breakfast—Michael's sleep returned to where it was after track #3: He fell asleep within 30 minutes of turning on the REI Program Sleep Track, and he and stayed asleep most nights.

Based on his parents' observations, his motor tics remained somewhat variable, but their overall frequency was down from the beginning of the Program. Stressful situations, as expected, increased tic activity. Because his overall anxiety was lower than when he began the Program, he seemed to be less bothered by situations that used to be stressful for him. There was no observance of vocal tics during Track #8.

With Tracks #9 through #12, Michael's tic behavior was variable but showed steady progress. The vocal tics were essentially absent and there were longer periods of time with few, if any, motor tics. At one point during this period he caught a cold and his tics increased. They reduced again once his cold was over. This demonstrated more overall improvements, but also suggested that stress on his system, both physically and psychologically, still had an impact on his tic behavior.

Michael's anxiety remained low and his sleep was good, with only the occasional bad night's sleep. Over the last six tracks or so he also improved in some of his ADHD symptoms—he seemed less restless and exhibited a greater ability to handle new situations and life's frustrations.

Overall, Michael made significant gains in his sleep, anxiety, and tic behavior during the 12-track Program, with minor changes in some of his ADHD-type symptoms.

Before beginning the REI Custom Program, Michael often took one to two hours to fall asleep. He awoke at night several times per week and many times was unable to fall back asleep again. By the eighth day of the Program, his sleep had improved significantly. This made an impact in many ways, including reducing his tics and lowering his anxiety and frustration intolerance.

At the beginning of the Program, Michael's day was ruled by anxiety. He was clingy with his mother and fearful of new and unexpected situations and events. Within just a few tracks, his anxiety was noticeably lower. He exhibited less clinginess and became more relaxed in general.

Before REI, Michael's tics were near-constant and impacted his life significantly. The vocal tics—grunting and throat-clearing—were especially bothersome because they impacted him negatively in social situations. With these gone and the motor tics much reduced, he was more comfortable interacting with his peers and was receiving less negative peer attention.

Even though the focus of Michael's REI Custom Program was not directed to his ADHD-type symptoms of restlessness, inattention, impulsivity, and frustration intolerance, he did show some improvements in some of these areas. As his tics decreased, his restlessness also appeared to reduce.

Michael showed some improvement in frustration tolerance. This coincided with his improved sleep and reduced anxiety, suggesting that this symptom was caused, at least in part, by his poor sleep and high anxiety levels. Likewise, as his sleep, anxiety, and tic behavior improved, so did his attention. There was no observable change in his impulsivity.

Michael and Nate both did well with their tics on the Program, though both followed very different paths. This uniqueness of each person and their REI Program consistently reinforces my decision to stick with custom-made and dynamically-adjusted drumming recordings.

Chapter Twelve
Sleep

I have a long history of not sleeping well, which is not uncommon for someone with ADHD. One of the pervasive stories from my childhood, and one of much embarrassment when I was younger, is that I used to sleepwalk. My father often related how he found me searching around—inside and outside—the house at seven or eight years old looking for what, no one knows.

The sleepwalking stopped as I hit middle school, to be replaced by night waking and night terrors. I used to wake up every night, without fail, often experiencing terrifying dreams and physical sensations. I spent time at a sleep clinic in my twenties. The best the sleep clinic could offer me was a list of good habits I could develop, like not drinking coffee before bed or taking medications that kept me awake and gave me a hangover. I began exploring ways to use the drumming to help with my sleep. It turned out that this is an area where I (again) have unique ideas.

Sleep is one if the most consistent areas where I see improvement from listening to my music. The listener's age doesn't matter. I've seen infants sleep better listening to the drumming, and I've seen people in their eighties develop more restful sleep by turning on the music when they turn off the lights.

The approach I take to induce sleep, and in many cases the approach I use to change overall sleep patterns, is very different than other music commonly used to help someone fall asleep.

Most music used for improving sleep involves one of two approaches. The first, and most common, is to listen to music that is relaxing, much like the music most people use to calm, which I described in detail in Chapter 9. With this approach, the goal is to psychologically soothe the listener in the hopes that he will relax and fall asleep.

The second approach involves binaural beats to entrain the brain (see Chapters 5 and 6). People using these beats are trying to entrain the brain to the delta level of consciousness, a state where the brain oscillates between one and three hertz. Delta is a deep sleep state; and though the logic to try to entrain a listener's brain to this state makes sense on the surface, it doesn't work as well as using complex rhythms to help a listener transition to sleep on their own.

Sleep is not a static level of consciousness. When you sleep, you are in and out of delta, theta, and alpha. Solely entraining to delta doesn't always make the most sense, as the delta state of consciousness neither replicates nor induces the normal cycles of a sleep state. I've found that if I help someone achieve an alpha state of consciousness, he will fall asleep on his own and will end up with a more restful night.

Alpha is often considered a pre-sleep state, the state of consciousness in which we begin our transition to sleep. It seems that helping someone calm to alpha lays a solid foundation for the proper cycle of brainwave sleep states. As well, difficulty getting to sleep is most often caused by an inability to calm the brain. Alpha induces a physiological calm, which can then lead to sleep.

This concept is something I stumbled on as I was playing around with my first REI recordings. An important part of my process in creating recordings for people after playing for them live involved listening to their rhythms to see how they affected me. This was critical to me, because hearing and experiencing the rhythms as I played them is a very different feeling than what I experience when I simply listen. And as someone with a different brain, an ADHD brain, I was, and still am, the first tester.

It wasn't long after listening to tapes I made for children like Stacey that I discovered that listening to calming rhythms at eight-beats-per-second would often leave me drifting off to sleep. Now, I know I was often tired during the day—mainly because I typically didn't sleep well at night—so drifting off while I was lying down and listening didn't seem that odd.

I've never really had a problem getting to sleep and didn't notice any benefit from these recordings at bedtime. But what did pique my interest in these fast tempos for falling asleep was that when I would wake in the middle of the night—and I'd be wide awake—I would often turn on one of these recordings and find that I was able to fall back to sleep. When I didn't turn on my high-speed drumming music, I could be up for hours trying to wind down.

I saw this pattern in my sleep-deprived brain and mentioned it to a relative who is a psychiatrist specializing in sleep medicine.

"So, why do you suppose that the fast drumming will help someone fall asleep?" I asked. "Is it just the calming?"

"You say that you're entraining the brain to an alpha state of consciousness?" Tim asked.

"That's the theory."

"Alpha is a pre-sleep state. The transition from your wakeful state of beta to Stage 1 sleep, which is in theta, requires a mild synchronization through alpha."

"Okay, relaxing into alpha could help with the transition to sleep."

"That's right."

"Wouldn't I be better off trying to entrain a listener into delta like the binaural beat CDs do?"

"No, that doesn't make sense. Delta level brain patterns are only present during Stage 3 sleep. Keep in mind that sleep is comprised of four distinct stages. Each stage has its own level of brain activity and you're cycling through them throughout the night."

He went on to describe that when we fall asleep, we first enter a theta-driven state called Stage 1 as we transition from a relaxed-alert state of alpha. Stage 1 sleep generally lasts ten minutes or so. Then we enter Stage 2, which is also in theta but contains short periods of higher-level activity called sleep spindles. These sleep spindles are short bursts of brainwaves in the lower end of beta (12-14 hz) that occur after a huge spike in some brain activity called K-complex. Both the K-complex and sleep spindles seem to be related to the process of becoming less responsive to external stimuli. Once these stop, we enter Stage 3 sleep.

Stage 3 is the delta level deep sleep state. Because we have gone through Stage 2 and are internally directed, we really aren't hearing, or at least responding to, sounds that may be trying to entrain us. We have successfully tuned them out, unless they are a threat to us, in which case, we may wake up.

Alpha is the perfect state to entrain the brain to in order to initiate sleep. Any deeper and we are able to tune the music out. My listener's responses have suggested that this is indeed the case.

Kids almost universally go to sleep while listening to my drumming, but some adults can't seem to stop their anxious or active thoughts. When I was developing my *Sleep Rhythms* CD, I experimented with some guided relaxation techniques and ended up adding a narration to help soothe anxious thoughts.

While helping someone fall asleep by calming their brain and letting them drift off seems pretty straightforward, changing nightwaking patterns is somewhat more difficult. Falling asleep to the REI drumming essentially requires entraining the brain, whereas helping someone stay asleep involves changing overall sleep patterns using a series of REI drumming tracks to gradually make the change. For most people this process also includes other areas of concern besides the sleep.

I describe one case, a four-year-old girl named Nancy, in detail in Chapter 18, but I'll offer a brief synopsis here. Nancy woke many times a night, anxious, and went into her parents room and woke them up. Following the philosophy of doing whatever it took for the most people in the house to get the most sleep, Nancy's father put a mattress on her floor and slept in her room with her. When she woke up, all she needed to do was climb into his bed and fall back asleep.

She did this, but it often took her hours to fall back asleep. Her father was awakened each time Nancy woke up and spent the next several hours trying to get her back to sleep. This arrangement at least allowed Nancy's mother to sleep through the night uninterrupted, but her father wasn't getting the sleep he needed to function at his best. The goal was to change this pattern by helping her sleep through the night.

This first week on the Program was a disaster. Nancy's sleep grew progressively worse as the week went on. It appeared that Nancy had become overstimulated by her recording.

There are three ways to become overstimulated by an REI drumming track. One is by playing the track more than once a day, which they didn't do. Another is from playing the recording too loudly. The last is due to the rhythms on the track being too stimulating. After talking with Nancy's father, I felt that Nancy's response was probably due to a combination of the latter two.

I should note that, in addition to the sleep, Nancy's parents' primary concerns were language and socialization. Even though I see this combination quite often, it is challenging to facilitate gains in these areas at the same time. The type of stimulation used for sleep is very different, opposite, actually, from what is necessary to help with language or socialization. So, even though Nancy's sleep deteriorated during the first week, her language improved noticeably.

Nancy's parents were happy with her language progress and wanted to keep that going; I felt there was no need to revise her track, as long as the volume was lowered. They were aware that we would be taking a slower path to better sleep this way, but the positives outweighed the negatives in their minds.

It took five weeks of adjusting the tracks to see a change in Nancy's sleep. It started with the occasional full-night's sleep, with the frequency of these good nights steadily increasing over the course of another month until it was rare that she didn't sleep through the night with her father happily sleeping in his own room and bed.

As I worked with people like Nancy who didn't sleep well, I learned a lot about how someone responds to the drumming; but when I met Marcie, I was delighted to gain deeper insights into a listener's process.

"I've had problems sleeping off and on for years, but the last several have gotten so bad that it's disrupting my life and my marriage. I'm depressed and anxious, and my husband needs to sleep in another room because I toss and turn all night," Marcie described in our intake interview.

Marcie was a 52-year-old psychotherapist with two masters degrees. As one may expect, she was very articulate and self-aware. Through working with Marcie I learned a lot about how the drumming affects sleep and eventually validated a change in protocol that I had stumbled upon with some other clients.

"I know this may seem odd, but I think you should play your recording in the morning. Try to listen sometime between 9am and 11am, if you can. Definitely avoid playing it after lunch, otherwise it may keep you up at night," I said.

"Why so early? How could playing it in the morning help me sleep in the evening?"

"I don't really know, but it's something I've seen with adults who develop insomnia in their forties or later. Try it for a week and let's see what happens."

Marcie called me after a week of listening to her REI recording.

"The first three days were kind of uncomfortable. My mood was better, but I just felt a rush of energy. I can't really describe it other than to say that I felt hypo-manic."

"Are you still feeling that way?"

"I still feel more energy, but it's not uncomfortable. My mood is better and I have the energy to be more social. I've actually spent some time with friends this week. I haven't done that in a very long time," she added.

"But the interesting thing is that I've been sleeping the last four days. I've noticed that I've had pleasant dreams every night. I don't remember dreaming like this for years."

"It sounds like we're on a good path. Keep doing what you're doing and switch to the next CD after another week," I said.

All was going well until I received a call from her just as she was going to transition to her next CD.

"I had a busy day the other day and didn't really have time to listen to my REI recording the way I usually do, so I played it while I was in the shower. I had turned it up pretty loud so I could hear. The weird thing is that I was agitated the rest of the day. Do you suppose it was because of the CD?"

"It could be. The volume needs to be low and if it was too loud, it could cause agitation. This is not uncommon for sensitive people," I continued, then suggested that it would be best to alter the week-three protocol to ensure that the transition from CD#1 to CD#2 would not over-stimulate her and cause her mood or sleep to be disrupted.

"I recommend that you alternate CD#1 and CD#2 during the week, slowly introducing the higher stimulus of CD#2."

This became standard protocol in the Custom Program, creating a supportive and smooth transition from the first to second CD. We did this for many years until we started creating more recordings at smaller intervals, allowing gentler steps between CDs or online tracks.

Marcie did this; and at the end of three weeks, she described that listening to CD#2 gave her more energy during the day and didn't disrupt her new deep sleep patterns. Aside from consistently having restful sleep, she was less anxious and her mood was elevated. She was also enjoying more social contact and wasn't tired during the day.

"I'm sleeping in the same room as my husband. I'm actually sleeping and waking up rested, my mood is improved and I am able to be more social. Thank you for giving me my life back," she said to me after ten weeks on her Program.

I was obviously gratified by her progress, but I was also surprised that listening to the drumming in the morning would help with sleeping at night.

This is a pattern I've seen time and time again, but I don't really have any answers to why this is the case. Some people have suggested that it has something to do with hormone levels or biorhythms, since most of the time women in their forties and fifties are the ones who respond to this protocol.

But it isn't just women who can sleep better by listening to the drumming.

Joseph was referred to me because he was having trouble at work and was recently diagnosed with ADHD. A fairly typical twenty-something software engineer, Joseph tended to sleep late and work all night, ignore household chores, and run himself ragged trying to meet a deadline.

Joseph listened to his REI CDs in the evening while he worked. He chose this time of day because he knew he should be winding down and felt that the drumming would help him do so.

I received a call from his REI provider after two weeks. She said that Joseph was a little disconcerted because he shifted to a more normal sleep/wake cycle. He was getting up early and going to bed before midnight. This thrilled his family, but he was kind of bummed not to be living the upside down life that he was used to. He liked being different and his change in sleeping/waking patterns removed his difference. But he was getting more done and was more engaged in his life, so he was willing to accept this change.

His focus was improving and he was more engaged in the world around him. But he still lacked motivation.

"When you started with Joseph," described Donna, his REI Provider, "he was extremely dis-regulated and had significant problems with attention and focus. Pre and post tests indicate that this has all improved dramatically."

This provider was unique in that she regularly conducted intake and follow-up tests to try to quantify the changes she was seeing in her patients. She did this partly to be able to show the tests—and the improvements—to her clients, but also to quantify the changes she was seeing and pass them along to me. I greatly appreciated her diligence and she quickly became one of my favorite REI providers.

"I'm glad to hear that. What's happening now?" I asked.

"At this point, his biggest concern is his lack of initiation. He wants to do things; he just can't seem to find the "start button". That, and his inability to build routines into his life. So I am wondering if tweaking his CDs is in order."

"Sure." I made a new CD and shipped it off to Joseph, asking that she let me know after four to six weeks how he was doing. Donna called me five weeks later.

"Hi Jeff, I just had to pass this on to you. I don't know whether you know that Joseph became my son-in-law."

"Congratulations," I said.

"Thanks. So, now I get the inside scoop on how things are going. Today my daughter said, 'Wow! Joseph got up and made breakfast, did a load of laundry and then asked if there was anything else I needed done—all before 8 a.m.!!'"

"I'm glad he's more motivated."

"Yes. He said to me that, 'this new CD is great! I put it in [the CD player] and it's like someone does this (picture turning brain around 180 degrees) to my brain.' I thought that was hilarious! The changes have been down right miraculous!"

"Thanks for letting me know." Joseph is a good example of the progressive nature of listening to the REI tracks. We start with sleep (and anxiety if there is any—there wasn't much with Joseph), then we tackle the core issues, which in Joseph's case were focus and attention.

Once these core issues begin to respond, subtler symptoms often appear, such as motivation for Joseph. We then focus on that while trying to keep progress going on the initial issues. It's a bit of a balancing act; but if I am in touch with either the client or the provider (or both), I can then adjust the tracks as necessary to keep moving in the right direction.

Sleep problems never exist in isolation. As these clients suggest, sleep deeply impacts other areas of their life. For Marcie it was mood, energy, and social interest, for Joseph it was focus and motivation, for Nancy it was language and socialization.

I write in a bit more detail about the balancing act of trying to affect change in more areas than one in Chapter 18. As I illustrate with
Nancy's experience, sometimes the type of stimulation needed to affect change in one area is very different than the stimulation needed
to make improvements in another area.

Chapter Thirteen
Mood

"Logan came home the other day from school, ran straight into his room, and turned on his CD. I asked him what he was doing and he said that listening was his reward for getting an A on his math test," described Kim, his mother.

"That's great. It's always a good thing when teens take the initiative to play their REI music on their own," I said. "That's a big change from last month when he wouldn't listen at all."

"Absolutely. He has taken ownership of the process. I can see his mood lifting. He cares about his schoolwork now and he's getting involved again in activities at school. Before he started listening to the drumming, he just wanted to come home and stare at the screen."

Logan was having difficulty in school, socially more than academically, when he began the REI Custom Program. He was slightly shy, though he had a couple of friends. Having recently turned fifteen, he had become moody and withdrawn.

Teenagers can be hard to reach. Whenever I run into a clients' resistance to listening to the drums, it's usually with teens. Logan was initially resistant, saying that he didn't want "anyone messing with his head".

Because Logan was not interested in the drumming—he often told his mother how weird he thought it was that she attended my drumming classes—we decided that I wouldn't play for him live. Instead, she and I would talk about Logan's issues and her goals for him. From that, I would make a recording that Logan would listen to before going to bed.

"He doesn't want to do anything. He used to be so bubbly and energetic, but now he is so lethargic and down. Getting him up in the morning is impossible and he just drags himself through the day. His grades have slipped and he is distancing himself from his friends," explained Kim during Logan's intake interview. "Do you think the drumming can help?"

"I don't know," I answered. This was fairly early in the process of developing the REI therapy and I hadn't yet worked with any teens with mood issues. I knew I could help with anxiety or attention, and I told her that, but the mood would be something we'd have to evaluate as we went along.

"If you're okay with feeling our way through this, I'd love to give it a try," I said.

"I usually feel so good after the drumming class that I can't imagine it wouldn't help Logan," she replied. Kim had been coming to my drumming classes for a few months. This was the reason she approached me about working with her son, even though he didn't have autism or ADHD, the conditions I would often talk about during class.

This wasn't an unusual request. Even from my earliest days of exploring how the drumming may work outside of its cultural context, people approached me and asked if what I was doing could help them or their children. This led me to work at Pathways, a center for people with chronic illnesses, where I played for people with a large variety of chronic conditions, from pain to HIV, CFS (chronic fatigue syndrome) to depression.

One client, Jamie, was recently diagnosed as HIV-positive and was feeling pretty hopeless about his life. He was 28-years-old, generally healthy and not symptomatic, but he felt that he really had no future. I was worried when I first played for him; the entire time I drummed, he sprawled on the couch and cried. These were not quiet tears, rather they were plaintive wails with full-body convulsions.

"Are you okay? Would you like me to stop playing?" I asked, as I stopped, concerned that I was making things worse.

"No, I'm fine. Please keep playing," he answered between sobs. "This is the best I've felt in a long time."

I looked at him, not sure what to say or whether to believe him. Jamie, I would learn, was a dramatic guy. He did everything in a big way and crying was no exception.

"Really," he sniffled, "I feel this deep well of grief and sadness purging from my body. Please keep playing."

"Okay, but tell me if you need me to stop."

I began playing again, searching for the most uplifting rhythms I could think of, careful not to deepen his mood. I understood catharsis and knew he had a great support system in place, so I wasn't concerned about him in general, but I was a little uncomfortable with such a dramatic show of emotion.

I kept playing until our session time was up. Jamie blew his nose, wiped the streaks from his face, gave me a hug, and left with a smile and a bounce in his step.

I met with him once a week for most of the summer, each session mirroring the others, with Jamie sobbing while I played and then leaving uplifted.

In mid-September he arrived at his last session and handed me an envelope. "This is my new address," he said. "I'm following my dream and moving to San Francisco. I'm not going to let this disease stop me from living my life. Wish me luck."

"Good luck," I said as he bounced out of the room. I never saw him again. I don't know what impact our drumming sessions had on his overall perspective and life choices, but I learned a lot about how to play for someone who was grieving and how to stay with someone as they moved through their emotions.

This experience was helpful a few years later when one of my REI providers called asking for a set of Program CDs.

"Could you do a Program to help with grief?" Helen asked. "I lost a child a couple of months ago, and I'm having a hard time. I'm unfocused, unmotivated, and sad."

"I'm so sorry for your loss," I said, not sure how to respond. "Why don't you send me an intake and I'll see what we can do."

I understood that grief was a process that she would work through over time. I also knew that Helen had a strong family supporting her. Based on this, the focus of her Program was on using uplifting rhythms to help her feel better as she listened, while also trying to get her brain engaged, hoping to help with her focus and motivation. I ended up using some pretty stimulating rhythms—rhythms I often use for people with ADHD, along with a bunch of the fun and bouncy rhythms I played for Jamie.

"I always look forward to listening to my CD," she told me after a couple of months. "I'm doing a lot better—more driven, more focused—and I can see light in my days."

Working with people who are working through their grief is only a small portion of the clients I see with mood issues. Many more are like Logan, teens who are struggling with the changes inherent in adolescence, while others are adults with histories of mood issues, mostly associated with anxiety, ADHD, or sleep problems.

One recent client, Roger, was a 67-year-old who had been suffering from depression for the previous several years. He also discovered that he had ADHD, the effects of which he spent his life struggling with without knowing it. He was a highly accomplished businessperson, something he managed by surrounding himself with people who could do the things he could not. This is a fairly common trait among people with ADHD. Many of us rely on others to accommodate for our deficits.

He recently sold his business and retired. Because he no longer had the work he was used to and was having a hard time filling his days, he began getting depressed. His wife, Brenda, called me because her grandson had done the Program—he had autism—and she felt that maybe I could help with Roger's mood issues.

"Roger was in the garage the other day and I heard him whistling," Brenda said about five weeks after Roger began listening to his REI Program CDs. "He used to whistle all the time when he wasn't depressed. I think the CDs are helping."

"I'm glad to hear that," I said. "So, the other day when he was whistling, what else was he doing?"

"He was sweeping the garage floor. It was the first time he has ever done that. He said he was restless and needed to do something, so he swept out the garage. This is a nice change; before he started the CDs, he just sat in his chair and read. It was good to see him motivated to do something."

Having motivation is often one of the signs that the drumming is helping. Marcie, whose sleep issues I described in Chapter 12, also had some mood issues. Her downcast mood certainly seemed related to not sleeping well—something that wasn't an issue for Roger—but one of the first things she saw when she was feeling better was an increased motivation to work and to socialize. Roger wasn't really social, but he had always been extremely active. When his mood became darker, he lost his desire to do things, even simple things like sweeping the floor.

Seeing this change was a good sign, especially since he was initially resistant to listen.

"What time of day has he been listening?" I asked Brenda, curious about the change in his interest in listening to his music.

"He's listening in the morning. He has gotten into the pattern of sitting in his car in the driveway and listening. He says he likes the peace and quiet. I think it's a bit odd, but as long as he listens, it's fine."

I find that the people most resistant to listening to their REI recordings are people with mood issues, regardless of their age. I don't really know why this is, though I suspect it has something to do with some of the rhythms that I often put on their recordings to address non-mood challenges.

For most people I work with, mood is just one of many issues that

I'm trying to address. The uplifting rhythms that I used for Jamie are unique to mood and energy. Issues like attention, anxiety, and sleep all require different types of rhythms, not all of which are necessarily uplifting to listen to. They tend to be more complex and variable. These more complex unpredictable rhythms seem to elicit strong feelings in some people.

As an example, I spent several years working with a 57-year-old woman who complained of anxiety, mood, and lack of direction with her life. She was very sensitive and described that she had the profile of someone with PTSD, though she has no memory of any particular incident causing the condition.

"I've never been able to balance my nervous system for more than a day or two, despite years of trying various healing modalities and a twice-daily practice of TM (Transcendental Meditation) and fairly regular qigong practice," Abby described to me during her intake interview. "I'm prone to anxiety and depression and am easily distracted—not able to focus well. I get overwhelmed easily and react to things more strongly than is appropriate given my current reality."

She also described that she had her first migraine headache at age five and had rarely gone more than a month without one.

Abby was exceptionally sensitive and articulate, two traits that gave me significant insight into how even the most subtle variation in the music impacted her. I quickly learned that my default beginning stimulation level was much too high for her. Abby, like Logan and Robert, was initially resistant to listening. Her daily tracking log showed quite a few notations of being irritated or frustrated while listening:

> Day 1: I checked the "I was agitated or didn't want to listen" box. That was a response that happened a few times throughout the audio. Agitated is perhaps too strong a word, but I definitely wanted the music to stop.
>
> Day 2: I even spontaneously kicked a few times and shook my arm a few times and called out "Stop it." If someone had been watching me, I don't think I would have done that, but no one was

watching me.
Day 3: I was intermittently slightly irritated by the music.

Based on this feedback, combined with checking that the volume she used was appropriate for her, it became clear that Abby's first track was too stimulating for her. So I significantly reduced the stimulation level, setting it lower than for anyone I had worked with in the past. I knew that this could potentially slow down the process; but in Abby's case, slow progress was better than a negative reaction.

Over the next 18 months, Abby and I worked to find a place where her anxiety was reduced and her focus and mood were improved.

"I'm less anxious and more hopeful. Happier, I think. I know I'm not getting stuck in my head as much. I'm more trusting of life," described Abby.

Most people with Abby's symptom make-up respond more linearly and positively than she did. Tara, a 48-year-old accomplished artist, began the Program with very similar issues as Abby. Tara, in contrast, was in and out of the REI Custom Program in ten weeks.

She listed her major issues on her intake as anxiety, feelings of despair, feeling locked up, and feeling stupid.

"I have a high level of social anxiety. I cycle in and out of despair regularly. I'm not able to sustain lighter, more positive feelings," she described to me. "I'm able to visualize in my mind what I want to do, be, create, but I can't find any connection to bring it into the world. It's frustrating after 30 years of personal process work."

Like with Abby, Tara, was articulate and sensitive. Unlike Abby, Tara responded right away, even while being thrown into chaos as she began the Program. I could go into a track by track description, but an email I received from her at the ten-week point illustrates her process and progress better than I can.

This process has had a deep impact on me. When I look back over the ten weeks, when I first contacted you, I am amazed at how much chaos and travel and family have filled up those ten weeks. I started the CD's while attending a sibling reunion for my family,

*from there I went to my partner's family reunion and the scatter-
ing of his mother's ashes. Upon returning home we started a house
project to move our hot water heater out of the bathroom and have
ended up doing a full bathroom remodel (and there is only one
bathroom in our house.) Then my mother was diagnosed with an
aggressive stage-three breast cancer. During all of this I started two
online training classes that have a tremendous amount of writing—
and writing, knowing that others will read it, can leave me feeling
anxious and vulnerable. This is all stuff that would have completely
jacked up my anxiety and avoidance and despair. This is all stuff
that would have put me so up in my head and so out of my body.*

*But I've been able to stay with myself in a way that is profound.
Sure, there is still anxiety and it arises, but I've been able to work
with it in new ways. The avoidance trigger is still hot, but I've also
been able to feel it and see it and sometimes make different choices
about it. The phone, however, still knocks me for a loop. But for the
most part, I've been able to just be with the stuff life is giving me
right now, and I haven't felt all the old stuff and headed to bed with
the covers over my head.*

*What I have felt is substantial and here and good. I wake up in
the morning and think I feel good. I have more energy to just do the
things I need and want to do. This is new. The sense of impending
doom around every corner has disappeared. I feel tender and new
and alive and I'm liking feeling all those things. These feelings are
all so new to me that I don't always have words for what is shifting
in me. But I do feel the shifts. My mind that works overtime has
relaxed. I'm not obsessing about every move I make, every word I
speak. I feel so appreciative to have some bigger space in me.*

*Thank you, Jeff. This simple listening has worked very deeply in
me.*

Articulate, self-reflective adults like Tara are fairly unusual for me,
though. Given that most people I work with are children or teens,
getting this level of insight from a client is rare. I am usually talking
with a parent or other caregiver and the feedback centers on behav-

ior rather than feelings. Or, in the cases when I do get to talk with the client, I get vague answers. This was the case with a 22-year-old woman, Catherine.

My first indication that I was going to have some difficulty getting her to describe how she was feeling was when I looked over her intake. Rather than offer a description of her issues and goals for the Program, Catherine's client description looked more like a personals ad rather than a list of issues and goals: "I am a 22-year-old female currently in graduate school. 5'3" 120 lbs. I have black hair, brown eyes. I enjoy singing, playing harp, and being outdoors."

The rating scale questions were pretty clear. She showed significant issues with mood, lack of energy and motivation, difficulty making decisions, and low frustration tolerance. Given her open-ended description, I thought it would be a good idea to talk with her to try to get a better sense of who she was. A phone interview used to be standard; but since developing the comprehensive online intake form, it wasn't necessary for most clients. It was for Catherine.

"I'm often moody. I can go from high to low in a nanosecond. I go through dark periods where it's hard for me to even get out of bed. I don't know what causes them and they can go on for days," described Catherine. "This is thing I want control of most. That, and managing the stress as I go off to grad school."

My goal with Catherine was to choose rhythms that had the bouncy, uplifting quality that Jamie responded to, rather than focus on anxiety, which draws from a different, almost opposite, set of rhythmic criteria where the goal is to settle someone down rather than raise them up.

I suggested that Catherine listen at bedtime. This is a common time for many clients to listen to their REI music; and given Catherine's difficulty falling asleep, it was the best time of day for her. I also suggested that, because the rhythms were uplifting rather than stimulating, she could listen any other time during the day when she was feeling sad or lost.

Catherine took a couple of weeks to settle into the music, and there were no observable changes during her first REI track. By her second REI track, though, she was sleeping better and reported that her mood had improved.

"This set of the Program really helped with anxiety, especially with getting out of the anxious thought 'loop'. It also helped somewhat, although not as obviously, with some obsessive-compulsive tics," Catherine explained. "I also began listening to the REI Program once or twice in the morning instead of the evening, which helped a lot with nervousness after waking up."

After eight weeks, Catherine hadn't had any of her dark periods, her mood seemed a bit more stabilized, and her anxiety seemed to be something she was learning to moderate, though it wasn't completely under control.

I decided to add more stimulation to help with the anxiety and her motivation. The transition wasn't easy for her, though.

"I had a brief anxiety attack on the 14th and had trouble motivating myself to finish assignments for school," said Catherine. "I was initially very resistant to listening to the new track and was agitated."

"It sounds like the shift in intensity of the rhythms was a little much," I said. "Perhaps I'll step the next track back a little."

"Okay, that might be good, especially since I have finals coming up."

Stepping back the stimulation can sometimes be a good thing if someone has agitation or other negative responses from listening. The trade-off, though, is that this can slow the listener's progress. Covering a period of six weeks, Catherine's, next three tracks left her with minor, if any, changes.

As she described to me, "I didn't see any marked improvements, but I generally feel more balanced. This wasn't a negative response, but I started having very bizarre and vivid dreams after the track change. It reminded me of the response I had when I used melatonin as a sleep aid."

And a few weeks later she reported, "It has been a stressful finals period, but I think the REI has helped manage (not eliminate, it was still an issue) the anxiety and help me focus on moving through tasks more effectively. These improvements were very subtle though."

Catherine continued to progress with her stress management, and her mood continued to remain stable overall. She ran into an issue, though, when she went through a two-week period of not listening to her REI music.

"During this period, I had a lot of obsessive thoughts where I returned to the events of an extremely stressful event last spring. I couldn't stop myself from thinking about it and re-experienced the anxiety I felt then," she described.

Catherine's experience illustrates the point that missing a period of time during the process can cause a regression in symptoms. Catherine quickly got back on track when she started listening again.

"How long will I need to listen in order to not backslide like I just did?" asked Catherine.

"Once we get to the end of the Program—you have two more tracks to go—it would be best if you can continue playing your last track until you hit a plateau in your improvements."

"How long does it take to plateau?"

"It can be anywhere from two to six weeks."

"Then I can stop listening? And my improvements will stay?"

"Yes, most people can stop and their gains will stay. If you see any mood or anxiety issues resurface, just start your last track again. Give it a couple of weeks, then try stopping again. At some point you'll be able to stop indefinitely."

Adults tend to take longer to plateau and need to listen longer than children, since their brains are less malleable as they get older. Therefore, adults will need to listen longer than children in order to see their improvements stick.

Regardless of how long someone listens, I've found that if symptoms start coming back, it often only takes a few days of listening again for the improvements to reappear. That said, there are many people who continue listening long after a plateau in progress. Most of the time they continue because they find listening supports their mood and they have gotten into the pattern of playing their music. In fact, it's often something they look forward to.

Chapter Fourteen

Language

I was about ten minutes into my session with Noah when he started humming, softly at first. I thought I was hearing things, so I looked over to his mom, wondering if she was hearing it too. She was smiling and mouthed to me, "Did you hear that?"

I nodded as I focused on what I was hearing—unmistakable utterances of a humming passage that seemed to roll through the vowels.

I took note of the rhythm I had been playing for the last couple of minutes. It was a stimulating double-tempo lick based on a Swiss drumming rudiment (core techniques based in military drumming) that I learned from a fellow student when I was studying at the Musician's Institute. This rudiment, nicknamed a flirta, was a quick three-beat passage using 32nd notes. I had incorporated this into a shuffling rhythm in the time signature of 41/16. The flirta happened every nine beats and was punctuated by a bass tone.

Using the flirta and bass punches as a motif, I built some other patterns to create an eight-bar variation, totaling 328 beats. Then I repeated it and added a sixteen-beat flirta crescendo. This passage took 84 seconds to complete at my eight-beats-per-second pace. By the end of it, Noah was making quite a racket. His humming had become a more song-like pattern of vowels at varying pitches and durations. It wasn't terribly musical, but it had a rhythm and a discernable form to it.

I tried to mimic his pattern by creating a somewhat melodic rhythm using combinations of bass tones, slaps and flirtas. He looked my way and continued vocalizing, adding in some consonant-type sounds. None of his vocalizations formed, or even approximated, words, but it was the first sustained series of sounds that Noah had ever uttered. He was six, a non-verbal child who had been diagnosed with autism a couple of years earlier.

Noah and I "sang" together for a few more minutes and then he suddenly went silent again. I took the cue and unwound my rhythms into some basic calming patterns, while slowing my tempo and dropping my volume.

I ended with a slow bass pulsation that faded into nothingness. Noah sat spinning a toy soldier in front of his face, a familiar pastime for him.

"Wow, so did you hear that?" his mother said, crying. "He's never made so many sounds. Do you think he'll start talking?"

"I don't know, but it sure was fun playing with him. I'll come back next week and see if we can do this again."

Vocalizing to REI rhythms is not uncommon. Because I rarely play live anymore, I don't get to interact with my clients in the way that I did with Noah; however, I often hear from parents whose children talk more with their recording.

One client, Jason, went through spurts of language activity whenever he received a new REI drumming recording. As part of his extended REI Program, we created a new track every four weeks; I usually got a call from his mom after two or three weeks asking for a new set of rhythms, because his language development had stalled. For two or three weeks at a time, Jason developed more skills and increased his vocabulary, with longer sentence structures and more meaningful content.

When Jason began the REI Custom Program, he was five-years-old and had limited language abilities. He could say his name and ask for things using one or two word phrases. Over the course of the first two months, his language blossomed to two or three sentence phrases and he was beginning to describe events in sequence.

Sequencing, by the way, is something that shows a higher level of communication skill and awareness. This was something I saw in Stacey, my first client with autism.

Stacey had a prodigious vocabulary and talked constantly. But if you were to ask her what she did at school, she wouldn't be able to describe it to you in a cohesive manner. She may cover some of the events, but they do not fit into a timeline or logical progression.

As I described in Chapter 1, after working with Stacey for seven weeks, her anxiety dropped to a barely noticeable level. I then received a call from her mother describing two milestones.

"Stacey slept over at a friend's house last night," Sharon said to me. "She was able to stay the entire night, which was a first for her."

"That's great," I said. "That's a major change from last month when you couldn't leave her side."

"Yes, she has been much calmer since beginning the drumming. But the exciting part is that this morning I asked Stacey how her night was and she was able to tell me what she did, from start to finish. She described it in a clear and logical fashion. It was amazing."

"Is the first time she has been able to describe things this way?"

"Yes, and Anna's mother told me that Stacey displayed a similar level of clarity last night when Stacey was over there."

With my experience with Stacey in my mind, I went to see Noah again a week after he sang as I played.

This session, however, was not as dramatic. Noah had a meltdown before I arrived and was agitated, so I spent my session calming him down.

He rocked and pushed away from his mother when I started playing. I had started with some rhythms that I like to think of as "round" rhythms (a nebulous descriptor kind of like Eddie Van Halen's famous "brown" guitar tone). These round rhythms are soft patterns (still played at eight-beats-per-second) that have a four-beat pulse with five and seven-beat transitions to keep them from getting repetitive.

Noah settled down after about five minutes and let his mother hold him as he twisted his toy soldier in his hands. I played for another fifteen minutes, and by the end he was playing quietly on the floor with a set of Legos. He made no sound.

This was a big difference from my previous session with him. Yet, not all live drumming sessions produced obvious, dramatic effects like Noah's first utterances. Still, his mother and I were glad to see him calm.

Trying to capitalize on my first session with Noah, I gave his mother a tape of the session from the previous week when he sang. You could actually hear him in parts of it. She played this recording for the next four weeks, since I was unable to come visit him during that time.

At the end of the four weeks, I came back and played for Noah again.

"Noah has been humming and singing to the tape you made for him," his mother told me. "He's also been carrying the tape around with him and he hands it to me to put in the tape player. When I turn it on, he gets excited. I think he likes it a lot."

"I'm glad he likes it." I said, as I got ready to play for him again. Noah stood at my side and pawed at the drum as I set it on my lap.

"Would you like to play the drum with me, Noah?" I asked.

He nodded as he tapped away at the head. I joined him and we played together. He started getting excited, though, and began pulling on the drum; so I had to stop, lest he wrestled it from my hands and it fell to the floor. His mom rushed over and tried to guide Noah away from the drum. He pulled away and began running around the room, with his mom chasing after him.

I started playing a calming rhythm, but it didn't seem to have any effect. After a few minutes, I decided to turn on the tape he'd been listening to for the past month. I hoped that the familiarity of the drumming and his singing would help calm him.

I stopped playing, put the tape in the player and turned it on. Noah almost immediately stopped in his tracks. He turned his head and walked toward the tape player.

I was here with my drum, but he was drawn to the tape. I'd never seen this before. My live drumming had no impact on calming him, but a few seconds of a recording and Noah was mesmerized. I looked at his mom in surprise while she was shifting her gaze between Noah and me.

Noah stood in place in front of the tape player for almost ten solid minutes, listening to his tape, smiling when he could hear himself singing.

My experience working with Noah was the first time I'd had someone vocalize while I played my drum. And watching him react to his own singing on the recording was exciting for me. Later, when I moved to recordings based on an intake rather than first playing live for someone, I didn't have the opportunity to see these beginnings; but I did hear from parents or providers who witnessed the surge in a client's vocalizations. In one dramatic case, 19-year-old Jim, who was also non-verbal, had a similar response to the drumming as Noah.

"We had the CD made. We put it in during a session with his CranioSacral therapist and he responded instantly," described Jim's mother, Linda. "His system was calming down: and to the surprise of his therapist, he started vocalizing. We were like, hip-hip hurray."

I was sitting with Linda and Jim's occupational therapist, Lena, and talking about his experience with his REI Custom Program for a video I was producing. Jim had been listening to his Program CDs for about nine months when I visited. This was the first of many interviews throughout the country where I met with REI Providers and their clients, seeking feedback and, hopefully, testimonials on the REI Program.

"He is now starting to put sentences together. I'm very pleased," Linda added.

Something clicked when Jim first heard his CD. It took us quite a while to build on his language, but his first words were pretty exciting. Many people who do the REI Custom Program have language or communication issues. Some, like Jim, are non-verbal when they start the Program.

Years before, in 1995, when my institute was conducting a series of placebo-controlled studies, I heard a similar comment. One of the subject's mothers, Martha, spoke about her four-year-old son with autism.

"At the beginning of the study, Jonah didn't even seem to realize that speech had a purpose," she described to me at the end of the study. "He has gone from saying only one or two words a day at the beginning to about 30 or 40 a day now. His pronunciation has also improved. He now seems to realize that speech has a purpose, and he has been putting a lot of effort into talking."

This was a marked improvement over what she described at the beginning of the study: Jonah was non-verbal, highly anxious, impulsive, exhibited frequent self-stimulatory behaviors, and had no interest in interacting with others. His progression followed a similar path as 19-year-old Jim, but happened at a much faster pace—twelve weeks instead of nine months.

Jonah's progress, even though it was faster and more profound than Jim's, was similar to Jim's in that calm was one of the first things his mother, teachers, and therapists saw improve from listening to his REI recording.

"Jonah's eye contact has improved a lot," she told me after Jonah had been listening to his REI recording for four weeks. "Overall, he is much calmer, a lot less impulsive and interacts with others much more frequently. I asked his preschool teachers if they were doing anything differently. They all said that they noticed a change in Jonah, but they hadn't changed their routine any. His occupational therapist also noticed that Jonah seemed calmer."

Jonah wasn't really talking after four weeks into the study, but Martha described that he did seem to become interested. "He's really trying to talk now, when before he didn't seem to have any interest. He sometimes responds verbally now. He still has some un-meaningful hand movements, but he has had no panic attacks and is much less withdrawn. His autistic behavior has lessened so much that I think his main problem now is his lack of speech."

Jonah wasn't the only person in this study to start seeing some increase in language skills. Garrett, also four-years-old, started the study with very limited language skills, often only using sounds, such as grunting, rather than words to try to communicate.

"Garrett is speaking more and more," said his mother Julie. "He began saying his brother's name, and he now can let us know 98% of the time what he wants. It is as if now that he is more tuned in, he expresses verbally what he wants."

I talked with Julie again at the end of the study and she mentioned that Garrett liked his recording and often carried the tape around with him. She also said, "He is now initiating conversation and initiating social interactions."

Jonah, Garrett and Jim each had anxiety and related anxiety-based behaviors when I started working with them. Across the board, I attribute our non-verbal clients' improvements in language to REI's ability to lower their anxiety levels so that the client can find the words that are trying to get out. Anxiety seems to be at the heart of nearly all symptoms. I feel if I can reduce the anxiety, a door opens for language to start developing.

Linda, 19-year-old Jim's mother, had an interesting way to view this. As she told me during her interview, "I've always approached it as his body is his worst enemy. If I can get his body to calm down and not be so fearful then he can approach his world in a friendlier way and feel more assured. Then he can be confident enough to speak."

Lena, Jim's REI provider and CranioSacral therapist, described that another goal was to eliminate Jim's emotional outbursts.

"Yeah, yeah," interrupted Linda. "We haven't had them at all." Jim had always been emotionally reactive, mostly, I felt, due to his inability to express himself. By reducing his anxiety and increasing his communication skills, he no longer reacted with an emotional outburst.

Not all my clients with language and communication issues are anxious. I recently worked with a highly educated speech therapist to help her with word retrieval, also called apraxia.

"Do you think REI can help with verbal apraxia?" asked Mary, a speech-language pathologist who had just completed one of my first live REI Authorized Provider training seminars. "I've always had difficulty remembering words. They're on the tip of my tongue, but I just can't find them. Do you think the Custom Program can help?"

"I don't know, but we can give it a try."

Based on her intake and the fact that she seemed to have no anxiety, the first CD I made for her focused on stimulating her brain in the same way that I would for someone like me, with ADHD. A recording of this sort is highly stimulating and is something that I wouldn't do early on for someone with even a slightest level of anxiety because it could heighten their anxiety.

After listening to her first CD for a couple of weeks and then moving on to a second CD with even more stimulation, Mary reported that the CDs were working—in some ways.

"I feel like my brain is in high gear. I'm clearer and my focus and memory are better, but I'm still having trouble finding the right words to say. I'm also a little agitated by the drumming. Could you add one of those other instrument tracks you sometimes put on the kid's CDs?"

She was referring to the ambient instrumental tracks that I occasionally added to a REI Program recording if we saw agitation or an increase in anxiety (I talk in detail about ambient tracks in Chapter 9).

"Sure, I can do that," I replied. "You may also want to double-check the volume you're using when listening. The second CD can be especially touchy in getting the right volume; the drum has very little resonance and can be annoying if played too loud."

"Okay. I wonder…" Mary paused, perhaps considering whether she should present her next thought.

"Do you think the higher frequencies of the ambient instrument would help with language? After all, the frequency people all talk about higher frequencies stimulating cognition," she added.

She was referring to other auditory programs that employ frequency-modulated pre-recorded music. A theory (one of many) common among these other programs is that the higher frequencies are more activating for outer cortical regions of the brain and, therefore, may improve cognitive abilities. These theories are not part of the basis for REI, because I use musical rhythm rather than frequency, melody or harmony. Ambient tracks, up to this point, were only used to moderate the intensity of the rhythms.

Given that we talked about adding a harmonic component to her REI recording, I thought it was worth considering adding a higher frequency component to stimulate as well as calm. After all, adding an ambient instrument track to help with her agitation is something I occasionally do when a client has the volume set correctly and I have reduced the level of stimulation in the rhythm tracks to the point were I cannot go any lower without adversely affecting the outcome of the Program.

For Mary, I could have reduced the stimulation and tried to approach the word recall and minor agitation from a different direction, but my gut told me that I was on the right track, so to speak, with the rhythms. I also felt that I didn't want to introduce a calming element to reduce the level of stimulation.

So her idea of a more stimulating ambient track intrigued me. I decided that I needed an ambient track that would complement rather than moderate the effects of the rhythmic structures I had chosen.

I spent several hours creating an ambient sound with a series of complex high-frequency overtones and harmonics. Then I coupled them with complex rhythms played on the Udu clay-pot drum, the most intense drum I use. (Chapter 7 has more about this drum).

Mary called me after listening to this CD for three weeks.

"I've noticed a big difference in my recall," she described. "My vocabulary has expanded, because I can finally find the words in my mind. My staff has even mentioned that I'm more fluid when talking with them. I'm stammering less in search of the words that I want to say."

"That's great," I replied.

She went on to describe that she still felt more clear and focused.

And she offered some anecdotes about how she had been communicating better the previous couple of weeks.

"Was this CD less agitating with the ambient track?" I asked

"Well, yes and no. I don't feel agitated when I listen like I did with the other CDs, but I did find that the ambient instrument kind of pierced my brain."

"Pierced your brain?"

"Yes, it's hard to describe exactly. At certain places in the CD, I feel pressure in my head. Maybe not pressure. Maybe something more like electricity. It's kind of like a buzzing, but it's not a sound. Then when the CD stops, I feel super-focused. It's almost uncomfortable."

"Uncomfortable? Would you like me to adjust the CD?"

"No, I like it. It makes me feel like it's charging my brain cells."

"Okay," I paused, thinking, not sure if it was the best thing that she was uncomfortable while listening. "Aside from listening being somewhat uncomfortable, have you seen any negative effects from this CD?"

"No. Not that I can think of. I'm not anxious. I'm sleeping well. People are noticing that my language is more fluid. I'm pleased with the results so far."

Clearly she was happy, so I said, "Well, if you're okay with it, why don't you continue using the CD until you see your improvements even out."

She listened to this CD daily for over a year. It wasn't because her language kept getting better and better—she was plenty articulate to begin with. With this CD, she hit a consistent level of focus and her apraxia essentially disappeared; so she kept listening because it made her feel good. When she finally did stop listening, she described that her gains remained.

Verbal apraxia is something I've seen more and more over the past few years. I've found that the ambient instrumental track isn't necessary for most people. Still, Mary was happy with it and it allowed me to view the ambient instrument tracks in a different light. This process led me to consider how to use the harmonic content in a way that can not only moderate the rhythm track, but enhance it as well.

This has become an important component of the music I've created for Brain Shift Radio.

Like all of the symptoms that I see, challenges with language don't exist in isolation. For Jim, Noah, and Jonathan, anxiety also played a role. Their anxiety limited their language. For others, limited language seems to contribute to other behaviors. In the case of the man I introduce in the next chapter, his inability to express himself resulted in his aggression toward others.

Chapter Fifteen

Aggression

I could hear the screaming as we pulled into the driveway. I looked with concern at Lloyd, who simply raised an eyebrow.

Knowing they were expecting us, Lloyd and I walked right into the house and were immediately confronted by Ty who was running through the entryway screaming and flailing his arms.

His mother was following behind, trying to catch him.

Lloyd motioned for me to set down the drum and grab a chair for him as he took stock of the situation. Then he sat down behind the drum and began playing.

He started with a loud slap to the head. The drum's shout filled the huge room and reverberated off the hard surfaces, drowning out Ty's screams. Lloyd paused then gave the drum another hard slap.

Ty turned to look, but continued screaming, hitting and pushing his mother away as she caught up to him and tried giving him a hug.

Lloyd tapped the head with the tips of his fingers, laying down a soft patter that was barely audible in the midst of the chaos in the room.

Once out of his mother's arms, Ty made another lap around the room then came running toward Lloyd and grabbed at the drum. Lloyd was unfazed and kept playing, holding the drum between his legs as six-year-old Ty pawed at it.

Ty's mother took advantage of Ty's focus on Lloyd and the drum and was able to get a hold of him. Ty squirmed, but didn't put up much of a fight as Lloyd raised his volume and began playing in earnest.

I was still stunned by the difference in Ty's behavior from the last couple of sessions with him. This was our third meeting with Ty; and although Lloyd had told me before we met Ty that he was prone to aggressive outbursts, I hadn't seen one yet. The Ty that I had observed up until that point was a quiet boy who was intent on occupying his own world, generally oblivious to everything around him. The screaming, running, and lashing out where new to me.

These behaviors, however, were something that I became intimately familiar with in the following decades.

I thought of Ty's screaming and physical aggression as I entered the yard of the residential facility where I was getting ready to conduct a study. Located in a rural area not far from where I was living in Arizona, this home for adults with autism had been profiled in a newspaper article. I called the home, hoping to be able to play for the residents. Only a year before, I had seen the remarkable calming effects of one of my tapes when it was tested at an adult vocational center. (I talk about that research project in Chapter 9). I was told that this facility was having troubles with its residents' anxiety and aggressive behavior; I hoped to make customized recordings for each resident to see if my drumming could help.

Once through the entry gate, I saw a man coming toward me. He started yelling obscenities as I approached, his pace toward me quicker than my pace toward the administrative office. I started to say hello and ask him where the director was, but he simply continued on in great detail about how he was going to hurt me—punch me in the face, kick me in the groin, elbow me in the chest—if I crossed him.

This was Charlie, one of the residents and one of the reasons I was at this facility.

His threats were directed to me at a high volume and without making eye contact. By my observation and experience with other men with autism, I didn't feel that he really intended to act on his threats. He had the characteristic monotone, lack of eye contact, and overall flat affect that characterizes many with this condition. He also lacked the usual intensity and in-your-face aggressiveness that typically precedes such an attack.

Nonetheless, given his history of unprovoked aggression, I was careful not to get too close or to upset him if I could avoid it. I did, however, sit down on the bench near the garden and pick up my drum, which he regarded curiously, and begin to play, which prompted him to watch me even more closely. I was pretty confident that he had never encountered anyone entering his space and drumming. The novelty of this situation seemed to disarm him, because he stopped talking and watched me.

I began by quietly playing calming-type rhythms at the characteristic REI eight-beats-per-second pace. Over the next few minutes, I slowly built up the volume of my drumming and before long he sat down next to me. A few minutes later he put his hand on the shell of the drum.

After approximately four minutes, I began a series of more intense rhythms to see if his behavior would change. This is what Lloyd used to do to invoke a response in a listener and to gauge their level of engagement in the rhythms. Within less than 30 seconds, Charlie grabbed the hardware lugs that tension the drum and tried to pull the drum from my lap. Because I have become accustomed to anticipate a reaction of this sort (I'd lost hold of the drum many times before), I pulled back and just barely managed to hang on.

After a short struggle, he let go of the drum and leaned away from it, though he stayed on the bench. Using the calming-type rhythms I started with, I began playing again. He settled back on the bench. I continued playing for another ten minutes or so, careful to not play rhythms that were too intense or chaotic. He noticeably calmed during this time and was sitting still, gazing off in the distance as I stopped playing and walked away.

Charlie's response was not unlike Ty's when Lloyd finally got into a groove. With his mother's arms around him, Ty stood holding the drum as Lloyd played. I stood in awe as Ty was drawn into the pulse and power of Lloyd's drumming. Lloyd played for almost ten minutes and all the while Ty stood and held the drum. Ty was calm and allowed his mother to hold him by the time Lloyd stopped playing, so we decided to call it a session and leave.

When we got to the car, I asked Lloyd what he did to calm Ty down.

"I hit the drum with intensity to get his attention. The first slap didn't do anything. So I played another," he described.

"That's when Ty looked at you," I said.

"Yes, but he was still out of control. I needed to do the unexpected, so I played exactly the opposite way next. Instead of yelling, I whispered."

"I could barely hear what you were playing. What rhythms were you using?"

"Nothing special. The whisper was the important thing. He needed to search for the sound."

"And he did. He came right over to you. It was amazing."

"He was still out of control, though."

"Yeah, I noticed you switched rhythms or something. The sound was so, I don't know, pleading."

"I was talking to him. Asking him to join me. To surrender his violence."

"Then he just stood there. His mom held him and he didn't move. Why did that happen, and so fast?"

"He surrendered," was all Lloyd said. I got nothing more out of him.

These experiences with my teacher and mentor Lloyd were exciting, and maddening. I couldn't understand a lot of what he was talking about at the time. I was only 20, after all, and my life experience was limited. But somehow I learned enough to use as the foundation to grow on my own over the years.

The drum was a curiosity and the soothing patter drew listeners in, shifting their awareness from the anxiety and aggression they were displaying while allowing their brain to entrain to the rhythms and into a calmer state (I talked about entrainment in Chapter 5 and about calm in Chapter 9). In both Ty's and Charlie's cases, calm occurred within a few minutes.

While I played for Charlie, Kathleen, the home's director, came out and watched me play. I walked over to her after I finished, and we talked as we meandered through the gardens.

"Charlie, the man you just played for, is the aggressive guy I told you about on the phone," she described. "He's a sweet guy at heart, but we've been having three or four violent outbursts a week where someone is injured."

"That's a lot," I said. "How badly are people hurt?"

"Not too bad, but we have to report them and we're getting pressure to find him a different home if we can't reduce the incidents. We've tried different medications and behavioral interventions, but nothing has really helped."

"Do you know what triggers his aggression?"

"Most of the time it's when he's asked to do a chore that he doesn't want to do. Other times he gets in one of the other guy's [resident's] faces. It's worse during mealtimes. We have to work hard to manage everyone while they eat. Dinner is the most stressful time of day here."

Kathleen described that Charlie has lived in a group home situation since he was 14-years-old. He was placed there due to his family's inability to care for him and manage his anxiety and aggressive outbursts. This facility was his fifth group home.

Due to his non-compliance and severe behavioral reactions, Charlie was not involved in many of the day-to-day activities that the other residents enjoyed. The staff reported that he did enjoy riding and brushing the horses; but they didn't allow him to do these activities often, due to his tendency to spontaneously hit the horse with a closed fist.

Aside from these aggressive behaviors, Kathleen described that Charlie's anxiety also manifested in the form of self-stimulatory vocalizations and sleeplessness. The vocalizations were often threatening in nature, but there didn't seem to be a correlation between his threats and his aggressive actions.

"His yelling and swearing seems to be a release mechanism for him," said Kathleen.

"It sure is disconcerting, though," I added. "When I first heard him, I thought he had Tourette's."

"No, he has autism."

Tourette syndrome is a condition characterized by involuntary repetitive physical or vocal tics (Chapter 11 has more on Tics). Charlie's verbal threats weren't the result of Tourette syndrome, because his vocalizations contained form and more closely resembled perseveration (the repetition of an action, word or phrase in the absence of a related stimulus). Perseveration is a common trait of autism and is an area where I tend to see marked gains; I was eager to see if reducing Charlie's anxiety would improve this behavior.

Charlie could speak clearly with excellent grammar and vocabulary, but he only talked in an aggressive manner. The fact that he could speak and had a vocabulary, albeit a nasty one, suggested that if I could reduce his anxiety, he may become more conversational in his speech. This wasn't a primary goal in working with Charlie, but it was one area I intended to keep an eye on as he used his REI recording. As in the case of Jim, who I discussed in Chapter 14, I have seen the spontaneous initiation of speech occur in adults with autism as a result of reducing anxiety.

Kathleen and I talked for a couple of hours, going over the details of the study I would conduct. The plan was to create a custom-made recording for each of the residents. Each recording would focus on areas of concern specific to each resident. I would also attempt to reduce the overall level of aggression and anxiety in the facility.

The focus of Charlie's recording would be his aggression, self-stimulatory language, and sleep.

Charlie had difficulty falling asleep and often woke during the night. The biggest issue was that, if not supervised at night, he would attempt to leave the facility. He liked to wander around outside. On several occasions, he was observed walking off the facility grounds and wandering onto neighboring properties. In one case, he entered a neighbor's house. Fortunately, the neighbors knew and recognized him and called the facility director to retrieve him. In order to avert an incident of this sort again, a staff member was positioned within eyesight of his door throughout the night.

Just as I was ready to leave for the day, we heard a ruckus in the dining room. Kathleen ran in and I followed. Charlie was wrestling with another resident and a third man, Billy, who was screaming and rocking. The staff was trying to separate the two wrestlers while Kathleen went over to the screaming man to try to calm him. I watched the chaos unfold and realized that I had my hands full with this study.

I began to doubt myself. Here I was in an established home with professionals, most with a lot more experience with these issues than I had. And I only had a drum. Sure, the school study went well and the tests at the vocational facility showed significant calming, but this aggressive behavior was different. The stakes were higher, and I began feeling the pressure.

The funny thing was, though, that even with my doubts and the pressure to perform, I felt compelled to try. I needed to see if my drumming could help. I'd seen too much with Lloyd to ignore the possibilities.

I watched as the two men who were wrestling stopped, and Kathleen expertly calmed the screaming man. I thought that if they would have me, I'd give it my all and play my heart out for these guys.

Over the next week, I played for all five residents. As with Charlie, I saw calm each time I played for a resident who was anxious (I go into detail with three other resident's experiences with my drumming in Chapter 16). I made recordings for each of the residents and asked that they each listen to their own recording once a day.

Four weeks later, I met up with Charlie in the corral where he was quietly brushing a horse. He had no reaction to me when I approached him—a much different experience than the last time I met him. He was clearly calm and focused on the rhythm of brushing.

I said hello to him and asked if he remembered me. He responded that I was the "funny drum guy". The drum I use is very usual and shaped unlike any other drum, so this observation intrigued me. Of course it could mean that any drum was funny to him. Or my playing was funny. Or I was funny. Or that he was observant enough to see the drum was different—this would mean he had some previous knowledge of drums and their common shapes. But I didn't explore this with him. I asked if he liked the drumming, to which he simply said, "Yeah". I asked if I could play for him again. His response was, again, simply "Yeah."

I found a log to sit on about 20 feet away outside of the corral and began tapping a calming rhythm for him. I noted no discernable response as he continued to brush the horse. After a while, I began playing a rhythm that employed a steady accented pulse. This rhythm was a traditional Brazilian Samba rhythm with 16th notes employing two quiet notes and two accented notes, the second accented note louder than the first every other time through this pattern, which makes the loud accent occur once every second. The rhythm created a pulsing, forward-moving feel. This rhythm is different from a traditional Samba, however, because every other time through the pattern I cut the rhythm short by two notes, changing the time signature of this measure into 7/8 and the entire pattern into 15/8.

After a few minutes I noticed that Charlie was brushing the horse to the rhythm, his strokes following the louder of the accented notes. I changed rhythms to something more typical of an REI rhythm (more complex and variable) and noticed that his brushing strokes slowly reduced in speed.

It is interesting to note that the more complex and variable the rhythm I play, the calmer most individuals with autism seem to become. I also find that if I play a simplistic rhythm for too long, my playing often elicits a negative response. The repetition of a simple rhythm promotes irritation, and this occurs more rapidly for individuals on the spectrum than for typical people. People with autism often crave novel stimulus and are quick to physiologically tire of a rhythm or pulse that becomes grating. Their low tolerance of repetitive patterns is often evident in their aversion to the cycles of refrigerators and florescent lights, for example.

I've heard many reports from caregivers that their autistic charges are attracted to the REI rhythms in a way non-autistic people are not. And many seem to be able to decipher even the most complex patterns. Given there is a subset of people with autism that have savant capabilities, there appears to be some innate ability to interpret or latch onto complex patterns in a way that others simply do not.

Another population that does not tolerate simple rhythms are people with ADHD, like me. Given my need to play complex rhythms, I was uniquely observant of this characteristic. I also think my brain-type allowed me to develop my Programs in a way that others would not have thought to do.

I stopped playing after approximately 15 minutes, packed up my drum and left. Charlie was still slowly brushing the horse and made no notice of my departure. The director, who had been watching me play, joined me to describe how things have been since I was last there a month before.

"This is longest he's brushed a horse," she described as she asked Charlie to stop and put the equipment away. Prepared for a meltdown, I watched with trepidation. Charlie offered some minor resistance, though he didn't put up a struggle or react aggressively.

As we walked away from Charlie, Kathleen said, "We have not had a single aggressive incident since the first week of his listening to the REI recording."

"That's great. I'm glad to hear that. How has he been overall since he received his tape?" I asked.

"He's much calmer," she paused, "More compliant. We noticed that he is more engaged in activities, especially those involving the horses. A month ago I wouldn't let him brush the horse for fear that he'd hit it."

I nodded, happy that he was calmer. Then asked, "How about his vocal stimming? He hasn't yelled at me today. Has he been better?"

"He still falls into his loop, but he's less aggressive with it and he'll stop when we ask him to. Because he is calmer, he is talking more. 'Conversation' isn't the right word, but he's trying to get his needs and desires met."

"We can get him to converse to a degree," she continued, "but it's not spontaneous."

I looked at the tracking log the staff had been completing to document Charlie's listening times and responses. I noticed that his recording was being played at bedtime. The notes described that he often asked for the recording before going to bed. It also looked like he was falling asleep much more quickly, usually sleeping by the time the REI recording ended (approximately 20 minutes).

"It looks like his sleep is better," I observed.

"Definitely. He hasn't gotten up at night and he hasn't tried to get off the property. That's been a real relief. We're still keeping a close eye on it, though."

I was pleased with this. These results were beyond what I expected, but I was nervous to ask about the rest of the men in the home. "And the overall anxiety and aggression in the facility over the last month?"

"It's been a lot calmer," she replied. "As I told you last time we met, dinner time is the most difficult time around here. So, at dinner we play the calming tape that you gave us. It seems to make a difference. Everyone is much easier to handle and there haven't been any incidents beyond a couple of minor scuffles."

This was a great success, I felt. But I also learned over the years that the path to reducing aggressive behavior wasn't always so linear. Many times I see an ebb and flow to a reduction in aggression. One recent client, who I worked with for nearly a year, is an example of the need to be diligent when trying to help reduce aggression.

Conrad was a three-year-old boy who had been diagnosed with autism a year before I first worked with him. He was highly volatile and in crisis when his REI Provider called me to go over his intake.

"Conrad has been really aggressive to his parents. They've tried everything and are at their wits end. I'm hoping REI can help," she said.

"The intake looks good. Given his outbursts, I recommend playing the first track at the time of day when he is the most volatile," I suggested. "It may give us a head start to getting these aggressive incidents under control."

"That would be right after school. He seems to hold it together at school, but he explodes when he gets home."

Conrad listened to his first track after school for the first two weeks and then his parents decided that it would be easier to have him listen at bedtime. He was also having a hard time winding down to go to sleep, so bedtime seemed like the best time for him to listen.

Conrad's first month on the Program went as expected. He showed improvement in his aggressive outbursts and in complying with requests. He was also sleeping better. His third track derailed his sleep, though, so I made a revision to see if it could help get his sleep back on track. It did.

Sandra, his mother, and I talked about three months into the Program because we seemed to be a bit stalled.

"So far Tracks 1, 2, and 3.1 have had the best results in calming him and in helping him transition into other things without the negative behaviors," she described. "Tracks 4, 4.1, 5, and 6 have not seemed to improve Conrad's behavior, but have actually made his behavior start to get worse."

"How different is his behavior since we started the Program?" I asked.

"He's a lot better than he was at the beginning. It's just that now he seems more willful than uncontrollable, if that makes sense. It's like he's testing us instead of just lashing out."

"It is possible that some of this is part of his development," I explained to Sandra. "When listening to my drumming music, children on the autism spectrum often play 'catch up' in their basic child development stages. As they work through the Program and grow in their development, the challenges and intense behavioral stages that typical children experience often appear."

As Sandra and I talked, I analyzed the progression of the tracks I had made up until this point and compared them with his responses so far. We decided that we needed to be more diligent in making sure that Conrad didn't listen to any one track for too long. It appeared that his behavior always got better as soon as he received a new track, but his tantrums and aggression grew more frequent if he listened to any particular track for more than two weeks, sometimes less.

I asked that Sandra email me every week and let me know how Conrad was doing so we could decide if he needed a new track. Things went well for a couple of months; but as we were approaching the last three tracks, we saw how even minor variations in a track had a big impact on his behavior and progress. Here is a series of emails Sandra sent me documenting this process:

Feb 14:

I was supposed to call you Wednesday. Conrad has done better with this last CD. He has peed in his bed twice this week but I'm not sure that this has anything to do with the CDs.

I think we can move to the next track. Thanks!

Feb 25:

Conrad has done well with this past CD, too. He is still having some wild reactions, but isn't as emotional and is way easier to talk down. I would certainly say he is better.

His morning tantrums are typically just a reaction to not enough sleep. Our fault, probably.

Mar 5:

We need to do a new CD for Conrad. He hit his wall and is melting down. This morning was a nightmare!

Can you do it today? He is also having trouble expressing himself. Just goes into immediate whining/crying. Constantly talking him off the cliff and talking him down.

I made a new track and received this email the next day.

Mar 6:

We got Conrad to bed by 7 last night, played his new CD and he was already a changed little guy this morning. Thank you! I guess we'll have to keep him at the weekly changes. It's amazing how much he is affected by the CD's.

Mar 18:

Conrad has done really well this last CD. Should we start the next one? Last time when we didn't, it backfired. We are at a week and a half with this CD.

Mar 31:

Hi Jeff. It's time for the next CD. Conrad has done well with this CD, but we have found that he is peeing his bed every night. The only [thing that changed was] the CD. It happened at school twice today.

Any tweaks that can help? I got up last night before his typical time of 1-3am and made him potty.

May 6:

We haven't done a new CD for Conrad in several weeks and we are certainly seeing the effects. He has been extremely irritable and has a lot of trouble going to sleep (screams and yells out from his room).

Once asleep he seems to be doing great with staying asleep and not wetting the bed. At the beginning of this CD, we were seeing the light at the end of the tunnel and felt like the end is in sight (this is a huge excitement for us).

Most of his tantrums now are age appropriate but he does still have difficulty self-soothing once he is upset. We have used a calming approach and tried deep pressure hugging to make him feel secure. It seems to have a calming effect.

By this point, Conrad had made some great improvements. Now all that was necessary was to solidify the improvements. This is generally accomplished by continuing to play the last track for six to eight weeks (I talk more about this process on Chapter 18).

I reflect on Charlie and the men at the residential facility and ponder why a 35-year-old would show a more consistent improvement in aggressive behavior than a four-year-old. Most of the time, the younger a client is when I work with him or her, the greater and more lasting the gains.

I think Charlie's anxiety and inability to express himself verbally contributed to his aggressive behavior. Calming him and helping him get the words out reduced his need to lash out.

Conrad, on the other hand, was still learning to navigate his world and hadn't yet developed the skills needed to consistently calm himself when he was having a hard time. Part of this is developmental, and I have found that continuing to listen to REI rhythms supports this developmental growth.

I called Kathleen about eighteen months after completing the study and learned that Charlie was still calm, having had no aggressive incidents that resulted in injury since the first week of listening. And he was still listening regularly. The rest of the residents (three of which you will meet in the next chapter) were only occasionally listening. The facility was still much calmer in general than before I played my drum for the residents, so I was happy.

In my experience, everyone reaches a point where they can stop listening and the gains all stay. Both Charlie and Conrad reached this point. It took longer for Charlie than Conrad, but that's typical as adults are more resistant to change than children.

Chapter Sixteen

Self-Stimulatory Behaviors

Kylie watched as I set up my gear, her face blank while she repetitively zipped and unzipped her sweater.

"She stims like this a lot," explained her mother. "I can't get her to focus when she does this. She just stares off into space and plays with her zipper or button. She can do this for hours, and when I try to stop her she has a meltdown. She'll pull away and scream."

I nodded as I began to play. Simple, quiet rhythms at first. Just testing the waters.

The slightest smile appeared on Kylie's face. It was gone as quickly as it came.

I settled into a groove with syncopated muted tones, creating a pulsing patter to try to engage Kylie. For about one minute she looked down toward the floor while zipping and unzipping her sweater.

I stopped for a couple of seconds, looking for a response. Kylie looked up at me. I started playing again, figuring that she was listening. She opened her eyes wide a few times as though she was trying to wake herself up.

I kept my syncopated patter going, interjecting a couple of rhythms I had found useful for stopping self-stimming. At about two-and-a-half minutes into this session, Kylie looked at her mom, who was sitting next to her on the couch. Over the next minute or so, Kylie looked at her mom and then away several times.

I switched to a nine-beat pattern, and Kylie moved over to her mom and leaned into her and closed her eyes. The stimming stopped.

I played for another minute and noticed that Kylie was asleep. I stopped and left the room.

Kylie had autism. She engaged in a fairly typical behavior of self-regulation through repetitive motor movements. For Kylie, zipping and unzipping her sweater was soothing. Hers was a relatively subtle, innocuous behavior, one that didn't seem to coincide with any outward stimulus or event.

This behavior was upsetting to her mother because when Kylie was stimming she was unreachable, having retreated into her own world. This is common among people with autism, though the stimming isn't always present, because being unresponsive is a defining characteristic of the condition.

From my perspective, repetitive and self-stimulatory behaviors like this take two forms. They are either internally-driven, possibly as a desire to self-regulate or retreat from the world, or they are in response to a disagreeable external stimulus. The stimming is a way to tune-out or modulate the stimulus. I witnessed a perfect example of externally driven self-stimulatory behaviors when I first met the residents of the facility in Northern Arizona, which I introduced in Chapter 15.

Kathleen, the facility director, was giving me a tour of the home when we entered the main living area where four of the residents and three of the staff were gathered. I didn't see the start of the incident, however a staff member reported to me that one of the residents grabbed an object from another resident and these two began wrestling over it (I was later told it was a granola bar).

I only caught a fleeting glimpse of the two residents who were wrestling because as soon as they started, Billy began howling and twisting back and forth. His howls and screeches grew louder and louder to an ear splitting level. This noise was enough to distract one of the residents involved in the wrestling to stop and let go.

Even with the other two residents no longer wrestling, Billy continued screeching and howling. Shortly, he began biting his right hand and intensely throwing his body back and forth. Kathleen quickly walked to him and put her arms around his shoulder and talked to him in a soothing voice. He seemed to calm a bit, and Kathleen was able to walk him outside. They spent about ten minutes out on the patio while he slowly calmed down. The screeching reduced almost immediately upon Kathleen's hug, but he remained rocking and twisting for close to ten minutes. After this event, Kathleen described that at least once a day Billy reacted just like this to other residents' behaviors.

"He is like the house barometer, always reacting to what others are doing. He's calm if everyone else is calm; but if anyone is anxious or aggressive, he stims," Kathleen described. "I think it's hard for him because he can't communicate well. This is his way of communicating with us."

"He came here when he was 21," continued Kathleen. "He's a really sweet young man and would never hurt or act out toward anyone, but he gets wound up and exhibits these behaviors."

I nod as I watch Billy wander around the patio. He was now calm and seemingly content in his own world.

"He can tell us 'yes' or 'no' for known activities, and he requests to go outside, inside or to the bathroom; but he can't let us know how he is feeling or express anything beyond basic needs. It's as if he doesn't understand feelings or reasons for others' anxious behavior. So, he reacts."

"Most of time, it's rocking back and forth. But sometimes it's what you saw, with the screaming and biting himself. This is when it's really hard; he'll bite hard enough to draw blood, and he's strong enough that trying to stop him is a challenge, especially for someone as small as me. The best thing I can do is try to get him away from the others so he doesn't have anything to react to. But even then, it can take quite a while for him to calm down. I'm hoping that the drumming will make this easier."

I stayed around for dinner and observed that he ate at a table away from other residents. A staff member accompanied him but didn't eat.

"He'll grab the other resident's food if he's not watched," explained Kathleen. "He is obsessive with it. He won't get aggressive, though. All it takes to keep him from grabbing other's food is to redirect him. It's easier, though, to have him eat by himself with a staff member to keep him company."

After this encounter with Billy, I wanted to make certain that he was calm at the onset of our first live session. I figured that if his first encounter with the drumming was a positive one, the association would help when a recording was turned on while he was stimming.

I met up with Billy on the patio when other residents were busy elsewhere in the building or on the grounds. When I arrived, he was sitting quietly. I approached him with my drum and asked if he minded if I played it. He made no response, though he did give the drum a good look. He continued looking at it as I tapped it a bit. Once I settled into a steady rhythm, his gaze drifted and he sat looking across the grounds toward the distant mountains.

At one point during my session, I noticed a slight lift in his mouth, a slight smile or an attempt to suppress one. I tried to recall the rhythm I had just played. It was a bouncy triplet-feel rhythm in 29/16 with syncopated bass hits and accented slap tones

I returned to this rhythm, and I saw another slight change in his expression. I cycled between this rhythm and others with a similar bouncy quality that I typically play for people with autism. I observed that whenever I played these bouncy triplet-based rhythms, he seemed to smile slightly.

I alternated between two syncopated triple-feel rhythms and, after about three minutes, he was beaming with a smile. After a short while longer, I stopped on those rhythms. He never looked my way the entire time I played; but once I stopped, he looked over toward me (in a way typical of people with autism: he didn't look at me, just my way, as if seeing me out the periphery of his vision). His smile faded to what I would characterize as a satisfied grin, and he turned away again to gaze out over the grounds toward the mountains.

I thanked him for letting me play and walked away as he sat grinning and looking out in the distance. Later, Kathleen told me that after I left she asked him if he liked the drumming. His response was a little smile and a nod as he said "boom, boom".

Because Billy didn't have any problems sleeping and because he often struggled with any anxious, agitated, or aggressive incidents that occurred during the day, I asked Kathleen to have his REI recording played at the time when he most often had difficulty. This was generally mid-afternoon. I later heard that Billy often requested his recording by asking for his "boom, boom" music. The staff generally played his REI music whenever he asked.

I returned to see Billy after four weeks. I found him in the garden watering the plants. Without saying anything, I pulled out my drum and could tell he was regarding me with interest, though he didn't look at me, only past me. He continued to peripherally look my way, seeming to be watching my hands on the drum, as I began tapping the drum lightly. He stood still for a few minutes while I played until Kathleen approached. She guided him over to a bench in the garden a few feet away from me and they both sat quietly.

Because they were both still and not reacting in any way to the rhythms, I began playing more stimulating rhythms to see if I cold get a response from Billy. These rhythms are chaotic and loud and can be annoying to some people. Billy, however, showed no reaction, positive or negative, to these rhythms.

I began playing a grouping of five with accents on the second and third beats played as slaps. These were high-pitched accents played by pressing my fingers into the edge of the head, just in from the rim. My five-beat rhythm then evolved to include the first beat of the phrase played as a bass tone, which involves hitting the middle of the head with the heel of the hand. This is an REI rhythm set that has been observed to often elicit an agitated response, especially with people on the autism spectrum.

Billy sat forward and began wringing his hands in his lap after a few minutes of this pattern. His reaction was what I was looking for and told me that he was engaged in what I was playing. I immediately switched to a rhythm traditionally used to uplift a listener's mood. A pattern in a 12/8 time signature with a triple feel, this rhythm contained a pulse with accented slaps on the second and fourth grouping of three. A bass tone was played on the first note of the third grouping of the first measure and played on the first and third notes of the third grouping of the second measure. This two-measure pattern continued for several minutes.

Billy sat back and stopped wringing his hands. Then he flashed the smile I saw on the first day I played for him.

I altered the rhythms slightly by eliminating the last beat of the second measure and varied the accent pattern to keep it from getting too repetitive. I played these variations for approximately five more minutes, and Billy progressively got more animated until he was sitting up in his seat clapping and rocking. Kathleen sat next to him smiling and clapping along. On this positive note, I stopped, packed up my drum and left.

I talked with Kathleen the next day and she mentioned that Billy was happy all afternoon.

"He kept saying 'boom, boom'," she described. "Then he got excited when we turned on his REI recording before dinner. He seemed happy after you played. The recording re-enforced that."

"I'm glad to hear that. He seemed pretty upbeat when I left." Then I added, "Aside from that, how has his self-stimming been going?"

"When his CD is playing, he is less bothered by others' behaviors. He doesn't engage in body rocking or twisting or in self-injurious behaviors."

"I will say, though, that because the facility is calmer overall, it's rare that there is enough going on for Billy to react to. And when he does get agitated and rock, we just turn on his rhythms. It calms him right down."

Like Billy, Jim, another resident of this facility, rocked when he was agitated. I saw this when I first met him.

When I approached and said hello, Jim didn't look up from a candy wrapper, folding and crinkling it in a repetitive manner. A staff member asked Jim to hand him the wrapper. Jim kept playing with it and after repeated attempts at getting Jim to stop, the staff member then removed it from his hand. Jim got upset and began rocking his body, gesturing in an aggressive manner with his hands, and making a groaning sound.

Seeing this, I sat down in a nearby chair and began playing my drum. Jim's attention almost immediately focused on me, particularly on my hands, as I played. Jim noticeably calmed down within a couple of minutes; and after approximately fifteen minutes of listening, he quietly sat in a chair about ten feet away, slowly moving to the rhythm of the drum. His gaze was not focused on either me or the drum, rather it was directed to a point on the ground in front of him. When I stopped playing, he glanced over toward, though not at, me and stopped his rhythmic movements.

I then went over to him and reached out my hand and thanked him for sitting and listening to me play. He reached up and we shook hands. His grip was soft. He made no eye contact and no sound.

Stopping a self-stimulatory behavior that happens in response to a stimulus is pretty straightforward. I treat the stimming with the same approach as I treat anxiety of any kind. I begin with some basic calming rhythms and then create a dialog between the progression of my rhythms and my listener's response. For both Billy and Jim, it required rhythms consisting of accents in time with their repetitive movements.

When Billy rocked, I used his tempo to drive my rhythms. This didn't mean that I played simple pulses to his rocking, though. I used the pulse of his rocking as a downbeat to play to. So if the rocking happened two times per second, I tried to choose a rhythm that had a bass tone in time with his rocking, while having other beats filling the space. I would also be sure not to have these beats repeat very much and instead keep a steady dose of variability.

When I play live, this dialogue is the key to stopping a repetitive, self-stimulatory behavior. But a rhythmic dialogue such as this is not possible when a client is using a recording. Instead, I must draw from the database of rhythms I have collected to help stop stimming behaviors. This is especially the case if I'm trying to make permanent improvements in stimming behaviors during the course of an REI Custom Program.

The process of stopping the stimming behavior is a fluid process. Rarely does the behavior stop outright. It's usually a progression, and many times the behaviors morph over time. For example, I recently had a discussion with one parent and her REI provider as we were working with six-year-old Colton. This discussion took place eight weeks into the Program.

"Colton is no longer flapping his arms. He will flick his fingers when he is excited, but it's not as frequent or as prominent as the hand flapping use to be," said Angela, his REI Provider.

"Before he started the Program, Colton stimmed most of the time," his mother added. "It was really distracting, and I had a hard time getting his attention. If I tried to stop him from flapping his hands, he'd pull away and scream. This is a huge difference."

"I'm glad to hear that," I responded, feeling pretty good about the results so far.

"But can we get rid of the finger thing?" his mother asked, bringing me back to the ground.

"Self-stimulatory behaviors tend to morph as we work through them," I answered. "Eventually we may be able to eliminate them altogether, but this path Colton is on is pretty typical."

"How long do you think it will take," asked his mother.

"I would expect that we'll be working on it for the rest of his Program. These behaviors take time. We need to reduce his anxiety and help him tolerate sensory input," I explained.

"His anxiety is definitely better, but he still gets bothered by sounds."

"Which is why he is still stimming," I added. "We'll work on the sound sensitivities next."

This is a typical path when working with self-stimulatory behaviors. Most times, if I can help reduce anxiety, we see a reduction in some self-stimulatory behaviors as well. Other times, if I can help with sensory defensiveness, then the self-stimming also gets better. And in some cases, like with Colton, it takes addressing both the anxiety and sensory issues for the stimming to cease.

Self-stimulatory behaviors are common in autism. Typical stimming behaviors are flapping hands as though shaking off water (of course there is no water in this case), finger flicking, (usually done in front of the eyes), and rocking or twisting the torso back and forth like Billy and Jim did. These are difficult to watch and look odd, but they are not a problem like some other behaviors are.

Self-injurious behaviors are a form of self-stimulatory behaviors, but these, as the name states, can cause injury. These include pulling out hair, picking at the skin, digging at body parts, or banging the head into objects, such as a wall or floor, in a repetitive fashion.

Russell, another resident at the facility with Billy and Jim, had serious self-injurious behaviors. He banged his head, scratched his forehead, and dug at his anus without provocation or in response to external factors. He was in his thirties, was largely non-verbal and was also diagnosed with bipolar disorder.

Russell scratched and dug to the point of bleeding, usually during his manic period, when he was very excitable. Getting him to stop his digging was difficult. When the staff tried to physically stop him he would become aggressive, as you might expect.

I approached Russell's anal digging the same way I addressed the more benign hand flapping that Colton was doing—by trying to reduce his anxiety.

According to his records, Russell had very limited communication skills and was functionally non-verbal. The facility staff described that his communication consisted of mostly pointing, directing and vocalizing (mostly with grunts and other non-language cues).

The staff reported that when he was depressed, he needed near constant redirection to keep him from engaging in these self-abusive behaviors. It was also difficult to engage him in activities such as doing chores and interacting with the animals.

Russell preferred to sleep during the day or to sit by himself and self-stimulate until asked to stop. He would generally stop when asked to, but approximately 30% of the time the staff noted that they needed to physically stop these behaviors. This was done by gently pulling his hand away from either his face or anus or by moving him from the wall that he was banging his head on.

Russell hadn't eaten yet the first day I met with him and had eaten very little in the past two weeks since his depressed cycle began: He had lost seven pounds already since the end of his last manic period.

I met Russell in the main group living area where he was sitting by himself. He made no response when I said hello to him and simply sat in his chair with his hand to his forehead. He wore a bandage and was lightly scratching at it as I talked to him. A staff member pulled his hand away and he fidgeted with it in his lap for a short while before returning it to his forehead, where he started scratching again.

I began playing the drum. Nothing in his behavior changed for a few minutes until I noticed he seemed to be scratching less on his forehead. After approximately ten minutes, he was no longer scratching his head and his hands were clasped in his lap while he sat nearly motionless. His gaze was fixed in front of him, and it didn't appear that he was looking at any thing in particular.

He continued to sit quietly with his hands in his lap for about 15 minutes after I stopped playing. At that point, one of the staff came to get him to take a walk outside, which he did without resistance.

I met with Russell a second time before making his REI recording so that I could observe him when he was in a manic state. The director called me about two weeks after my first visit, informing me that he was now manic. When I arrived at the facility he was agitated—evidenced by his pacing back and forth while wringing his hands. I was informed that he hadn't slept well the last few days and had, in fact, had been under constant supervision for the past two days for fear of him hurting himself with his self-abusive behavior.

I quickly got out my drum and began playing. His reaction was immediate—he stopped pacing and turned to me, frozen. He stood nearly still for the duration of my playing (approximately 12 minutes). When I stopped, he turned and quietly left the room. One of the staff members remarked on how calm he seemed at that moment.

The director related that his bipolar cycles where pretty regular—the manic period lasted about two weeks and the depressed period lasted between two and three weeks. He currently wasn't taking any medication for this because none seemed to be successful.

Russell received his REI recording three days after my last visit, while he was still in a manic period. Because he was having trouble sleeping, I recommended that he listen at bedtime. Upon my follow-up visit after four weeks, his daily REI tracking log reflected that he fell asleep while the recording played the first night and, aside from three nights during the first two weeks, he fell asleep before the REI recording ended (this is within 20 minutes, a much shorter time than was typical for his manic periods).

When his cycle shifted to a depressed mood, the staff continued to play the REI recording at bedtime because it was the easiest time of day for them to play it. He continued to fall asleep while the recording played, though it wasn't unusual for him to fall asleep within this timeframe when he was depressed before using the REI recording.

Russell was shown how to turn on the recording himself at bedtime and, except for a few days during his depressed cycle, he did so without prompting.

The staff had also taken to playing his REI recording during the day during his depressed period (in addition to playing it at night), and they noted that his mood seemed to elevate and he became more active throughout the day. His self-abusive behavior also lessened. This change in self-abusive behaviors was noticeable within five weeks of beginning REI.

For the next few months Russell continued listening to his REI recording at bedtime and during the day during his depressed cycle. His frequency and intensity of self-abusive behaviors was progressively lessening. When I went to see him at the twelve-week point, he had no sores or scabs on his forehead, a state that was unheard of before starting REI.

By the sixteen-week point, Russell's manic and depressed cycles were less severe. When he was most recently manic, he was much calmer and was sleeping every night. Likewise, when he was depressed he was less lethargic and easier to engage in activities. He was also eating three good meals a day.

After six months, Russell showed an overall improvement in his symptoms of bipolar disorder—his cycles were not as deep, the lows were not as long, and he was better able to handle the depressed side when it did occur. The director said that he no longer listened to the REI recording everyday, but when he did listen before bedtime he seemed to sleep better and wake more rested. After talking with the staff, they agreed to try to be more consistent playing his recording and in helping him remember to turn it on before going to bed.

Self-stimulatory behaviors are a form of self-regulation, often in response to some sensory input. These behaviors can be from anxiety over an event or a change in activity or they can be from an overwhelming sensory stimulus, such as a loud noise or restrictive clothing.

My goal when reducing self-stimulatory behaviors is to reduce the internal anxiety over these events or stimuli. And over time, to help the person be able to handle the stimulation or find another way to moderate their response.

For Colton, I worked with both his self-stimulatory behaviors and his sound sensitivities. It took another sixteen weeks and several new custom-made REI tracks to get the better part of them under control. Colton developed the skills to self-regulate without needing to stim. At the end of his Program, he was able to stop listening to his REI recordings and he rarely self-stimmed.

Colton was able to achieve a long-term improvement in his self-stimulatory behaviors partly because of his young age, but also because I was able to create a series of progressively-stimulating recordings to help him learn to moderate the effects of sensory stimulus and become less sensitive to them.

Billy, Jim, and Russell could likely achieve similar results, even though they were adults, if they listened for sufficient time for their brains to change. Only Russell listened consistently over a long enough period of time (in his case, 18 months) to see an overall reduction in anxiety and self-stimulatory behaviors that lasted when he wasn't listening. Billy and Jim, on the other hand, only saw reductions in their anxiety-based self-stimulatory behaviors when their recordings were playing (and for a short while afterwards).

I mentioned the difference between the anxiety levels of these three reidents to Kathleen and she agreed to resume playing their drumming recordings regularly.

Chapter Seventeen
Sensory Processing

Sensory processing issues are common among the people I work with. In fact, sensory challenges are part of nearly everyone who falls into the developmental disability spectrum, including people with ADHD and autism. Sensory processing issues come in three basic forms: sensory-defensive, sensory-seeking, and poor sensory discrimination.

Sensory defensiveness is characterized by being easily overstimulated by sensory input. This is the child who recoils to touch, won't wear shoes, covers his ears in response to loud noises, gets dizzy easily, or throws up in the car.

Easily overstimulated people constitute most of my clients with sensory issues. I work to reduce their sensitivity to stimulation by giving their brains more stimulation.

"What do you mean by stimulation?" Laurel asked. "Emily is always overstimulated. Why would you add more, and how could it calm her down?" This was one of the first questions she asked me after I began to work with her daughter, Emily.

From her very first track, Emily responded immediately and decisively to the drumming. After just one listening, her emotional outbursts increased and her sleep, already poor before the Program, deteriorated further. Upon her first night on the Program she needed to be held by her mother to calm down.

Laurel and I quickly discovered that Emily needed less stimulation, far less than a Program usually begins with. In fact, I had to step down the level of stimulation on her tracks to a point lower than what was on our 'stimulation low enough for anyone' *Calming Rhythms* CD. Once we determined a stimulation level she could tolerate, we were then able to slowly begin adding more stimulation and progressively build her tolerance to address her sensory issues.

"Stimulation is related to the complexity of the rhythms on the track," I described to Laurel. "I have built a series of rhythmic structures, varying in their length and complexity, for each symptom.

"By complexity, I mean the difficulty needed to decipher the rhythm's pattern. Think of the brain as a computer whose central job, when dealing with sensory stimulus, is to decipher and categorize the stimulation.

"Emily takes in sensory stimulus at a very high level. It's as if her volume control is turned way up. Everything comes at her with an intensity that is higher than for you or me. And she can't turn down the volume. A light touch may feel like a hard squeeze, or a normal voice level may sound like a shout. Our goal with the REI tracks is to teach her sensory system to turn the volume down and to learn to distinguish important from unimportant sensory input.

"With each track, we want to increase the level of stimulation we can give her so that she becomes used to it. Over time, she'll develop the skills to be able to moderate the stimulation she receives."

Before I made her first Program track, Emily, who was four at the time, wouldn't wear clothes, preferring to only wear undies. Sometimes she would wear shorts or a skirt but she was never okay with a shirt. And don't even think about a coat. She also slept poorly, often waking at night or early in the morning, unable to get back to sleep. Emily was also anxious, and Laurel needed to be with her at all times lest she have a melt down.

Laurel was one of my favorite parents. She was engaged and inquisitive. And the two years I spent working with her extremely sensitive daughter was one of the most satisfying—and sometimes perplexing—experiences of my career.

Emily mirrored many challenges exhibited by a six-year-old boy I worked with a few years before. Gerald had both tactile and auditory sensitivities. He wouldn't wear shoes or socks and would cover his ears, or sometimes cry or scream, when someone turned on music, even if the volume was low.

He also tended to isolate himself from his family, preferring to be in his room alone, playing with toys by himself. If a sibling or cousin came in his room, he'd have a meltdown.

For Gerald, the Program was pretty straightforward. He responded within the first two weeks in all areas.

"Gerald is doing great with the Program," said Jenna, his REI provider. Jenna, an occupational therapist in south Texas, was our first active provider and this was one of her first clients. We were both excited by Gerald's progress, especially by his quick response to REI.

"He's been wearing socks and shoes everyday, since the end of the first week. Yesterday he joined his extended family outside and played with his brothers and cousins. He now lets his mom turn music on in the car and he has also been rocking out to his own pop music in the house."

"That's pretty quick progress. Is he using CD #2 yet?"

"He just started the other day. So far the transition is going well." The transition from CD #1 to CD #2, at this time in the history of the REI Custom Program, was sometimes difficult because of the jump in stimulation.

The first CD (and first track with the current Program) generally focuses on reducing anxiety and sets the foundation for improving sleep issues, if there are any. The subsequent tracks progressively build stimulation and broaden their focus to include other areas of concern.

When sensory sensitivities reduce during the first track, it usually means that they are related to anxiety. This was my assumption with Gerald.

I had no such assumption with Emily when she started the Program. This is because, even though she had a similar symptom make-up, she also had sleep issues and a more heightened response to over-stimulating environments.

"We'll start with trying to help Emily's sleep," I said to Laurel when we started the Program. "If she can fall asleep more easily and not wake up, we may also see some improvement in her sensitivities. Sometimes being tired, especially chronically, can increase the presence of these symptoms. Her overreaction to things in general suggests that this may be the case."

"So, do I play the track at bedtime, then? Can I play it all night long to help her stay asleep or turn it on again if she wakes up?" asked Laurel.

"Yes, turn it on at bedtime. Just play it once through. If she wakes up, it's okay to turn it again, but only once. With any luck, she'll be able to stay asleep after a couple of weeks of this pattern."

Many of our clients wake up at night. In fact, falling asleep is often not a problem. It's the night waking. And this is probably one of the most difficult things for a parent to deal with. Having your night interrupted, night after night, becomes wearing and leads to a host of problems.

The kids who wake up at night often wake up ready to go for the day. Getting them back to sleep can be exhausting. So, the first and most important thing for us to focus on is to help the child sleep so the parents can sleep, too.

"Emily slept all night the fifth night," Laurel told me at her two week check in. "She slept through the night for the next week and started waking up again the last couple of nights. Do you think we need to change tracks?"

"It sounds like it." I made a new track and waited to hear from Laurel again in another two weeks.

"Emily slept through the night again when we started the new track, but she started waking up again the last couple of days."

And so a pattern started to emerge for Emily. Sleep was a barometer to how a given track was working for her. Every time I made a new track, Emily would sleep well for a while and then she'd start waking up again.

"How are her anxiety and sensory issues?" I asked after the third track, hoping that we'd now start seeing some changes there.

"Oh, I forgot to mention this because I've been so focused on her sleep, but she's now letting me put on a shirt," Laurel added, sounding like it's not a big deal.

"Wow, that's great! When you started, she'd melt down if you tried that," I added, trying to help her see what a big change this was. When we first talked, Laurel was much more concerned with Emily's tactile sensitivities than she was by her sleep, but our focus on the sleep issue seemed to make her not as aware of Emily's tactile improvements.

"Yeah, I guess it is a big change. And come to think of it, she hasn't been melting down as much," she said as we talked about where Emily was before the Program started.

This isn't uncommon. Many times people are so focused on playing the track and dealing with whatever is up that it's hard for them to see the big picture, unless it's pointed out to them.

This is one of the most helpful things about our REI providers. Since they can't make the CDs or even mix-and-match pre-recorded CDs as is common in other auditory programs, many providers feel like they don't have an important role in REI. The key to their role is their relationship with their clients: It is valuable not only to help me see what the real issues are, but also to help the client gain perspective on how much progress they've made.

Laurel didn't always need to be reminded where Emily started. She became keenly aware. In fact, she was one of the most astute observers of her daughter's progress with the REI Program.

"Emily has been weepy the last few days in this track," Laurel told me a few more weeks into her Program. "She did fine for the first week then she started crying for no reason. It's not like a melt down. She's not reacting to anything going on around her. She'll just stop and cry. Could it be the track?"

"I don't know. It could be, I suppose. How is she sleeping? How are her sensitivities?"

"She's sleeping okay. She has been a little fussy about clothes. She'll only wear one particular shirt and she doesn't want to wear shoes anymore. Do you think we should try a new track?"

"That's what I'm thinking. I'd guess that this track is probably too stimulating for her."

I made a new track. Laurel called a week later.

"She's not weepy anymore and she wearing shoes again. What did you do with the new track?"

"I went back to rhythms we used in Track #2 and rearranged them. I looked at your current track (#3) and noticed that it had changed databases and drums. The Udu drum is much more stimulating than the Gonga, and I'm guessing that had an impact on her."

"I noticed it sounded like a different drum. Why would that matter?"

"The Gonga drum has a pretty soft, rounded tone. The Udu is really sharp. As well, on the Gonga I tend to use rhythms that are less complex and carry a longer structural flow than those played on the Udu. The Udu tracks tend to be much more stimulating than the Gonga tracks because the drum's sound is more pointed and the rhythms more complex. Someone as sensitive as Emily may find the Udu uncomfortable to listen to."

An REI Custom Program will draw from eight databases and switch back and forth between the Gonga and Udu. Even though the Udu drum rhythms tend to be more stimulating, the stimulation is presented on a scale. So a particular database of Gonga rhythms may be more stimulating than another database of Udu rhythms. In fact, each database used for the Custom Programs are progressively more stimulating;, so even though database two is an Udu, the rhythms are less stimulating than the rhythms played on the Gonga in database three.

We discovered that Emily was never able to handle the Udu tracks. I had to alter her Program so that we never drew from the Udu databases. She could handle fairly high intensity Gonga rhythms, but not lesser stimulating Udu drums. Fortunately, I was able to accommodate her.

Over the course of almost two years, Emily made significant progress in her anxieties and sensory issues. Then Laurel offered me another opportunity.

"Are you ready to work with my other daughter?" she asked. "Lila is the polar opposite of Emily. She is a sensory sponge. She could spend all day in the swing."

"Okay, let's give it try."

Like Emily, Lila was four-years-old when I started working with her. Unlike Emily, who withdrew from sensory stimulus, Lila was a classic sensory seeker. She was high energy, high activity.

Her response to her Program was also harder to track than Emily's. For instance, Emily's sleep would change when she was ready for a new track. She also made steady progress, as long as we changed tracks on her schedule.

Lila, on the other hand, could stick with the same track forever without showing any negative effects. With Lila, we needed to be more vigilant in changing her tracks on time in order to move her forward. She soaked up all the stimulation her Program would offer.

In some ways, a client like Lila is easy because I never have to contend with, or even worry about, overstimulation. Overstimulation generally causes sleeplessness, anxiety and agitation. Once we see overstimulation in a client, we tread pretty carefully from that point forward to ensure that she doesn't become overstimulated again.

Someone like Lila, though, doesn't react as strongly. Because she can handle so much stimulation, it takes more intense rhythms and more frequent changes to the tracks to ensure that she makes progress. If I'm not seeing tangible progress by Track #3, then I step up the stimulation further. If progress doesn't happen even after adding more stimulating REI tracks, I'll sometimes also ask that the REI tracks be played more than once a day.

Lila didn't need these contingencies. Her sensory-seeking became less pronounced during her second track, about three weeks into her

Program. She was sleeping better and was less anxious overall. Other than that, Lila was a hard to read. She didn't react strongly to a track like Emily did. She showed a slow, steady pace. Laurel was used to reacting to Emily's response to a track and felt a little lost when it came to knowing how Lila was responding.

"Lila is different than Emily in many ways, but the curious thing about the REI is that she just goes with the flow."

"Sensory seekers tend to be more consistent than sensory defensive people," I described. "I think that someone who is seeking sensory input tends to run at a pace that keeps them stimulated. They may not react to sensory input as much because they are still seeking more.

"A sensory defensive person, on the other hand, has a threshold that may change depending on how they feel. Different types of stimulus have different effects on them. So, unless they experience the same type and level of stimulation, you're going to see some variability in their response to stimulus and, in turn, in their behavior."

"That makes sense. I really see that with Emily. There are days when she can handle going to the grocery store, but there are other days when she melts down. Same thing with school. That's the most difficult thing about Emily's sensory issues: I can't predict how she is going to respond to something. Just when I think she'll be okay with going somewhere, she'll have a meltdown.

"Lila, on the other hand, is always busy. This consistency, although it's hard, is easier to handle because I can plan for how she'll react to something."

Though I see quite a few people who are sensory-seeking like Lila, more clients are on the sensory defensive side, like Emily. Either way, because I can fine-tune the stimulation for each person, I can accommodate their sensory needs and hopefully help them learn to more efficiently process sensory input.

• • •

"I like to crawl inside a sleeping bag and put pillows on top when I get home from work," Megan described to me as I was setting up my drum and recorder.

"You can climb in a sleeping bag now if you want," I told her. "I'll just play while you get comfortable."

"No, I think I'll just sit and listen. When I heard the *Calming Rhythms* CD, it felt comforting to me."

"Okay. Please feel free to let me know what my playing makes you feel, physically, emotionally, whatever," I said as I started playing. Megan had severe sensory issues. She was 34-years-old and had always been easily over stimulated, often to the point of physical distress. She drove a school bus for a living and would often come home and spend the evening wrapped up in her cocoon, trying to relieve the stress of the day.

Things had gotten worse for her recently because a change in her job description required her to do heavy work in addition to just driving. As part of the bus company downsizing, Megan was now also tasked with cleaning her bus, inside and out.

This heavier labor was stressing her system, leaving her physically fatigued and in pain. She was also having difficulty with the smells of the cleaning products.

Wrapping herself in a sleeping bag, especially with the extra weight and pressure from the piling of pillows, helped her feel the boundaries of her body, calming her nerves. But she couldn't very we'll spend her days wrapped up this way, so her occupational therapist recommended that she meet with me.

I started with a bass-tone-heavy pulse at regular intervals, separated by muted tones in an odd grouping of seventeen. My goal was for her to feel, more than hear, the drum, as she was easily overstimulated by sounds.

Megan was a fairly rare case for me. As an adult with a sensory processing disorder, she had the ability to tell me how she was feeling as I played. Most of the people I work with that have sensory processing disorders are children and most of them are also on the autism spectrum. Self-awareness and communication skills are not their strong suit.

This is why, even though I rarely see clients in person anymore, I agreed to meet Megan and play for her live like I used to when I was just starting out.

Megan shifted in her seat as I increased my volume and pounded out the bass beats. My goal was to give her the same basic sensation with the drumming that she was craving with the sleeping bag and pillows—help her learn the distinguish where her body ends and the sensorially overwhelming world begins.

This part of sensory processing is referred to as proprioception. Proprioception is the awareness of your physical boundaries, where your body sits in space, and the ability to physically move in an appropriate manner.

One of Megan's issues was that she often bumped into things, used too much or too little force when doings things, and occasionally injured herself.

It's a bit ironic that she drove a bus for a living. Driving requires coordination, the ability to use the feedback from the steering wheel and foot pedals to react to unpredictable events. She was able to drive safely and confidently, but it required a concerted effort and taxed her system, leaving her tired and much more sensitive than if she were engaged in a job that didn't put so much stress on her system.

I was about five minutes into her session, still playing bass-heavy notes, when I raised the complexity of my rhythms and the overall volume and intensity of my playing to a level where the objects on tables and walls were rattling.

Megan had curled up on the couch and was lying there with her eyes closed and a smile on her face.

I switched to a triplet-based rhythm in 49/16 using bass tones in a kind of circular pattern. Megan subtly rocked to my beat. I continued this rhythm for several minutes then began to alternate between variations on this triplet feel and the bass and muted tone rhythms I started with.

This brought the volume and intensity down considerably. I also saw an increase in her rocking motion. She was still smiling when she looked at me with satisfaction as I settled into a somewhat repetitive pattern. I dropped the volume to barely audible as I repeated the pattern.

The switch from a loud, almost all-encompassing drumming experience to a more subdued patter gave her sensory system bit of a break. Because the volume was low, the shift went from physically feeling the drumming to actively listening. For someone with sensory sensitivities, especially with regards to proprioception, this was a welcome transition that also required her to mentally focus to really hear the rhythm.

Megan sat up and watched me as I played. I tried not to look at her as I slowly switched to overtone-rich sounds. These are created by using the knuckle of my right thumb against a point half way between the edge and center of the drumhead. This creates a fairly quiet, but piercing, tone on my Gonga drum.

Megan closed her eyes and leaned her head back. Pleased that she shifted, I added in muted tones on my left hand using three fingers playing a ruff-like pattern. A ruff is one of the American Standard drumming rudiments consisting of a three-beat-rhythm with two quiet notes immediately followed by a third louder one. The two quiet beats, called pick-up beats, act as a prelude to the third beat which lands on the intended pulse.

This is all to say that my left hand ruff beat, coupled with the overtone thumb-tap, gave the rhythm a light and playful forward movement. I often use this type of pattern as a transition between a low muted passage and a louder, more rhythmically intense passage.

Megan happily sat with her eyes closed and head back as I started bringing in bass and open tones. The tempo never varied, but the orchestration and accented notes increased, giving the drumming a sense that it was speeding up.

I use this approach a lot. When I play this way for students, inevitably one of them will insist that I speed up. Yet every time I play the recording back and count out the pulse, the tempo has indeed remained the same.

Whether the rhythms actually sped up or not, the effect was as though they did. In this case with Megan, she opened her eyes and sat up again.

I wanted to see how far I could push her (in a good way), so I stepped up the rhythmic intensity another notch.

Now I was playing at full volume, heavy on bass and slap tones in quick succession. I was waiting to see if she would get up and move around. Sure enough, after a few minutes of this tirade, Megan stood and moved around the room.

She didn't look distressed and she didn't say anything to me. She was simply walking, almost dancing, around the room as I played. I continued this pattern for a few minutes and then settled the rhythm down again, returning to more muted tones. Then I slowly integrated the first rhythms I played, reducing the volume until I was just playing a single bass tone every second or so.

By this time Megan was back on the couch, sitting with her knees against her chest and a slight smile on her face as she watched my hands come to a rest.

I breathed and let silence fill the room. Neither of us said anything for a while until she let out a sigh.

"How was that?" I asked.

"That was nice. At first I kind of dozed off. I felt safe. Then I was really alert. When you played the loud section, I felt restless so I needed to walk around. Toward the end I could feel tingling, or maybe it was my pulse, in my fingers."

I felt that what I had played would be the right rhythms for her to listen to, so I gave her a copy of the tape I made during our session. I asked that she play it once a day for four weeks. Many times, I would use the recording of my playing as a guide to make another recording that would be used for a month. But in this instance, I felt that what I played was as good as anything that I could come up with later.

My decision was confirmed when her occupational therapist called me after about three weeks. "Megan is doing amazingly well. She says that the rhythms make her feel safe. She's been more organized in therapy, more aware of where she is in space. Less overstimulated and in less pain."

"I listen to the music and it makes me feel like I do when I'm in the sleeping bag," she told me when I called her. "I feel a sense of pressure on my body. It's like I'm being massaged in some way."

"So, it's a pleasant sensation?" I asked.

"Yes, it's like I described when you played for me. I can feel my pulse in my fingers and toes. It's a grounding sensation. I am also less tired. It's like I can do more out in the world and not get over-whelmed by everything."

"She's been coming to therapy much less stressed," her therapist told me. "I am spending less time in session just getting her stabi-lized. We can actually work on her proprioception issues."

"I feel more capable, if that makes any sense," Megan added. "I'm not as reactive to things around me. Oh, and I'm not bumping into things as much. This has made a huge difference."

Proprioception is a common sensory issue for the clients I work with. Megan's challenges highlight some of the most common issues: The lack of awareness of her body in space and the desire to have pressure against her, reassuring her.

The desire for pressure is something that Temple Grandin talks about in her book, *Thinking in Pictures*. She describes how she made a squeeze machine inspired by the devices used to hold cattle in place for branding. She would climb in her machine and pull a lever to put pressure on her own body. She describes this as being very calming.

This is what Megan described with her sleeping bag and pillow routine. The fact that the drumming gave her a similar sensation means that she was free to find this calm without needing to go through the ritual of the sleeping bag and pillows. It freed her up to find this calming place whenever and wherever she needed, without being confined to only have that security when she was at home with her gear.

An astounding number of kids I see have a similar craving. In fact, this tendency is so common that we ask about it in our REI Custom Program intake form.

• • •

"Brandon can hear the Fed Ex truck coming from miles away,"

his mother, Jules, told me. "He has super hearing. On the flip side, he is easily overstimulated by the noise. It's good that we live in the country, otherwise he'd probably be screaming all the time. Is this something you can help with?"

"A lot of my clients have sound sensitivities. So, I think I can help," I said. Brandon's sound sensitivities reminded me of Steven, a child from my study at the public school I described in Chapter 2. Theresa, one of the teachers helping with the study, had warned me that if I played my drum in the small room where I had successfully played for every other kid, Steven would run out of the room screaming. He didn't. In fact, he was less bothered by sounds after listening to a recording of me playing for two months. I was confident that I could help Brandon. This is why I was willing to drive forty miles to his home in a tiny town on the St. Croix River in Wisconsin.

I arrived and Brandon was standing on the porch, dancing excitedly on his toes.

"Hi Brandon. Do you like drums?" I asked.

Nothing.

I handed him a case and had him follow me into the house.

We went into the living room and I started to set up my equipment when a plane flew overhead. Brandon's hands flew up to his ears and he started rocking and groaning. Jules grabbed him and held him, soothed him. I sat by my drum and watched as Brandon reacted to the sound of the airplane. It was flying low and it took a while for it to get far enough away for Brandon to calm down.

"Does the airplane scare you, Brandon?" I asked.

He looked at me and didn't say a word, though I thought I detected a slight nod.

"The planes don't come very often," Jules told me. "There is a small light aircraft terminal a few miles from here and sometimes a plane will land or take off over us. When it happens Brandon gets anxious."

"Do any other sounds bother him?" I asked.

"Anything sudden or unexpected will do it. He also hates the vacuum, lawn mower, and hair dryer."

"How about loud noises? Are they a problem in general or is it only unexpected or droning noises?"

"Not all loud noises bother him. He can handle loud music. He actually prefers his music loud. I think it's mostly sounds that carry on."

I turned to Brandon. "Do you mind if I play the drum?" I asked.

"Brandon, why don't you sit down next to Mr. Jeff," said Jules.

Brandon came over to me and sat as I started to play. As you might expect, I started slowly and quietly, using mostly muted tones with some soft open tones and bass punches thrown in as I built the volume. I wanted to see how loud I could play before he began getting uncomfortable.

For about five minutes I increased the volume and added slap tones, which are the loudest most piercing sounds this drum can make. By the end of these five minutes, I was playing as loudly and intensely as I ever had. Brandon sat next to me watching my hands hit the drum. He was not bothered in the slightest.

This has been my experience with the live drumming for people who are extremely sound sensitive. In every case, they could tolerate what I was playing and none showed any signs that they were uncomfortable. No covering of their ears, no screaming or crying, no recoiling or shying away.

This is often not the case with a recording of the drumming. If the volume is too loud for someone with a sound sensitivity, he will cover his ears, complain or leave the room. But with the live drumming, this has never happened.

So, knowing that my drumming wouldn't bother him, I settled down a bit and focused on playing rhythms that I have used for other kids who had similar sound sensitivities. I played a series of rhythms with more subtle differences between the lower and higher notes, creating more of a droning patter. Brandon shifted in his seat. I increased the repetitive nature of the rhythm and Brandon shifted again, this time leaning away from me.

More repetition and Brandon stood up and left the room. I increased the volume; and, as Brandon brought his hands to his ears, I dropped the volume and played a five-beat rhythm heavy on bass tones. These rhythms and textures were in large contrast to what I had been playing. Brandon dropped his hands from his ears.

Next, I switched to a 73-beat rhythm that I played once before when a young girl was covering her ears as a plane flew overhead. This rhythm settled her down. And now, I wanted to see if it would relax Brandon as well. Testing a rhythm this way is what allowed me to develop the databases of rhythms related to symptoms.

After a minute or so with this rhythm, Brandon was next to me again. I eased off on the volume a bit and added a few more muted tones to the pattern. Brandon sat down. I added some more bass tones and played for several minutes before Brandon put his hands on the side of the drum.

It is common for kids to place their hands on the drum when I play a combination of bass and muted tones. The bass is deep and resonant. And it's inviting. The physical sensations of the drum are palpable. You feel it in your chest.

Brandon held onto the drum as I played for several more minutes. Then I stopped. He continued holding the drum. I tapped out a simple bass pulse and asked if he wanted to join me. His hand slowly moved from the side of the drum to its head. He held his hand on the head as I kept pounding the bass pulse.

Soon he tapped in time with me. I kept the bass pulse going with the right hand and with my left added simple syncopations, encouraging him to keep playing with me. We played together for a while before I stopped again. His hand remained on the drum for a minute or so. Then he lifted his hand, got up, and walked out of the room.

Satisfied with the session, I packed up and left. I made a tape for him and sent it to his mother the next day. I also asked her to specifically note how often and how severely he reacted to sounds in his environment.

I checked in with her after four weeks.

"Brandon is much calmer than he used to be. He is less bothered by the lawn mower and vacuum cleaner. The other day I forgot he was in his room when I turned on the vacuum and went down the hall with it. When I had done this in the past he would come screaming out of his room with his hands over his ears and run outside. This time he stayed in his room and kept playing.

"I was surprised, because after I finished vacuuming I went into his room to get his dirty laundry and there he was, playing on the floor. I asked if he heard the vacuum and he said he did. I asked, 'Didn't it bother you?' and he said, 'Yeah'. I asked why he didn't leave the room and he said he was busy playing. I was shocked because any other time and he would have been crying and screaming. This is just one example of how he seems much less bothered by the noises that used to drive him crazy."

Brandon is not unusual. I see a lot of people with sound sensitivities who are less sensitive after listening to their REI recording.

Sensory processing issues are common for our clients, and most of our REI Authorized Providers are Sensory Integration professionals. As a result, I worked with a few providers to develop a set of CDs to aid them while working in session with their clients. The set, called the *SI Series*, includes eight CDs covering four sensory areas: auditory (hypo- and hyper-sensitive), proprioception (grading of movement and hypo-sensitive), tactile (hyper- and hypo-sensitive), and vestibular (hyper- and hypo-sensitive).

The goal of these CDs was not to do what the Custom Program does, which is help reorganize the sensory system, but to support the work an SI therapist does in session. This is accomplished in two ways. First, the therapist can play the appropriate CD and track during an SI session as an added stimulus and, second, they can "prescribe" certain CDs and tracks be played between SI therapy appointments to support the therapy session work between sessions.

One clinic in New York has implemented the SI series to great effect.

"We play *Calming Rhythms* in the sensory room all day long," described Karen. "The *SI Series* CDs are used with each client."

"How do you isolate them?" I asked as I toured the sensory room, a large open room with swings, hammocks, mats, and balls. It was a loud room with a lot of activity and I wondered how a child could hear a recording in the din without it being so loud that it was disruptive to others in the room.

"We generally use the CDs to organize the child's brain before we work with them in this room," she said as we walked to a series of small rooms equipped with bean bag chairs and assorted toys. "For the beginning of each session, and for many sessions in general, we work one-on-one in rooms like this. We have six of them."

She opened a door where Ben, an eight-year-old boy, was being brushed on the arm by a therapist. I could hear one of the *SI Series* CDs playing in the background.

"Which CD did you choose for this child?" I asked.

"This is the first track from the *Tactile Hypo-sensitive* CD," Karen answered.

"Why did you choose that one?" I asked, trying to see if she grasped the logic of these CDs. Brushing is used to help with proprioception, tactile, and sensory discrimination in general, and often used as a way to teach a child to calm.

"We started with the *Tactile Hyper-sensitive* CD and then moved to the *Proprioception Grading of Movement* CD, then to this. He seemed to need help with distinguishing not only where he was a space, but also in being able to even identify where we were brushing him. Is this a good choice?"

"Yes, it's common to move through different CDs in the set, even those that work opposite ends of a sensory issue like the hypo- and hyper-sensitive CD of a particular sensory area. In this case, it sounds like Ben had tactile sensitivities when you began the brushing. Then as he became less sensitive, you noticed that he couldn't discriminate where you were brushing him, so you chose the Proprioception CD followed by the Tactile CD to deal with discrimination."

She nodded and we watched Ben for a while as the therapist finished her protocol and stopped brushing him. He sat quietly as the CD continued playing in the background. After a minute, his therapist led him out into the sensory room where he climbed on a tire swing.

"He has made remarkable progress," said Karen. "When he started with us, he was often out of control. He'd run from one area to another, treating this room as a playground. We weren't able to success-fully engage him for very long each session. In fact, as I think about it, once we started playing *Calming Rhythms* in this room, he would calm down without our having to constantly redirect him."

"When was that?" I asked.

"About a year ago, right after I took the training." She was refer-ring to the REI Authorized Provider Training. In this training we teach professionals how to use our CDs and to facilitate the REI Custom Program.

"Every client listens to *Calming Rhythms* when they're here, and most listen to at least one *SI Series* CDs during the time we work with them."

Karen and I talked for a while longer before I moved on to the next clinic I was visiting that day. I don't do this as often as I used to, but talking with therapists at their clinics was helpful in teaching me the subtleties of sensory processing issues and the way they unfold as a client responds to our therapy. This had been an important part of the *SI Series* protocol development and has also allowed me to approach sensory issues more systematically within the REI Custom Program.

Chapter Eighteen
Dynamic Path

The development of REI coincides with the knowledge I gained along the way. Early on, there was much more variability in how someone responded, because I didn't have as deep a grasp of the subtleties of the rhythms I used. This meant that the gains were not as dramatic or predictable, but it also meant that there was more room for error. If I had the wrong rhythm, or the right rhythm in the wrong order, I might only see a stall in changes; now, because I'm using much more sophisticated rhythms and techniques, I see more dramatic changes overall, but when I get the rhythms wrong I see more obvious reactions.

As I have refined the rhythms and protocols, I have also discovered that I need to balance the stimulation required for one area against the needs of another. This has made the dynamic track creation and listener feedback much more important.

Nancy was a case in point. Because I was asked to help with a large variety of symptoms—anxiety, sleep, language, social interaction, and self-stimulatory behaviors—I needed to make a plan where

I could work with all of them over the course of her Program.

Each symptom area requires a specific type and level of stimulation. For example, sleep, anxiety and anxiety-based behaviors require a calming approach. The rhythms need to be softer and less jarring, in other words, less stimulating. On the other hand, language requires high levels of stimulation. More complex rhythms, more slap and overtone rich sounds. Less predictability.

Nancy's symptom make-up required stimulation levels at two ends of the possible spectrum. If I tried to include both of these ends in one REI track, the track would likely be unproductive, or at the very least, unpredictable.

The trick, in this instance, was to create a path where I prioritized the symptoms I wanted to work with and tackle them one or two at a time. The problem was that sometimes my client had a different priority list. In this particular case, I felt sleep was the primary concern, because Nancy couldn't sleep alone and she couldn't sleep through the night.

According to the intake assessment, Nancy's father needed to sleep on a mattress on the floor in her room. She had difficulty falling asleep and also woke up at night, often between 3 and 4 a.m., and stayed awake for several hours. As well, she rarely slept past 6 a.m., if she fell back asleep at all.

Nancy's lack of language and social skills were the primary reason her parents wanted to do the REI Custom Program. Her parents described that Nancy had difficulty knowing how to engage with others, especially other children. She was often unresponsive when spoken to, she preferred to play alone, and when she did interact, she often displayed verbal outbursts and inappropriate laughter. She also rarely looked at people or made eye contact unless prompted. She would also get anxious and upset if someone she didn't know approached or, often, even looked at her.

Her language development was below her age level. Nancy was only able to communicate using single words or short phrases. Complete sentences and meaningful language was nearly non-existent. Her receptive language was better, as she understood what was said to her, but she needed significant processing time when given multi-step instructions. She also tended to lose focus often when asked to listen to instructions.

Before beginning the REI Custom Program, Nancy's diagnosis was autism, due to her limited language and lack of interest in playing with other kids. Her parents wanted the language and socialization to be a priority, since she was soon going to kindergarten and her parents wanted her to be mainstreamed. So, I tried to help with both the sleep and language and social development. Nancy's response illustrates the delicate balance between the opposing REI rhythms that this approach requires.

Nancy showed immediate improvements in language and social engagement; but as the first week wore on, her sleep and behavior got progressively worse. According to her father:

> *Today, she is really wound up. There have been several vocal outbursts and periods of out-of-control behavior. Over the course of the last few days, the vocal outbursts have continued at home, although she has been more affectionate than usual with my wife. Nancy has been able to engage for longer, continuous periods of time with my wife, 1-2 hours of doing various preferred and non-preferred activities. She is also using names more frequently to gain our attention.*

Sleep disruption is the most common indicator of an REI recording being overstimulating, so it appeared that the stimulation on Nancy's first track was impacting her sleep. However, the level of stimulation contained in this recording provided noticeable improvements in language, anxiety and social interaction, as her reports showed:

> *On the positive side, Nancy is doing more self-talk, especially conversational self-talk. She is also being more social with people outside of our family and exhibiting less anxiety outside of the home.*
> *Last night we took Nancy to an event for kids with autism and their families. Nancy had one brief verbal outburst in line while we*

were waiting 15+ minutes to enter the building, but no additional outbursts for the next 2 hours. There were a LOT of people and there was a lot of waiting in confined areas. She was patient and engaged the entire time with no further outbursts, only communicating with words about what she was seeing and what she wanted to see next. We were nervous when we saw the crowd of people because she was very excited to go to this event and we were worried she was going to have a meltdown since it was in the evening and she was tired, but she did a great job!

Nancy's parents we ecstatic about her improvements and wanted to continue seeing progress, while at the same time they wanted Nancy to sleep better. We talked about the trade offs—making sleep the top priority meant little to no progress of language and social skills, whereas continuing a brisk pace in language and social meant the sleep may not improve until much later in the Program.

We choose a path that would continue the gains they were seeing while slowly trying to get her sleep under control. Ordinarily, with sleep degrading like Nancy's, I'd reduce the stimulation on her next recording, but I felt that in order to keep the language and social in the mix there was some room to reduce the level of simulation she was receiving by simply lowering the volume. This represented a trade-off between Nancy's unimproved sleep and her improved language and social participation.

After another week on her first recording, her parents reported that her meaningful, pragmatic language was continuing to improve, as did some of her impulsive behavior. As they described:

We continue to hear an improvement in Nancy's language. She is using meaningful language more regularly in sentence format. We are also hearing more verbs, adjectives, and adverbs, as well as more pragmatic language. We are playing the music softer and her sensory has improved. She still has bouts of excitement when she tears through the house, but it is in shorter increments (10-15 min) vs. 30 min+.

Regarding Nancy's sleep, she was still waking up at night, but she was falling asleep easier. Her parents noted:

There is little to no improvement in Nancy's sleep. She continues to wake between 3-4 a.m. each night and has been up regularly at 5:30 a.m. for the last 4 days. ...One great thing is we are continuing the same bedtime routine, playing the track while she hears a story, and she is falling asleep faster than in the past.

At this point, even though her language was improving and she was listening at an appropriate level for her, it appeared that this recording was still too stimulating for Nancy. This was evidenced by a decrease in eye contact and no change in focus, anxiety, and impulsive behavior. Again, according to her parents:

Nancy's eye contact is getting worse. She needs to be constantly prompted to look at our eyes when she speaks. There is no improvement with her turning toward us when her name is called and she continues to exhibit poor focus. Also, she continues to have occasional verbal outbursts and it has now begun at school. She also has times when she bursts into laughter for no apparent reason and cannot control herself. She falls on the floor laughing hysterically at very inappropriate times. Nancy has also been very short-tempered and is getting upset easily. Her anxiety level is still high, especially if anyone she doesn't know looks at her. She is still very disorganized, too.

Based on this feedback, I reduced the level of stimulation for her next several REI recordings, hoping that her anxiety, impulsivity, and behavioral outbursts would diminish and her sleep would improve. After six weeks on the REI Custom Program (four tracks) Nancy's parents reported that:

I just spoke with Nancy's teacher. She called to tell me that Nancy has seemed different at school the last week and a half—that Nancy has been more "huggy" and nurturing, but also sad. She said Nancy hasn't been her usual happy-go-lucky self and has instead been more sensitive and has been asking for hugs. The teacher has noticed that there are times when she expects Nancy to get upset and yell, but Nancy catches herself and does not. Perhaps Nancy is experiencing and discovering new feelings from the latest track. This is a good thing!

Overall, Nancy was still showing improvements in language, however her sleep had not improved and she was still exhibiting impulsive behaviors and poor focus.

Due to her behaviors, I made the next track, #5, even less stimulating, as I tried to put the focus on calming her nervous system. Her response was initially somewhat negative. However, after a few days she began to calm down and many of her issues improved, as her parent's feedback documented:

She exhibited increased negative behavior over the first several days of the track (sensory, aggression, anxiety, etc.), but her sleep, behavior, mood, focus, and language suddenly and dramatically improved over the past 7 days.

She is still having moments of uncontrollable and inappropriate laughter at home and at school, as I've described before, but it is for shorter periods of time. It's easier to redirect and calm her behavior within 5-10 minutes versus 20-30 minutes. Her eye contact and language have dramatically improved and she is spontaneously asking questions with appropriate eye contact. We still see anxiety and moments of 'weepiness'. Yesterday she suddenly burst into tears. I asked her what was wrong and she said, 'I remember something.' I asked her what but she wouldn't tell me. She cried for 2-3 minutes, then wiped her tears and said, 'I better. I happy now.' She has also expressed to me this week that, 'I scared of people sometimes.' I am then able to talk her through it and comfort her. When she feels better she'll look at me, smile, and say, 'I happy now.' It's an unbelievable break through! She had the best day of her life on Tuesday—great day from start to finish.

Sleeping has also improved. She has slept all night for the past 3 nights; but if she wakes up alone in the morning, she is afraid and screams.

The next several tracks again focused on calming Nancy's nervous system in the hopes of continuing the positive path we were on and to further stabilize her sleep. After sailing through three new tracks over the next four weeks, Nancy showed considerable improvements in language, social interaction, and problem-solving (her parents gave an example of her figuring out how to navigate the monkey bars from end-to-end).

Her sleep was improving, but her father still needed to stay in her room in case she woke up. Nancy was also making great strides with more social engagement, focus and attention, and language skills. As described by her parents:

Nancy has been talking more and focus has improved. She is actually able to sit and watch a full 90-minute movie. She is also able to sit and play with her Littlest Pet Shop toys quietly for 15-20 minutes doing pretend play. She is also beginning to ask family members to play with her! She still has bouts of impulsivity related to sensory, but she is much calmer than in previous weeks. Nancy has recently been able to sit and play quietly with toys for 1-2 hours during her brother's baseball games. It's great!!

At this point, I chose to focus her next track on her sensory-seeking and body awareness. Initially, this wasn't a positive experience.

She became increasingly anxious about the potty during the last track and has begun screaming about the potty and several days in a row last week she had multiple accidents each day. This has not happened in months.

Her next few tracks focused on increasing her sensory processing with a particular focus on potty training. This appeared to work, as described by her parents:

> *Nancy has turned a corner with potty training! We are thrilled!!!! She is doing a great job urinating on the potty, although she has gone in her pull-up once or twice in the morning (she sleeps in a pull-up each night)—we don't even need to ask or remind. Nancy also defecated on the potty for the first time this weekend all by herself. She has no interest in wiping at any time.*

The other area of focus for her last tracks was making sure that she was sleeping well and that her parent could sleep together in their own room. According to Nancy's mother:

> *Sleep has improved and my husband is no longer sleeping on a mattress on the floor of her room. The last two nights she has been able to sleep by herself; she does need the light to be on the whole night. However, there have also been two nights over the last week when she has woken up multiple times during the night and needs someone with her to get back to sleep.*

Thus was Nancy's progress on the Program. It was a balancing act between social, language, sleep and anxiety. Over the course of twenty weeks, Nancy began sleeping well and blossomed in her language and social skills. At this point we began working on helping her focus better.

This too, was a long road because she still had some sensory challenges that tended to run in conflict with the stimulation needs for attention.

She moved to an extended REI Custom Program, staying with a track for four weeks instead of the two week pace of the regular Program. This allowed me to offer a higher level of stimulation for her attention, since she had time to get used to it before moving to the next track.

Nancy had been a success mainly because her parents were clear about their goals and relentless in keeping in touch with me to ensure we adjusted Nancy's track if her responses were not going in the directions that we anticipated.

For Nancy, balancing between the high and low stimulation needs of her symptoms made her path meander, causing some difficulties along the way. Most clients follow a dynamic path that is more like peeling away layers. Obviously, this path is easier on everyone.

Tommy is a case in point. Tommy was ten-years-old when he started the REI Custom Program. His main issues were sensory and attention-related; both are areas that require a high level of stimulation to address, though I often ramp up the stimulation over time with these symptoms rather than jump right into a high level.

Tommy also had some anxiety and OCD (obsessive/compulsive disorder) symptoms, the most significant were thoughts such as "If I don't blink five times in a row something bad will happen" and tics related to these thoughts. Sleep was also a minor issue for him—he often had a difficult time winding down to go to sleep, tended to wake up at night, and was slow to get moving in the morning. These issues are usually the first ones I work with because they generally respond to lower levels of stimulation and, therefore, are easier for a new listener to tolerate.

Because of his anxiety and sleep issues, I advised his mother to play his REI recording at bedtime, hoping to help him calm down and fall asleep quicker. She did this the first two nights and reported that Tommy said, "This music is very soothing".

The third day he became agitated by some homework, so his mother played his REI recording for him to try to calm him down, which he did within a few minutes of turning it on. Playing an REI recording while a behavior is happening offers two benefits. First, it generally stops the behavior, and second, it helps the listener learn what it feels like to make the shift out of the behavior. This can lead to learning how to self-regulate.

Tommy's first track went well overall. His mother reported that he "Seems a little better with recuperating from upsets".

His compulsive tics continued and he wasn't yet showing any signs of improved attention, but this was expected since my goal was to address the anxiety first.

Tommy's next five REI recordings focused on anxiety and self-regulation, and he showed consistent improvements in both. His mother described that he "continues to show consistent moods and even when he does get upset, the intensity and duration is more normal. He has been putting his dishes in the sink after meals without being asked, has been putting toys away instead of leaving things all over the house."

His compulsive behaviors were not improving by this point; so starting with Track #8, I shifted the focus of his Program to see if this issue could be improved. Because his compulsive behavior wasn't being improved with the lower stimulation level used for anxiety, I also thought it would be worthwhile to add in some rhythms for attention.

The next several REI recordings slowly improved both the compulsions and attention. After Track #8 his mother reported:

> *Tommy is really taking responsibility at school and home more often—working hard and doing extra or trying to stay caught up at school without complaint. Still a few compulsions, like leaving toys in the middle of the floor and not allowing them to be moved. But, he is walking in front of the mirror he was avoiding since summer and is sitting in the bean bag chair he was avoiding.*

Tommy was making progress. His mother reported:

> *The only remaining issue I see right now is his sensitivity to certain sounds, metal on metal or ceramic, pennies on a table top, whisks in a bowl, silverware touching or placed in a drawer. Thus issue was put on the back burner while the attention, compulsions, and moods were prevalent.*

Based on this feedback, I again shifted the focus of Tommy's Program. This time we worked on his sound sensitivities. For the next two recordings Tommy showed improvements in sensitivities to certain sounds, particularly metal on metal. According to his mother:

> We made breakfast together, French toast. As I whisked the eggs in a glass bowl, I expected Tommy to cover his ears and make a quick exit from the room. He didn't. He made no reaction at all! I kept whisking more vigorously just to see...it didn't bother him. He never reacted or even moved away from me.

During the last few recordings he also made progress in his schoolwork. His mother reported:

> Tommy's report card is great: Social Studies—A, Science—A, Lang Arts—B, Math—C. Teacher states it does take Tommy a long time to process and finish his work, which has always been the case. And, may always be the case.

Tommy and Nancy both did well on their Programs because I received a lot of feedback from their parents. This allowed me to dynamically-adjust each track to focus on the areas that were at the fore.

This high need for feedback was a point of concern at the beginning of creating the REI Custom Program and one that I have taken seriously each time we adjusted the Program. When we started training providers, we quickly weeded out the ones who were unable to keep close tabs on their clients. When we built our online Program with feedback forms, we learned that we also needed to keep in touch. Our first online tracking system didn't provide close enough contact, so we stepped in personally to fill the gaps until we were able to create a system that worked. In fact, I've found that if I can personally be involved in following up on a client's progress (either directly with the client or his provider), people tend to be more engaged. I suppose if they know the Program's creator is available, they feel more secure in knowing they are not just a number, but an individual and valued client.

This is why, even after all these years, I still try to be the one who answers the phone. I think there is something reassuring that the person ultimately responsible is also intimately available.

Chapter Nineteen

From Traditions to Technology

"What was that rhythm?" asked Lloyd. "I felt like you were massaging my brain."

"Well, let's see," I said, pausing to reconstruct the rhythm. I tapped around until I found the last pattern I had been playing. "It starts with a syncopated triplet-feel, then adds three two-beat bass pulses embedded in five-beat patterns, followed by a seven-beat turnaround."

He nodded as I grooved on this rhythm for a minute.

"That's nice," he added.

"Is it okay?" I asked. "I completely butchered the traditional rhythms."

"No, it's fine. This isn't like playing for ceremony. The Orisha don't matter."

I was trading rhythms with Lloyd as he was teaching me how to play one-on-one for someone. This process draws from traditional ceremonial drumming, where the drumming honors Orisha (spirits) who appear to help fulfill the goals of the ceremony. Lloyd assured me that when playing one-on-one for someone the Orisha didn't matter; the rhythms were the key, and my inspiration drove the creation of the rhythms.

"There is always room for something new," he continued. "Remember that you're creating a dialog between your drum and your patient. As long as you listen, you won't play the wrong rhythms."

Lloyd explained that nothing is static in this tradition. Since the beginning, drums, rhythms, and techniques have evolved and morphed to fit the needs of the community. For example, when the African Orisha tradition moved from West Africa to the Americas, the Orisha were often replaced by Catholic saints, with each island or region utilizing a different saint/Orisha relationship.

As well, drums, which were often thought to have souls of their own, changed. The drums used in Trinidad where Lloyd was from were different than those used in West Africa. Likewise, the drums we used for ceremonies in L.A. were not the drums used in either Trinidad or West Africa. In each case, the drums employed were the ones that were most available.

I played some more. Lloyd nodded and swayed to the rhythms, and I began noticing that what I was playing took on a life of its own. I would start with a traditional rhythm, but found that it would twist into an unrecognizable form. I found that if I tried to stick with the original pattern, I'd soon be making mistakes.

"Follow the rhythm," he'd often instruct. "Mistakes are the spirits telling you to change the pattern."

"But why do my rhythms always end up so strange?" I asked. "You don't go so far out."

"You're hearing music that I don't. Remember, this is a dialogue, one between you and your listener. When I play it's a different conversation. Your voice is unique. Follow that voice and you'll play what's right for you and your patient."

"Your voice is strong," he continued. "Keep listening and pushing the bounds of what you think the rhythms should be. Carry the drum forward and the traditions will walk with you even as the rhythms change. Only by doing this will you truly find your voice."

This was one of my last conversations with Lloyd. I didn't plan it that way. It's just how life worked out. I got busy finishing my studies at the Musician's Institute and moved from Hollywood to the San Fernando Valley.

During this time Lloyd took a trip back to Trinidad. When I tried getting in touch after getting settled, he was gone. I don't know if he returned to L.A. or if he stayed on the island. It didn't really matter, because I was newly graduated and ready to start playing professionally again.

His last words stuck with me as I moved on. Not in the context of playing for people—I wasn't interested in that at the time—but in the popular music world where there were hundreds of drummers trying to make their way in a cutthroat industry. I worked hard to find and define my style. At first, I played in a couple of cover bands playing other people's music. One band played blues, the other the worst of the top-40, both at clubs where I'd earn about $50 per gig.

It was soul-sucking work for me; so when an opportunity came along to take a gig playing more interesting music in Minneapolis, I took it. One of my main reasons for leaving L.A. was that I wasn't a metal drummer or a seasoned session player, so there was little work for me aside from low-paying club dates. Minneapolis offered R&B and commercial session work, both of which were more aligned with my skills and experience.

As it turned out, the band I moved to play for quickly petered out. As I scrambled to keep money coming in, I ended up getting a teaching job at the hippest music store in the city. This job not only led to a lot of gigs, but also kept me on the edge of technology.

The music store, Knut Koupee, carried the latest and greatest tech goodies. My fellow employees and I were enthusiastic about exploiting the tech any way we could.

My employee discount kept me knee-deep in the latest tech, and the manufacturer clinics the store often hosted allowed me to become proficient in its use. This led to my first recording engineering gig, countless tech support gigs for drum machine, sequencer and electronic drumset programming, and opportunities to produce singers and bands exploiting the latest production techniques.

My deep experience in—and love of—tech became integral in the development of REI and Brain Shift Radio. And Lloyd's encouragement to follow my voice and find what works for me gave me permission and confidence to eventually let the tech take center stage.

It wasn't entirely my love for technology that put tech out front. My choice was also born out of my trepidation of people's reaction to the tribal sound of the drum, evidenced by my experience with Lily from Chapter 3.

I figured if I could remove the drum from the conversation and instead focus the conversation on musical rhythm, I would be able to reach more people, particularly people with a similar background to mine where the tribal aspects of the drumming were thought to be associated with spirits.

Even from the beginning of my studies with Lloyd, I sought a better explanation to the effects of drumming beyond spirits. Therefore, my research focused on what was happening with the rhythm and not the cultural aspects of the traditions I was studying, such as the rituals and superstitions.

Essentially, I removed the shaman's hood and replaced it with a lab coat. From my observations of improved focus from playing syncopated rhythms at eight-beats-per-second, I knew there was more to drumming than some spiritual cause.

So, when I began my clinical research, I took great pains to remove the cultural influences. A large part of that process was to remove the expectation, good or bad, that accompanied the drums.

The problem, though, was that I was a drummer, and I quickly learned that the most effective way to deliver musical rhythm was through drums and percussion. This meant that I needed to downplay the drum and accentuate the rhythm. Using technology in the delivery helped me do that.

• • •

"Why don't you put your CDs up on a streaming music site, like

Pandora?" asked Michael. "Streaming is the future of music," he added, as he searched for music to listen to on his iPhone.

I pondered this for a moment. "I like Pandora but I don't know how prescriptive music would fit there. Their genome project is limited."

We drove along in silence taking in the vast emptiness of the landscape off the highway. We were in the northeastern corner of New Mexico, driving from Santa Fe to Denver to pick up some stereo speakers my friend had bought over the Internet.

Michael and I had been playing music together off and on for the past ten years, and in that time we have spent countless hours talking about music and technology. He was an audiophile who loved vinyl and vintage tube amps, and I was a technophile always trying to push the limits of whatever technology was at the edge of practicality.

Even from my earliest days after graduating from the Musician's Institute, I embraced the latest tech. In 1983 I took out my first business loan and bought a Simmons SDS 5 electronic drumset, inspired by a clinic given by drummer Bill Bruford (of the bands Yes and King Crimson) where he played one of the earliest versions.

In 1985, for my first audio engineering job, I used an Apple computer to sequence music (using Performer by Mark of the Unicorn). And in 1986 I was using a Korg DSS-1 digital sampling keyboard and a pieced-together electronic drum set to make some of the first cutting edge drum sounds, going so far as to use breaking glass as a cymbal crash, a baseball bat smashing a garbage can as a snare drum, and a toilet flush as a sound effect.

By 1990, I'd switched from analog to digital recording, ecstatic to trade the noise and degrading sound with the ability to edit without having to cut and splice tape, though the earliest versions were a bit cumbersome for editing. Then I moved on to a first-generation CD burner that cost over $10,000 for making client recordings.

My push for new tech went on and on, so when Michael mentioned streaming music, I was already thinking beyond just putting up static tracks to play.

I had just built software that would both compile our custom-made recordings from an online intake form and adjust the music based on the feedback we received from our clients (Chapter 6 explores this development). My company had become known for our custom-made programs, so when my friend talked streaming, I thought custom.

How could I make our CDs more personalized in an interactive way?

"Pandora is a good model," I said, thinking out loud. "They have their music selection algorithm where you choose a song or artist and the system chooses music with similar traits. What if we took it a step further and use mini-intake to select the music for someone?"

"We could have categories of music—focus, calm, sleep—stuff like that. And when someone chooses a category we could ask a question that would help us refine a selection to meet their needs."

"Say you want to start a project. You choose 'focusing for a project' or something like that and we choose focusing tracks for getting going on something. Or you're really anxious, and when you tell us what your anxiety level is we are able to choose a more intensive anxiety reducing track than if you were only slightly stressed. Then, instead of a simple thumbs up or down, we use a five-point rating system so you can tell us how much you like a track. Oh, and we could also ask how the music is working and adjust the music based on the feedback."

"I like that idea, but it sounds complicated," he replied. "Could you make it intuitive and easy to use?"

"Yeah, sure. And you know what would also be cool?" I said, beginning to get wound up. "To deliver my music in two separate music streams so the listener could mix the music themselves."

"What do you mean?" Asked Michael.

"As you know, one of the challenges I face is that people often have a hard time tolerating the rhythms, so I sometimes add an ambient-type instrument to push the rhythm in the background and make it easier to listen to. It would be really cool to split these two instruments and give the listener a slider so they can adjust the balance between the two tracks."

"Hmm," he intoned skeptically.

"While we're at it, let them swap the tracks. And rate the mixes. And save them to share with the community"

"Now, that sounds complicated. How do people choose tracks for a mix?"

"Provide tips and tutorials. Make it an option for people who want to dig deep into the program."

"Yeah," he said getting into the spirit of the discussion, "like a game or program that has basic functions for most people and "power-user" functions so hardcore people can stay engaged. You could call it Brain Radio."

"Yeah. Or Brain *Shift* Radio. This would draw from the *Brain Shift Collection* CDs I did a few years ago."

Brain Shift Radio became a reality after about a year of development. The process, though difficult, was extremely satisfying and reaffirmed my commitment to harnessing technology to enhance my music.

The REI Custom Program and Brain Shift Radio represent ways of making my recorded drumming rhythms more closely encompass the infinite variability of my live playing. A static CD is just that, static.

Just as I couldn't have predicted the form my music would take twenty years ago (or even ten), I can't begin to guess what form it will take in another decade.

Regardless of where it goes, I will continue to follow the rhythm, as Lloyd always advised.

Afterword

Thank you for reading. This is my eighth book, but the first one that I chose to publish without the aid of a major publisher. I did this for two reasons. First, this offered complete narrative freedom – I could write the book I wanted, not the how-to book that nearly every committe of editors thought the market wanted. Second, the publishing landscape has changed dramatically since my first book was published in 2001, offering opportunities that didn't exist back then.

Historically, major publishers, such as Wiley (mine), were able to reach distribution avenues small publishers and independent authors could not. However, this is no longer the case. Small, independent publishers and self-published authors have largely the same distribution outlets available to them as the biggies. As well, sales now seem to be driven by reader reviews and recommendations rather than brute marketing force (though brute force still happens with big name authors, of which I am not).

After a long discussion with my agent, I decided to embrace the possibilities in this new landscape and forego an established publisher. As a result, I am more dependent on readers to spread the word. This is all to say that I could use your help. Please take a few minutes and write a review of this book or make a comment on your social media platform of choice.

• • •

Martin Mull is attributed to saying, "Talking (writing) about music is like dancing about architecture." There is a lot lost in the translation. Therefore, me writing about my work doesn't do it justice. You really need to experience the drumming for yourself. If you found yourself interested, engaged, or just plain curious by the possibilities I present in this book, I can't recommend highly enough that you get your hands on some of my music.

Luckily, I have made this opportunity available for free in several ways at differentdrummerbook.com

• • •

My work is ongoing. Since I wrote this book, I have continued to develop and refine my music and Programs. You can discover the latest at the following:

For this book: differentdrummerbook.com
REI Custom Program: reicustomprogram.com
Brain Shift Radio: brainshiftradio.com
General information: stronginstitute.com
My personal blog: jeffstrong.com

About the Author

Jeff Strong is the creator of Rhythmic Entrainment Intervention™ (REI) and the Director of the Strong Institute, a research center and provider of custom auditory stimulation programs for individuals with neurological disorders. He is also the co-founder of Brain Shift Radio, a streaming music site containing personalized music to enhance brain function.

As a musician and composer, Jeff created the REI Custom Program, more than 50,000 hours of music for Brain Shift Radio, and over 30 CDs, including the *Brain Shift Collection* 8-CD set (Sounds True, 2008).

As a researcher, Mr. Strong has published numerous articles and has been a member of the faculty for two International Society for Music in Medicine (ISMM) Symposiums as well as over three-dozen other professional conferences. His work has been featured in numerous books and journals including *Insights into Sensory Issues for Professionals, The Mozart Effect for Children, The Autism Treatment Guide, The ADD Checklist, Open Ear Journal,* and *Sound Connections,* among others.

As a sought-after expert on music, rhythm and sound healing, Jeff has made frequent media appearances including two documentaries and numerous radio and television programs.

Also by Jeff Strong:

Selected Books

AD/HD For Dummies (with Michael Flanagan, MD), Wiley, 2004
PC Recording Studios For Dummies, Wiley, 2005
Pro Tools All-In-One Desk Reference, Wiley, 2004
Woodworking For Dummies, Wiley 2003
Home Recording For Musicians For Dummies, Wiley 2002
Drums For Dummies, Wiley, 2001

Music (all formats)

Focused Attention, Sounds True. 2015
PowerNap Rejuvenator, Sounds True. 2015
REI Custom Program, Strong Institute, Inc. 1997-2015
REI Sleep Rhythms, Strong Institute, Inc. 2010
REI Sensory Processing Program, Strong Institute, Inc. 2010
REI Sleep Program, Strong Institute, Inc. 2010
REI Focus Program, Strong Institute, Inc. 2010
REI S.I. Series 8-CD set, Strong Institute, Inc. 2009
Transition to Sleep, Sounds True. 2009
REI S.I. Auditory Hyper-Sensitive, Strong Institute, Inc. 2009
REI S.I. Auditory Hypo-Sensitive, Strong Institute, Inc. 2009
REI S.I. Proprioception Grading of Movement, Strong Institute, Inc. 2009
REI S.I. Proproiception Hypo-Sensitive, Strong Institute, Inc. 2009
REI S.I. Tactile Hyper-Sensitive, Strong Institute, Inc. 2009
REI S.I. Tactile Hypo-Sensitive, Strong Institute, Inc. 2009
REI S.I. Vestibular Hyper-Sensitive, Strong Institute, Inc. 2009

REI S.I. Vestibular Hypo-Sensitive, Strong Institute, Inc. 2009
The Brain Shift Collection: Ambient Rhythmic Entrainment, Sounds True. 2008
REI Focusing Rhythms, Strong Institute, Inc. 2007
REI Calming Rhythms, Strong Institute, Inc. 2007
Calming Rhythms 3, Strong Institute, Inc. 2005
Revitalize Your Body, Strong Institute, Inc. 2003
Calm Your Mind, Strong Institute, Inc. 2003
Calming Rhythms 2, Strong Institute, Inc. 2003
Rhythms for Learning, Strong Institute, Inc. 2003
Calming Rhythms, Strong Institute, Inc. 1997
NBD Calming Aid, Strong Institute, Inc. 1996
REI for the Immune System, Strong Institute, Inc. 1995
REI for Neurobiological Disorders, Strong Institute, Inc. 1994
Healing Journeys, Bone Mountain Records. 1992

21633896R00180

Made in the USA
Middletown, DE
07 July 2015